T0014017

"A taut, chilling novel about the weaponization of language as a tool of oppression."
—*KIRKUS REVIEWS*, starred review

"*Tongueless* shocked me as much as any masterpiece I have ever read."
—CHAN HO-KEI, author of *The Borrowed*

"*Tongueless* is a riveting horror novel that explores the psychic depths of two desperate secondary school teachers struggling to navigate a merciless society. Set against the backdrop of post-1997 Hong Kong, amid shifting social norms and language politics, Lau's striking debut novel compels readers to confront the voices of dissent that have been polished into excessively smooth, mirror-like surfaces. In Feeley's brilliant translation, Hong Kong's cultural and linguistic nuances are vividly brought to the fore."
—DOROTHY TSE, author of *Owlish*

"With fervor and aptitude, *Tongueless* portrays characters that are guileful and defenseless, repressed and vigorous. No matter what happens, they hold together both themselves and a world that is being wrenched apart by multiple forces. An enthralling novel."
—YAN GE, author of *Strange Beasts of China*

"Darkly gleaming with claustrophobic terror and pitch-black humor, *Tongueless* picks away at the surface of Hong Kong to reveal the festering tensions that lie beneath, and skillfully depicts the relentless pressures that ordinary Hong Kongers come under."
—JEREMY TIANG, translator of *Rouge Street: Three Novellas*

"A manifesto of language and morality. A psychological unraveling that reveals the ways we deceive ourselves and others. *Tongueless* is a slow-burn social horror that deftly captures the way human cruelty always returns to destroy its originator."
—MOLLY McGHEE, author of *Jonathan Abernathy You Are Kind*

"Insightful and investigative, Lau Yee-Wa explores the searing politics of a threatened tongue in Hong Kong with tact, terror, and empathy. She evokes a dangerously competitive world fueled by success, shopping, inflation of housing prices, educational hierarchy, and social status. It's a timely portrayal of a city that has experienced a seismic shock and is grappling with the consequences of irreversible change."

—KIT FAN, author of *Diamond Hill*

TONGUELESS
LAU YEE-WA

TRANSLATED BY JENNIFER FEELEY

THE FEMINIST PRESS
AT THE CITY UNIVERSITY OF NEW YORK
NEW YORK CITY

Published in 2024 by the Feminist Press
at the City University of New York
The Graduate Center
365 Fifth Avenue, Suite 5406
New York, NY 10016

feministpress.org

First Feminist Press edition 2024

This book is made possible by the New York State Council on the Arts with the support of the Office of the Governor and the New York State Legislature.

ART WORKS.

This book is supported in part by an award from the National Endowment for the Arts.

First printing June 2024

Cover design by Sukruti Anah Staneley
Text design by Drew Stevens

Library of Congress Cataloging-in-Publication Data
Names: Yee-Wa, Lau, author. | Feeley, Jennifer, 1976- translator.
Title: Tongueless / Lau Yee-Wa; translated by Jennifer Feeley.
Other titles: Sat Jyu. English
Identifiers: LCCN 2024003354 (print) | LCCN 2024003355 (ebook) | ISBN 9781558613188 (paperback) | ISBN 9781558613195 (ebook)
Subjects: LCGFT: Thrillers (Fiction). | Novels.
Classification: LCC PL2972.3.E49 S3813 2024 (print) | LCC PL2972.3.E49 (ebook) | DDC 895.13/6--dc23/eng/20240312
LC record available at https://lccn.loc.gov/2024003354
LC ebook record available at https://lccn.loc.gov/2024003355

PART 1
WAI AND LING

I t was as if nothing had happened.

Summer vacation had passed, and Wai's cubicle remained untouched. Even the custodian hadn't asked about it. A perfectly ordinary seat, a desk full of exercise books, a pen holder packed with red pens, a partition tacked with scattered notes in Mandarin pinyin romanization, reminiscent of a poor bird whose feathers had been plucked from its body. What stood out was that the area was extremely neat, the exercise books on the desk arranged by height from tall to short, each angle precisely ninety degrees. Similarly, the pens in the pen holder were categorized by color: red in front, black and blue in back, resembling a national flag from a distance. Although it had been two months since anyone had sat there, there wasn't a speck of dust on the surface of the desk. Another peculiarity was that Wai's desk and bookcase were covered in mirrors—a small round convex surveillance mirror, a mosaic-studded vanity mirror, a small mirrored decorative box, and on and on, all of them connected like one mirrored sea. Even the four sides of the computer screen were besieged by mirrors, leaving only a small rectangular frame. Ling had always wondered: when Wai turned on the computer, what else could she see other than her own image?

Wai had died by suicide on the first day of summer break. News of Wai's suicide had generated a lot of buzz. Facebook comments flew everywhere, and the foreign media scrambled

3

to report it. It was absolutely spine-chilling, bloodier than a family massacre—surely it would be selected as one of the top ten news stories at the end of the year. There were people online using the incident to promote their own views, calling for the government to advocate for smaller class sizes and abolish the territory-wide system assessment and contract teacher system . . . The teachers' office, however, was like a sealed-off structure; no one mentioned Wai unless they absolutely had to. At the start of the new school year, as she'd done previously, the head of the department reviewed past papers of the International English Language Testing System (IELTS) exam during her free period. Miss Wu and Miss Ip huddled together to browse the gossip pages, information on group buying, and pet photos. The other Chinese-language teachers had their hands full teaching classes, issuing announcements, disciplining students, contacting parents, grading homework, and planning lessons. No one had time to think about what had happened to Wai—everyone had long forgotten this person, except for her mirrors.

In the Sing Din Secondary School teachers' office, colleagues who taught the same subjects sat together, forming their own communities. None of the colleagues in the Chinese department could bring themselves to look at Wai's mirrors. The array of mirrors reminded the head of the department of the Eight-Trigram battle formation, giving off an evil aura that made her scalp tingle at the very sight. Miss Au, who sat behind Wai, was separated from her cubicle by a corridor. Whenever she sat down, she scooted her swivel chair forward, unable to feel at ease until her body was pressed tightly against her desk. The other teachers steered clear of Wai's seat whenever possible, as though something ominous would happen if they got too close.

Ling was the one who sat closest to Wai. Their seats were

divided only by a partition the height of half a person. Each afternoon, Wai's sea of mirrors reflected the piercing glare of sunlight. Whenever she passed by Wai's seat, even if she avoided looking at her mirrors, Ling nevertheless felt countless oncoming blades dismembering her entire body. Even on cloudy days, she deliberately kept her head down, but the light from the mirrors still flashed in her peripheral vision like the useless tail of a gecko that remained in place even after the gecko had scurried off, giving a false impression of power.

But no one ever considered clearing out Wai's cubicle, Ling included. They just wanted it to be out of sight, out of mind.

At the end of August, the principal attended lunch with the Chinese department as usual. Ling hadn't seen her all summer break; the principal's mood didn't seem to have been affected by Wai's suicide. The school was on a hill, with only a public-housing-estate shopping mall nearby. There used to be many dining options, including a cart noodle stall, a cha chaan teng, and a Chinese restaurant, but several years earlier the shopping mall had been acquired by Link Real Estate Investment Trust, leaving only a Western and a Japanese restaurant from which to choose. The other eateries had all been replaced by chains. However, the mall renovations had little impact on colleagues in the Chinese department. All along, they'd solely patronized the Western restaurant, because the principal preferred Western food. As each lunch cost at least 80 HKD, students rarely ate there, so they could let their hair down and talk freely. They sat in the innermost corner of the restaurant, chatting about students, stocks, and the property market, their laughter rising and falling. The principal poured a glass of red wine as she told them about a new real estate project in Huizhou.

"Rumor has it that Huizhou City will merge with Shenzhen, and the Huizhou property market will continue to rise." The principal was in her fifties, with short hair, the flesh around her mouth sagging down to her chin, the Valentino studded sheepskin handbag placed on the seat softly slouching against her waist—just by glancing at it, it was obvious that it was the latest model.

"Congratulations, Principal! You must be raking in the dough!" The head of the department raised her glass and clinked it against the principal's.

"Just a few hundred thousand, not that much."

While the head of the department was talking to the principal, the other teachers' perpetually smiling mouths quickly finished chewing so that they could join the conversation once the principal was done speaking. Ling rushed to interject, "Principal, do you have any interest in land speculation? Recently, it's been more lucrative than property speculation. One piece of land can change hands for more than two million dollars. I heard that the land in Hangzhou is the fastest-rising among all the major Chinese cities."

Ling had learned this tidbit from her mother. The principal liked real estate, and it so happened that Ling's mother ran a subdivided flat business and was familiar with a number of real estate brokers, who often slipped her inside information that even people paying attention to the property market may not have known. Ling had hoped the principal would say, "You know so much." Then her colleagues would chime in, surprised, "Ling really knows everything." But that day, everyone just bowed their heads and ate, the scraping of knives cutting back and forth on plates as clear as a scream.

After a while, the principal broke the silence. "The lasagna is delicious."

The head of the department said, "It tastes so different from ordinary lasagna."

The principal and head of the department took turns

speaking, discussing the cheese in the lasagna. Everyone shared which brands of cheese they'd tried. No one paid attention to Ling. Ling smiled and nodded at each statement, replying *mm-hmm*, but her smile was like ice-encrusted meat that had been hidden at the bottom of the freezer for so long that people had forgotten it.

It was as if nothing had happened, but things kept following the trajectory of the past. Since Wai's death, Ling's life had changed drastically. She felt as though Wai's words and actions were enshrouding her like a fog. All she saw was a vast expanse of white, without a starting or ending point.

Ling wanted to forget Wai, but the sea of mirrors, the blood, and the electric drill with the flashing red light would reappear in the blink of an eye, crossing over the half-person-high partition. Ever since Wai died, she rarely got a good night's sleep. Gazing at the orange light halo projected on the ceiling from outside the window, she recalled the thick ripples that spattered when Wai collapsed into the pool of blood. Even when she was sleeping, the rumble of the electric drill just before Wai died still echoed in her ears, startling her awake.

Wai clearly killed herself. She was her, I am me—what do I have to do with any of it?

SUNLIGHT DARTED THROUGH the transom window, fanning across Ling's and Wai's seats, slanting to the floor. The air conditioner didn't have enough horsepower—Ling couldn't stop sweating, the test papers on her desk wrinkling with wet spots. She wanted to go to the kitchenette to pour a glass of ice water. The kitchenette was far away from her seat, requiring her to pass by Wai's cubicle. Carrying a water glass, Ling took a roundabout route, heading toward her colleagues in the math department, then turning toward the kitchenette.

She came back the same way. As soon as she sat down, she leaned into her desk, lowering her head to avoid the reflected sunlight.

She took a sip of water. It had become hot before it even reached her throat. This semester was going to be brutal. It was only September, and the principal had already announced that she wanted to do an assignment check, reviewing teachers' grading of student homework. Last time she'd checked, the principal hadn't been satisfied, criticizing Ling's sloppy work. She had to do well this time. Her desk was cluttered with test papers from her Form 4 class and essays from her Form 5 class, her computer screen displaying the lesson plans for her upcoming course observations. Ling was a wreck—half of her two free periods had passed, and she'd only written two sentences in the teaching objectives column.

She couldn't concentrate. Her gaze shifted from the computer screen to her desk. Exercise books were strewn everywhere, the keyboard surrounded by papers, a few red pens tossed on top, the mouse swallowed up among all the papers, nowhere to be seen. There was too much work, too much multitasking, and her desk was an absolute mess. Ling decided to set her work aside, neatly stacking the exercise books, tucking the red pens back in the pen holder, and placing the papers on the file rack. After a while, the desktop returned to its original off-white color.

After all this physical activity, Ling was even hotter. The sun had shifted westward, and the sunlight projecting from Wai's mirrors was unavoidable. Ling's head was throbbing. Suddenly, a staff member informed her that someone was calling for her. It was a call she didn't want to answer.

"Hello. May I ask, is this Miss Ng Tsz-Ling?"

A young-sounding female voice was on the other end. She assumed it was a parent calling.

"I'm a reporter for the *Mango Daily*. I'd like to ask you about Miss Yu Bat-Wai."

At the sound of Wai's name, her whole body trembled as though an electric current coursed through her. "I'm sorry, I'm rather busy—"

"It's only a few questions. I won't take much of your time. I just want to learn more about Miss Yu."

"I'm sorry, I'm really very busy—"

"Rest assured, your interview will be anonymous."

When the reporter said the two words "rest assured," she deliberately raised her tone, so it was similar to the tone Ling used when comforting parents. Ling hesitated. The reporter continued, "What kind of teacher was Miss Yu?"

"Hmm . . . a good teacher, very hard-working. She gave everything her best," Ling responded coldly, hoping that the reporter would pick up on her impatience, but before she'd even finished the reporter followed up, "For example?"

"She graded essays on time. Look, I'm rather busy—"

"What else?"

"The students said she finished grading their test papers very promptly . . ."

The handset emitted *uh-huh* sounds, and a keyboard simultaneously clickety-clacked. Ling had a hunch that the reporter was recording her. In fact, these things she'd mentioned were simply part of a teacher's job. You had to submit graded work at regular intervals for the principal to do assignment checks—not submitting on time was unacceptable; student achievements reflected your teaching progress—not preparing for class was unacceptable.

"Was Miss Yu on good terms with her students?"

"I don't know."

Ling had taught senior secondary, and Wai junior secondary, so they rarely worked together. But Miss Au, who also taught junior secondary, said that many students disliked Wai's class because it was boring, and she was fond of punishing students by keeping them after school to do their homework, and . . . she was *weird*. The Hong Kong students made fun of her and teased her. Only the mainland students liked her. Rumor had it that Wai was especially kind to them.

"Was Miss Yu on good terms with her colleagues?"

"I wasn't close to her."

"Was Miss Yu . . . particularly unhappy before her suicide?"

"Can you ask someone else? I'm sorry, hold on."

The more she spoke, the hotter Ling felt. She set down the handset, stood up, and aimed the wall fan directly at herself. She took out a tissue and dabbed the sweat from her forehead, light brown foundation staining the paper. The handset emitted *uh-huh* sounds. She was annoyed and just wanted to hang up. How was she supposed to answer the reporter's questions? Say that Wai was a serious and boring person? Say that no one liked Wai when she was alive? Why did the reporter have to ask *her*?

Wai was a weirdo. Last August, on her first day of work, the head of the department had escorted her to her cubicle, which happened to be next to Ling's. The department head was in her forties, clad in a Céline blouse and pencil skirt, the typical outfit for a Chinese-language teacher. Ling wondered whether she'd recently undergone a thread lift—it was as if her facial expressions were propped up by metal needles, like a newly opened folding fan, her smile buried among the folds, giving the impression of someone who held her cards close to her chest. A short woman trailed behind her.

"This is Miss Yu." The department head moved out of the way, allowing Ling to size up her new colleague. A mushroom head. A wide gap between her bangs and eyebrows. Two drooping brows. Thick-rimmed glasses perched on the bridge of her nose. A black suit paired with leather shoes similar to the ones worn by schoolgirls.

"Ling's been teaching here for ten years. She's very experienced. If you have any questions, you can ask her."

Ling waved her hand and briskly said "Hi" in English.

"I'm Wai. It's a pleasure to meet you." When Wai spoke, her eyebrows drooped so much that they looked like they were about to slide right off her face.

The department head said a few words and set down some folders. Wai was deferential, nodding in agreement, as was common for newly hired faculty members. Ling already knew

11

that this new instructor would be teaching junior secondary and there wouldn't be many opportunities to work together in the future, so, after the department head left, she didn't strike up a conversation, and instead kept her eyes glued to her computer screen. Wai sat down. Soon, the partition between Ling and Wai started shaking, and Ling heard the rustling of plastic bags. She was trying to organize her notes for her senior secondary classes and couldn't help but be distracted. Glancing over, she saw Wai holding a slip of paper in one hand, the other hand picking up a thumbtack from a small dish filled with them. At first, Ling assumed it was a school calendar or family photo. Upon closer inspection, she realized it was a slip of paper inscribed with Mandarin pinyin romanization.

Wai firmly pinned the paper to the partition and, slightly embarrassed, said in Mandarin, "I'm studying Mandarin."

What a weird opening. New hires usually tried finding common ground to get to know everyone, but this teacher clearly didn't plan on saying much to her—she only told her a fact, and an awkward one at that.

When Ling didn't say anything, Wai lowered her head and softly spat out, "Are you okay with Mandarin?"

"Huh?"

Wai's throat twitched. "From now on . . . can we speak Mandarin?"

Ling didn't understand what was happening. Before she could respond, Wai had already continued, still speaking in Mandarin.

"You can only learn a language well by creating an immersive language environment. I often tell this to my students." But Wai's voice quivered. She'd used the wrong tone for "creating" and hadn't curled her tongue.

In her ten years of work, Ling had never encountered a new

colleague who asked her to speak Mandarin on the first day of employment. Wai rubbed her hands and kept on talking. "Whether studying English or Mandarin, Hong Kong people are always in a *female* . . . no, I mean an *in*—yes, an *infer-ior po-position*. We have no opportunities to listen or speak, so we always study . . . It's not good. If possible, I'd like to create a Mandarin-speaking *en-fry*—no, *en-vi-ron-ment*. This is the only way to speak as well as those whose mother tongue is Mandarin." Wai spoke extremely slowly, repeating the words she had difficulty pronouncing multiple times, as though she were coughing up each syllable from her throat.

Ling struggled to understand her.

"Oh . . . I'm not used to speaking Mandarin."

"Then I'll just speak it and you can speak in Cantonese." Wai peered at her, her eyebrows knitting together and furrowing into an upside-down V shape.

Not wanting to get involved with her, Ling said, "You . . . really know how to crack a joke."

"I'm not joking. I'm serious."

"But I'm really not used to—"

"So, it can be just me who speaks it."

Ling wanted to protest that her Mandarin wasn't good. She didn't teach in Mandarin at school—mainland students would ask her questions in Mandarin, and she'd answer in Cantonese. But as a Chinese-language teacher, how could she admit that her Mandarin wasn't good? She uttered a perfunctory noise, then turned around and resumed staring at the screen on her desk. Wai clearly assumed Ling had agreed, and kept telling her thank you. She was such a weirdo—Ling decided it was best not to engage her.

The partition shook for a while and then stopped. Ling thought that Wai had finally settled down, but before long more noise floated over the partition. This time, it was a continuous stream of a sharp, thin voice. It was grating on Ling's nerves. She raised her head, and was taken aback: Wai had tacked up notes in pinyin throughout her cubicle, English letters and the four tone marks stretching as far as she could see. And there was a Mandarin textbook on Wai's desk. She had covered the phonetic portion with her hand and was reciting the words aloud.

"Am I bothering you?" Wai asked.

Ling wanted to say, "Please keep it down a little," but she thought, they'd only just met, and it wouldn't be very polite to say that, plus she had to sit beside her for the next year, and she didn't want to make their relationship awkward. When Ling didn't reply, Wai quickly said, "Sorry, sorry . . ."

High-heeled shoes click-clacked behind them. The department head had returned, to inform Wai which classes she'd be teaching and where the reference books were located. Wai stood up. "Okay, okay," she said—in Mandarin, but the department head didn't seem to notice. After she'd finished speaking, the department head picked up her folders. Before leaving, she asked Wai, "Is there anything you don't understand?"

"No. Thank you."

Stunned, the department head squinted at her. Wai hastened to add, "Um . . . um . . . my Mandarin isn't good, so I want to practice speaking it more often." Looking perplexed, the department head muttered, "Do as you like" in Mandarin, then returned to her seat.

The head of the department had graduated from the Peking University Chinese department. She spoke the most orthodox Mandarin of all the teachers, scoring a grade of Level 1-B on the Mandarin Proficiency Test (PSC), perfectly pronouncing that single phrase "Do as you like" in a standard Beijing accent. By contrast, Wai's Hong Kong accent was jarring.

After a while, the head of the department came back. "I

thought you should know that Sing Din Secondary School doesn't use Mandarin to teach Chinese."

"I know . . . I'll use Cantonese in class. My Mandarin isn't good, I can't use it to teach. I just want to practice . . ."

The department head left before she could finish. Wai watched her retreating figure with admiration in her eyes, waiting until the department head was far away before she took her seat. Upon seeing this, Ling was dumbfounded. Wai shyly smiled at Ling, then sat down and continued studying. Ling exchanged glances with her other colleagues. Miss Au, who taught junior secondary, sat with her mouth wide open, and Miss Wu, who taught senior secondary, covered her mouth and snickered, but Wai didn't notice.

The Chinese department planned on having a welcome lunch for Wai. Half an hour before it was time to eat, Ling asked everyone in the WhatsApp group if they were going to the "usual place." The principal only patronized that one Western restaurant, so she didn't need to ask, but she did so anyway to be polite and seem democratic. Ling posted the latest OpenRice food reviews in their WhatsApp group chat—recently, many diners had recommended the restaurant's escargot. Ling encouraged her colleagues to order it that day, "So that our new colleague can try new tastes." The principal sent two thumbs up, and her colleagues followed suit.

Shortly before lunchtime, Ling turned off her computer and stretched. As soon as the bell rang, she picked up her handbag and walked over to Wai, illuminating the photo of the snails on her iPhone screen. "Let's eat together. The food is really good."

Wai didn't hear her. Her hand was still covering the pinyin romanization in the textbook, her mouth humming as though she were chanting sutras. Ling tapped her on the shoulder and repeated, "Let's eat together."

Wai shrugged her shoulders and turned to face Ling, her expression frozen. After a while, still speaking in Mandarin, she said: "I . . . want to stay at school and study."

"You can study any time, but you have to eat."

"No. I brought my lunch."

No new colleague had ever brought lunch on the first day. Each person would first assess the situation, seeing whether people tended to dine out or stay at school, before making a decision. Although this didn't sit well with Ling, she didn't let her smile fall. "On the first day, everyone gets to know each other . . . the food is really good. Even the *principal* likes it." Ling deliberately emphasized the word "principal."

"No thank you."

Before Ling had even dropped her hand that was holding the phone, Wai had turned her head away and resumed studying, not appearing the least bit sorry. Ling couldn't help but feel angry. She spun around and walked away. Up till the moment that the door closed, Wai remained hard at work, and didn't even say goodbye to her.

From that day on, Ling couldn't stand her. A know-it-all, different for the sake of being different, stubborn to the core, a pain in the neck.

LING GOT ALONG well with everyone at school. In an office full of women, name brands were a world language. The principal was fond of Valentino, the department head liked Céline, and other colleagues had their own preferences. Ling often prattled on about famous brands, such as where to score the cheapest handbags, where to resell them for the highest price, and the like. Her mother had previously been a hawker and had specialized in selling knock-off handbags, so, since childhood, she'd soaked up knowledge about all the major brands from Europe and the United States, from vintage to the latest style—there was nothing Ling didn't know. Moreover, her mother often asked her to buy designer handbags for her, and she always had a way to find the cheapest reseller. A group of women gathered together could gab about name brands all day.

Ling had her own views on name brands. Unlike the principal and department head, she didn't stick to the same brand. Yes, a brand could represent a person. Every time she walked into a Céline store, she thought of the department head. As soon as she learned that Valentino was launching their newest style, she'd inform the principal at once. However, she'd long believed that it wasn't the clothes that wore her, but that she was the one who wore the clothes. As long as they were complementary, different brands could look good together. It was all about taste.

In her spare time, Ling studied fashion magazines. She felt herself to be the best-dressed teacher in the school. School rules stipulated that female teachers could only wear closed-toe women's shoes, and slacks or skirts that were at least knee length, but even with these regulations Ling could still dress to the nines. She'd wear a floral dress paired with pointed-toe shoes, a khaki blouse with a vest and long skirt, a floral jumpsuit with French ballet flats . . . Students often compared her clothing combinations with those of other teachers. Whenever students she knew told her, "You're the only one who can carry off these clothes," she was in seventh heaven.

She was aware that there were people in the teachers' office who thought she loved dressing up too much, but clothes made the person. Who didn't like good-looking people? Besides, Ling wasn't naturally a beauty—she had to work at it. Clothing was a person's second skin; you had to package yourself well before you could sell yourself. After working for ten years, Ling had come to understand the perks of dressing up. Although she hadn't been promoted or given a raise, if she dressed smartly people would subconsciously have confidence in her.

However, the deeper reason why Ling liked dressing up was that her job was tedious. Day after day of teaching, grading assignments, attending meetings, on Monday looking forward to Friday, at the start of the semester dreaming of summer break, one batch of students after another graduating, their faces the only thing changing. The daily grind chipped away at teachers until they were reduced to only one type. Since life was so monotonous, why not add some color? Ling's motto was, *you are what you wear*. Whether you were mature, nonconformist, dull, or old-fashioned was reflected in what you wore—you could only stand out from the crowd based on how you were dressed.

Yet Ling never flaunted her fashion sense. When colleagues complimented her on how well she dressed, she gently brushed it off, pretending to be coy, and changed the subject to talk about food, wine, or travel. Rather than deliberately stick out and make others feel threatened, she tried her best to build strong relationships. Cultivating good interpersonal relationships was more important than a hard day's work on the job. Instead of showing off, she preferred discussing topics that everyone liked so that her colleagues would like *her*.

Aside from name brands, in recent years beauty and skincare were all the rage. Most of the teachers in the Chinese department were over thirty. They all understood that, no matter how fashionable their clothes or how expensive their handbags, such things only looked good when matched with a young face. And so, every time a new course of treatment was launched, such as HIFU, Sculptra, or hyaluronic acid injections, Ling would try it out and share her experience with everyone.

She still remembered how, just a few days after Wai had arrived at school, she'd been discussing her HIFU procedure with her colleagues. At the time, HIFU had just launched its first generation of treatments and many celebrity spokespersons raved about its lifting effects, so Ling went to the salon to try it out. Colleagues from the Chinese department gathered around to listen to her talk, as did curious female teachers from other sections.

"It hurts, it really hurts, the kind of pain that spreads from the skin to the roots of the teeth. I kept asking the aesthetician to be gentler."

"Was it effective?" the department head asked.

"See for yourself: The lines in my neck are much less visible." Ling stretched her neck. "However, you have to endure the pain. While it was happening, I was worried about getting burned. I heard that some people do HIFU for their cataracts." Although it did hurt, it wasn't as painful as Ling made it out to be—she'd intentionally exaggerated. Everyone "wow"ed in awe.

Wai happened to pass by at the time, and upon overhearing Ling's words, she squeezed into the crowd, her eyes widening. "Why do you . . . *ha-hat-hurt* yourself?"

Everyone looked at Wai and then back at Ling. Wai's reaction was over the top, and her Mandarin was so weird. Ling paused. "Are you worried I'm going to kill myself?"

One of her colleagues burst out laughing—she wasn't sure who—which made everyone else double over with laughter. Wai's face blazed so red that a rash broke out on her neck.

After everyone had been laughing for a while, Miss Chan, who taught economics, suppressed her laughter and tried to ease the awkwardness. "I couldn't do it. I'm terrified of pain." After she said that, she returned to her seat, and everyone else followed her lead.

Ling glared at Wai. "I'm just doing beauty treatments."

"I'm sorry . . . I always feel . . . it's not good to hurt your-self . . ."

Wai's hair is sticky, and her black-rimmed glasses look like they've been smeared with a coating of fog. She's a teacher who's as unkempt as a student. Where does she *get off criticizing* me *for doing beauty treatments?*

Wai glanced at Ling, lowering her head. "It seems *dung-arouse . . ."*

Wai's mispronunciation of "dangerous" made Ling even more impatient. Forcing herself to bite her tongue, she walked away without saying a word.

AT FIRST, Ling thought Wai only spoke Mandarin when making small talk. Then, a week before the start of the semester, the Chinese department held its first meeting of academic affairs to discuss the work arrangements for the coming year. The head of the department drew a chart on the whiteboard, with the Chinese department's annual activities written on the left, the column on the right awaiting the names of the corresponding teachers in charge. "Dear colleagues, please sign up," she said.

As soon as the department head finished speaking, Ling's hand flew up, volunteering for the Joint School Oral Exam. Ling had been in charge of this activity for five years. It only entailed one long day, unlike the debate team, special education tutorials, and school publications, which lasted more than half a year, plus the workload wasn't heavy—as long as students helped out, there wasn't much to prepare. Other colleagues signed up one after another, resuming their responsibilities from the previous year. In less than three minutes, the chart was full, except for the debate team. Everyone counted the names on the whiteboard and, discovering that Wai's was missing, they all turned to her. Wai lowered her head, avoiding their gaze.

"Wai, can you be in charge of the debate team?" the department head asked.

Wai started to wave her hand in refusal, then withdrew it. "I'm not good at *dupe-bait* ..."

The department head peered at Wai, whose face blushed crimson. "I must've misspoken. I don't know how to say *dupe-bait* in Mandarin—"

"Just speak Cantonese," the department head interrupted. Everyone howled with laughter.

"No ..." Wai stumbled over her words, unable to speak.

The department head cut her off. "Wai, you're in charge of the debate team."

Wai shook her head, but the department head ignored her and wrote down her name in the space for the debate team. The head of the department had always been in charge of the debate team. The workload was heavy, and the procedures were tedious. Naturally, the department head was eager to palm it off on someone else as soon as possible—now that someone new had arrived, wasn't this the perfect opportunity?

After going over each person's job, the department head snapped a picture of the whiteboard, then picked up her folders and left the conference room. As soon as the door opened, the hot air rushed in from outside. Seeming to regain her senses, Wai couldn't help but gaze out the door; then she turned and looked up at her other colleagues, unsure of what to do.

Wai deserved being placed in charge of the debate team—who told her to immediately refuse and then sit there tongue-tied for an eternity? Her colleagues stared at her, speechless. Ling piped up, "Actually, during meetings, can you not speak in Mandarin? You can't express yourself, and we can't understand you clearly."

"I want . . . I want . . . to force myself to speak Mandarin all the time, except when in class . . ."

No one knew how to react. Wai took a breath. "It's not a problem. I believe that, as long as I speak Mandarin every minute and every second just like a *main-man-man-lander*, I'll be able to speak it well."

If she was going to be so insistent, it was useless to say anything. Ling shrugged, and turned around to leave. Other colleagues filed out with her, Wai's calls of "wait, wait" fading away.

From then on, the whole Chinese department disliked her. If she wanted to practice Mandarin, that was her business—why did everyone else have to bend over backward to accommodate her? Speaking Mandarin was fine, but she couldn't speak it well, and had to rely on sign language; she clearly had working ears and a working mouth, so why act like a deaf mute?

What irked Ling the most, however, was that she spoke Mandarin not only in meetings, but also with the principal. Once, the principal showed up in the teachers' office with several folders, looking for the head of the department. The head of the department was busy writing down key points and seemed to be dealing with an urgent matter. Wai happened to pass by and saw the principal. She patted her on the shoulder, speaking loudly in Mandarin and bowing ninety degrees. "Hello, Principal." The principal couldn't help but be taken aback, exchanging glances with the head of the department. She quickly pasted a formulaic smile on her face. "Miss Yu, have you adjusted to school life?"

The head of the department impatiently thumbed through the files on the desk, explaining to the principal in Mandarin,

"Miss Yu is practicing her Mandarin." Then she turned to Wai and asked, "Have you finished the work in hand?"

"I have. I came over to say hi to the principal."

"To be a Chinese teacher, knowing how to speak Mandarin is certainly a must." The principal smiled, smoothing things over.

"Yes. I'll give it my best."

The principal no longer paid Wai any heed, and resumed her conversation with the department head, but Wai stayed put until the principal left, bidding her farewell, and focusing on her departing figure until the door of the teachers' office closed.

Teachers didn't salute the principal, only students did. And what did she hope to gain by speaking Mandarin all day long—was she angling for a promotion? Better classes next year? Ling had to keep her eye on this one.

At 3 p.m., the sunlight stretched wider and wider, but the heat never waned. Ling sat beneath a fan, her chiffon Céline blouse drenched with sweat. She couldn't resist unbuttoning it to let the air flow in.

Sounds of *Hello? Hello?* still rang out from the office phone. Ling had nothing more to say to the reporter.

Everyone knew that what the principal cared about most was the reputation of the school. She'd explicitly said that teachers weren't allowed to discuss Wai, and that neither teachers nor students were allowed to accept interviews, let alone teachers or students giving interviews to the media. Even if the reporter claimed to keep her anonymous, if she kept on talking, the reporter would link Wai's suicide to the school and make a big deal out of things, which would be of absolutely zero benefit to the school. If the principal suspected Ling had been in touch with a reporter, she'd have even more misgivings about her. She couldn't afford to lose any more of the principal's trust—she'd emerged from her office just fifteen minutes earlier. "I'm concerned about your career . . ." Recalling the principal's expression and how she didn't say goodbye before she left, Ling shook her head, not wanting to think about it any longer.

In any case, it was better to look the other way than to stick her nose where it didn't belong. Wai hadn't committed suicide at the school, nor had she left behind a note—who knew why she'd taken her own life? As long as no one said a word, it wouldn't circulate. Hong Kong people were very forgetful.

Ling took a deep breath and picked up the phone, determined to hang up. The tapping of a keyboard drifted through the microphone. Probably the reporter had been waiting so long that she was doing other work. "I don't have time," Ling said.

"I'm sorry, but my deadline's fast approaching—can you help me?" The clickety-clack of the keyboard sounded loudly as the reporter spoke.

If I help you, who'll help me? The principal will certainly be displeased if she finds out I gave an interview. "Why me? Why not another colleague? I'm sorry, but I can't help you."

"I've phoned all the teachers. No one was willing to be interviewed. The head of the department, Lo Syut, said you were close to Miss Yu. Please . . ."

The head of the department.

Ling glanced in the direction of the department head's cubicle. The department head had just gone to the kitchenette. Her desktop was empty, a Starbucks tumbler on the left side, two picture frames in the middle—one displaying a photo of her daughter, the other a photo of her with the principal. Two IELTS books of practice papers were placed near the computer screen, the English letters on the spine extremely conspicuous. Ling felt something was off—here she was working herself to death, while the head of the department had time to brush up on her English. Did the department head have so much time on her hands that she'd ratted her out—

The reporter's voice broke her train of thought. "This is my first feature article. My boss is very demanding. If I can't write it, I'll be sacked. I don't want to lose my job so soon."

Ling wanted to say, *That has nothing to do with me—I can't even take care of myself.* However, upon hearing "I don't want to lose my job so soon," she felt a pang of sympathy. Over the last ten years, though it hadn't completely been smooth sailing, she'd never encountered a tempest in the workplace. Even though her workload doubled this semester and the principal suddenly raised the requirements, she had been confident that she could survive. But just now, after leaving the principal's office, she suddenly felt that keeping her job wouldn't be easy.

Ling was reluctant to hang up the phone. Before she could say anything, the reporter asked, "Was Miss Yu on good terms with school faculty and staff?"

"So-so."

"So-so." The reporter repeated her words, then resumed typing.

"Before Miss Yu committed suicide, had the principal reprimanded her?"

"I have no idea." Ling's hand holding the receiver was sweaty. She switched the phone to her other hand.

The keyboard kept clickety-clacking in the receiver. She didn't directly answer the questions but instead made the reporter search for clues. What was there to write about? Was she just making up fake news? The *Mango Daily* was a notoriously unreliable news source. "I didn't say anything. Why are you typing?"

"Uh . . . I'm adding supplementary information."

"Are you trying to imply that Miss Yu killed herself because she didn't get along with other teachers?"

"No. I'm just trying to figure out what happened. I haven't found enough information to write the piece."

"I don't like reporters making up fake news. If you end up fired, I can't help you."

"We have journalistic integrity. If I were making up fake news, I wouldn't need to interview you."

The reporter had a point, but on second thought, even after

the interview she could still distort interviewees' statements and make false claims. But this wasn't what concerned Ling.

"You're anonymous. How do I know you won't disclose my identity?"

"Of course I won't. Everyone's just trying to make a living. I don't want you to get in trouble with the principal. If I write something incorrect, you can file a complaint with the Hong Kong Journalists Association. My name is Wong Wai-Yee. 'Wong' with three strokes, as in 'king,' 'Wai' as in 'favorable,' 'Yee' as in 'demeanor.' My phone number is 9856376."

Ling jotted the reporter's name and number on a notepad. She really knew how to talk. Subconsciously, Ling found her a bit slippery. "Once the article's out, what's the use of filing a complaint?"

The reporter named Wong Wai-Yee deliberated for a moment. If she wasn't making up fake news, she could've confidently refuted her. Was she feeling guilty now?

"After I finish writing it, I'll send it to you to proofread before it's published. Would that be okay?" the reporter said.

Although Ling had never worked as a reporter, she knew that a reporter wouldn't share a draft with an interviewee. If the interviewee disagreed with what the reporter had written and asked for additions or deletions, it would slow things down. Who would unnecessarily hold themselves back? Hong Kongers were clever. Ling was also clever.

"I'd be a fool to trust you." Ling hung up the phone.

The reporter named Wong Wai-Yee reminded her of Wai. Like the reporter, Wai had been a newcomer. When she came to Sing Din Secondary School, she'd only been in her second year of teaching. Young people just entering the workplace always strived to show off at all costs, eager to maintain their position and gain recognition from others.

Even as early as September, no matter whether it was a small break, lunch hour, or after school finished, Wai constantly shuttled back and forth between the teachers' office and the classroom, never sitting down for a second until 6 p.m. when she finally returned to her cubicle, where she proceeded to memorize pinyin for a bit, then grade homework and tackle various chores. Ling finished work at 6 p.m. every day, passing by Wai's drooped head, her hair fluttering underneath the desk lamp; according to the custodian, Wai didn't leave until eight thirty each night, and she had to be the first teacher to arrive at school each morning. Was that an exaggeration? When Ling first started, she didn't work overtime in September— it wasn't until October and November that she put in more hours. Likewise, none of her other previously new coworkers worked frantically in September.

Not only did Wai devote herself to her work, but Ling noticed her cubicle was extremely tidy. The notes in pinyin on the partition board were all the same size, with no gap between them. The thumbtacks were all red, from a distance resembling hundreds of cabinets in a medicinal herb shop. The exercise books on the desktop were arranged from tallest to shortest, each group the same height. No matter how many exercise books there were, she could always make space on her desk. In contrast, Ling's desk was a mess, with papers piled everywhere, files on her bookshelf tilting every which way. There were two bags of unpacked miscellaneous items crammed beneath the desk, leaving only a narrow slit for her to squeeze in her legs.

Every time Ling passed by Wai's cubicle, she was disgusted, always feeling that the person sitting beside her was a cleanliness-obsessed geek. After completing a task, Wai would line up the exercise books and tidy up the pens in the pen holder, putting everything back in its original place before moving on to the next task with confidence. Whenever the principal came into the teachers' office, Wai would pick up her glasses cloth and wipe the top of the desk, checking over and over that the exercise books were neatly stacked and arranged according to height. When the principal passed by, Wai would stand up and put her hands behind her back, like a shop clerk showing merchandise to a customer.

From large tasks to small details like her desktop, Wai was constantly showing off. *Pfft, the principal won't like you just because you work hard and keep your desk neat!*

However, what Ling hated the most wasn't Wai showing off, but her pretentious attitude, which was so fake. During her free periods, when Wai would correct assignments, or practice Mandarin until she was too tired, she'd tidy up her desk again, poking her head out of the partition and mumbling, "It's *horde lurk*. Being a teacher is really *horde lurk*."

Even her complaints were in Mandarin, as though she were wearing armor at all times, always ready for battle.

Ling glanced at her, then stared at the computer screen.

Wai continued, "Damn the education system! Damn the Secretary of Education!" Excitedly waving both hands, she accidentally knocked over the exercise books on her desk. Frazzled, she rushed to pick up the exercise books, repeatedly checking to ensure she hadn't left anything in disorder.

Not wanting to pay her any attention, Ling simply uttered a perfunctory "It is what it is."

"Why are Chinese-language teachers so much busier than other teachers?"

Ling thought to herself, *If you spent less time studying Mandarin and tidying up your desk, it wouldn't be such "horde lurk." Besides, it's your choice to be a teacher—how can it not be hard work being a Chinese-language teacher in Hong Kong?* For a math or science teacher, grading homework was simple: checking against the answer key, tick the right ones and cross off the wrong ones. For Chinese teachers, there were countless essays to grade, typos to circle, comments to write . . . Each essay took at least five minutes, and during testing week you had to take your work home, plus the Education Bureau changed the curriculum from time to time, and you had to prepare new lessons from scratch. But what could be done? Now that she had a teacher's salary, she'd have to bite the bullet and keep doing it.

Ling said nothing, hoping she'd shut her trap as soon as possible, but Wai heaved a sigh and said, "How many classes do you have today? I have seven. Tsui Siu-Hin in my 1D class got into a *vie-vie-fight*. I spent the whole class *hand-handling* it. After class, I had to call his *pah-pah-parents* and talk for an hour. It's really *horde lurk*. You teach senior secondary—there should be fewer problems maintaining order . . ."

In fact, Ling only had four classes that day. There were always fewer senior secondary classes, and as the students progressed to senior secondary they concentrated more on studying, so keeping order wasn't a big problem. It took Ling a while to answer her. "Everyone has their own hardships."

Teaching senior secondary was also stressful. The pass rate for the Diploma of Secondary Education Examination, also known as the DSE, had to meet a certain level every year in order to satisfy the principal's requirements. But Ling understood how to allocate her time, knowing when to work hard and when to relax. Not like Wai, who complained that things were hard and that she hated the education system, yet strived to show off—how hypocritical.

Ling fished her iPhone from her handbag and plugged in the earbuds to block her ears, but just when the earbuds were almost to her ears, Wai added, "Actually . . . don't I teach the most classes in the Chinese department?"

Was she done talking?

"Miss Au and Miss Ko both teach junior secondary. I know they are very busy—everyone works hard."

Before Wai's arrival, Miss Au and Miss Ko had selected the elite and better-behaved classes, but Ling didn't say that.

"Everyone *lurks horde*. But I have to work even harder . . ." Nodding her head, Wai turned her swivel chair back to her desk.

Wai was too unsophisticated, as was usually the case with newcomers in the workplace. From a young age Ling's mother had taught her that, to succeed in life, she needed to be clever and resourceful, and not rely on strength alone. Ling still remembered how after her very first week at work, she'd learned from the department head that the principal was a foodie, so every day she read food magazines, and after work tried out various restaurants, feeling this to be part of her teaching prep. Every time she went to the principal's office, she studied the storage cabinet behind the principal. Noticing it was always stocked with dried fruit, she ordered expensive

Japanese ones online and invited the principal to have some, and also shared them with her colleagues. In the WhatsApp group she was in with the principal and her colleagues, every now and then she shared food reviews from OpenRice. Sometimes when the principal came to the teachers' office in search of the department head, she'd drop by and chat with Ling, and Ling would always gather her colleagues around to join in. Since Ling's arrival, the principal and the Chinese department had gotten along better and better, and over time the principal began dining with the Chinese department whenever she was free.

Cultivating a good relationship with the principal was essential. Everyone saw that the principal was fond of Ling, and no one dared make her a scapegoat. Whenever she put forward suggestions during meetings, no one dared to oppose her. In her second year at Sing Din Secondary School, the head of the department assigned her to teach senior secondary classes, and they were all the cream of the crop, with a much lighter workload. Sometimes she left school before the end of the day, and no one dared to say a word. Of course, it was likewise important not to neglect building good relationships with her colleagues. She was careful not to let it go to her head—otherwise, everyone would just resent her. She wanted everyone to like her so that, whenever she ran into trouble, they'd be likely to help her.

How could Wai understand any of this?

Wai had been at Sing Din Secondary for two months and had never eaten a meal with the Chinese department. At first, Ling was irritated by Wai's ignorance of the ways of the school, but later she came to think of it as a good thing. Even now, she still recalled how last September, when the principal was dining with the Chinese department, she joked with her about Wai: "Today when I went to the toilet, Wai stood behind me, holding a piece of garbage, asking: 'Where do I throw it?' I thought it was strange, so I said, 'There's a garbage can right in front of you.' She told me, 'I don't know if I should say *garbage can* or *rubbish bin*.'"

Everyone laughed for a long time, and the principal even almost spat out her food. "I wanted to say, 'Are you asking, am I a pile of garbage, or a pile of rubbish?'"

She still remembered when she and Wai were standing next to the trash can in the women's bathroom. Ling was using the hand dryer when she happened to see a cockroach heading toward Wai. She intended to warn her, but before she even opened her mouth the cockroach had already crawled up the leg of Wai's pants, rubbing its hairy insect legs together, waving its two antennae from side to side. Wai stretched out her leg, and the cockroach played dead, but Wai was oblivious, fixated on the pronunciation of the word "garbage." Ling gasped, muttering, "I'm in a hurry," then ran out of the bathroom, the farther away from Wai the better.

"Wai's lost her mind." The department head dabbed at the tears in the corners of her eyes.

Everyone went on discussing other things about Wai, while the principal fell silent, cutting the steak on her plate into small cubes. She then pricked the steak cubes with her fork, putting them into her mouth. As she chewed, she spat out, "Working hard is always a good thing." At the time, everyone was too busy laughing and didn't pay attention to what the principal said; Ling heard it, however, wondering what she meant, but quickly let it go. Now, Ling often thought about this sentence, along with the cockroach crawling up Wai's pants.

WAI'S DILIGENCE WAS extremely over the top. The inter-class debate competition that she was in charge of wasn't a factor that affected her promotion, but nevertheless she began preparing three months in advance. Sometimes, Ling passed by Wai and saw her searching for information online, formulating topics for the students, and even writing up the pros and cons.

One day after school, at six in the evening, when half the fluorescent lights in the teachers' office were already turned off, Ling looped her handbag around her arm and got ready to leave work; but then she saw Wai standing next to the head of the department, holding a small notebook and frantically writing something down. The department head slung her bag over her shoulder, standing with her hands on her hips, helplessly watching Wai. Ling deliberately slowed her pace to eavesdrop on what Wai was saying—she was asking the department head about her experience organizing the debate team. Wai spoke slowly and inarticulately. The department head kept saying, "The details are up to you." But Wai ignored her and continued firing off questions.

Ling cast a sympathetic glance at the head of the department and left the office.

In the days that followed, Ling noticed Wai leaning close to the computer screen, squinting, searching for information about debating, her thick-framed glasses reflecting a greasy blue glow, sliding off the bridge of her nose every now and then.

Ling didn't want to meddle, but she couldn't bear seeing Wai work so hard on something so trivial. One day when she was heading out, she walked up to Wai and patted her on the shoulder. As though she'd seen a ghost, Wai let out a loud scream. Ling immediately regretted approaching her, and reluctantly said, "You don't have to work so hard."

Wai looked at her quizzically.

"It's not an important project at all. You should focus on grading essays."

Wai finally understood, and couldn't stop giggling foolishly. "Today I have to deal with the task of the *dupe-de-bate* team, so *lass-last* night I didn't sleep. I stayed up *owl-all* night grading essays. I'm touched you care so much about me."

Ling shrugged and waved goodbye to her. When she left, there were no students on the school grounds. The sports field, surrounded by school buildings, was lost in the darkness, the lines on the basketball court unrecognizable. Ling walked toward the school gate, her handbag swaying. She glanced back at the transom windows still lit in the teachers' office, and couldn't help laughing. Would the principal really like Wai just because she put on a lively and colorful debate competition?

In the past, the head of the department had never prioritized debate competitions, only advising students, reserving classrooms, and purchasing trophies in her free time. When she met with students, she'd merely talk to each group for five minutes on Fridays after school, briefly giving a few suggestions. Last year, some students on the debate team had complained on the school's secret page that the head of the department was lazy and didn't carefully prepare them. They even went so far as to doctor a photo of the department head to mock her. The post received three hundred likes, and many students left comments, with some offering to provide dirt on her that would force the principal to fire her. When Ling read the post, she didn't dare forward it to the department head, afraid she'd be upset. Besides, most students used anonymous accounts, so there was no way to track them down. Other colleagues in the Chinese department also said nothing— Ling didn't know whether they'd seen it or not. It was Miss Chan, who taught economics, who uploaded a screenshot to the Chinese department's internal network group, seemingly to inform everyone in good faith. The students' parody image was a mash-up of the department head and a pig. Instead of being offensive, it made the serious head of the department look cute. At the time, Ling had wondered whether the department head would be embarrassed or angry. One day after school, the Chinese department gathered around the department head's cubicle for afternoon tea. The department head said, "The students are so foolish, thinking I'd be shocked by them making a picture."

Everyone exchanged glances. Miss Au, who taught junior secondary, was the first to speak. "I bet this was Tsui Siu-Hin's doing, talking like this is some insurrection. What an idiot."

Ling took a sip of milk tea and stole a glance at the department head, only to find her seeming calm and collected, her black silk Céline skirt without a single wrinkle. She tentatively asked, "The principal . . . Does she know?"

"Yes, of course she knows. I reported it to her myself." The head of the department took a bite of French toast, keeping her eyes fixed on the plate so the melted butter wouldn't stain her clothing. "After the principal saw it, she just laughed. It was no big deal. School activities won't win any awards—why would the principal care?"

Recalling the department head's intimidating way of responding to her, Ling couldn't understand why Wai was working herself to death. Wai had bought several books on debate, including *The Complete Works of Refutation*, *Five Lectures on Logic*, and *Introduction to Debate* . . . They were stacked higher than the partitions, blocking the light from the fluorescent tubes. Each day after grading assignments, Wai would open one of the books, highlight key points on the page, and jot down notes in a notebook . . . Was this person sitting next to her a teacher or a student?

But what was even more incredible was what was yet to come. One month later, posters were plastered all over the school, the words DEBATE COMPETITION printed in the middle of the white A4 paper, a few flowers added on the side for decoration—at first glance, it seemed normal, but the shocking content was at the bottom of the poster. Wai had divided the debate competition into Cantonese and Mandarin sections. All of the classes in the Cantonese section were required to participate, whereas students in the Mandarin section could freely choose whether or not to participate. The Mandarin section was obviously for mainland students, but the ratio of mainland to local students at Sing Din Secondary School was two to eight. How many people would actually participate?

Although Wai was responsible for all of the administrative work of the debate competition, the other Chinese teachers would still act as judges. Now that there was a Mandarin section, didn't that mean more work for the teachers for no reason? Moreover, Ling worried that, if she were assigned to be a judge for the Mandarin section, wouldn't she have to read out the results in Mandarin?

Upon seeing the posters, everyone crowded around, murmuring cries of "Is there a mistake?" one after another. Wai had taken too much initiative. It was one thing for her to strive to perform her best, but why drag other colleagues into this? After venting, everyone calmed down, but no one could come up with a solution. The posters had been circulated, all of the students knew, and the principal must've seen them by now.

The department head tapped Ling on the shoulder. "You sit closest to Wai. You know her best. Help us take care of this."

Ling glanced in Wai's direction. At the sight of Wai's mouth opening and closing as she silently recited pinyin, Ling had no desire to take even a half-step closer to her, but the other teachers stared at her expectantly. Miss Au and Miss Ip pushed her forward. Ling had no way to back down. Holding on to the poster, she walked over to Wai. "I saw you're holding a debate contest in Mandarin."

Wai looked taken aback, but when she saw it was Ling, she grinned. "Yes . . . It's fairer this way. Both Hong Kong and mainland students will be on *e-call-call-equal foot-footing.*"

For the sake of being "fair" to those two out of eight students, she's making herself and us suffer, Ling shouted in her mind. Most of the mainland students could speak Cantonese. Since they were living in Hong Kong, shouldn't they learn Cantonese? Why make special accommodations for them?

"The judging arrangements . . ."

"I'll take sole responsibility for *juh-juh-ding-judging* the Mandarin section. I was thinking, since I'm going to be *juh-juh-judging,* I can practice . . ."

Once again, it was about learning Mandarin!

Wai looked at Ling, who stared, tongue-tied. She scratched her head and laughed, then turned her attention back to her desk, flipping the pinyin textbook to another page.

The fan shattered the afternoon sun, scattering shards of light. Ling felt a sheen of oil on her face. Her foundation was melting off, so she pulled out her makeup bag for a touch-up. The woman in the mirror had powder stuck in her pores, the fine lines around her eyes spreading to the surface of the mirror like ripples, the liner on her left eye smeared and staining her lower eyelid. Ling poured out the contents of her makeup bag, the compact, blush, mirror, blotting paper, hydrating mist, and eyeliner spilling onto her desk. She spritzed on the hydrating mist, used tissue to wipe off the smudged eyeliner and powder, picked up the eyeliner pencil and lightly fixed things, then dabbed on some loose powder with a puff and added a little orange-red blush.

After touching up her makeup, Ling studied herself in the mirror. Whether viewed from up above, below her chin, or a 360-degree panoramic view, her face was unsatisfactory from every single angle. The bags under her eyes couldn't be concealed. Even with extra blush and contouring, the apples of her cheeks were soft and saggy, lacking any definition; moreover, her skin was too dry, the fine lines around her eyes even more prominent now that she had applied powder. Alas, the more makeup, the more flaws. It was no wonder—this year, her workload had increased greatly, and she wasn't getting enough sleep at night. It would've been strange if she *didn't* look older.

Ling had always felt her appearance was ordinary, but she'd never felt inferior. There were few truly beautiful women in the world, and not many ugly ones—you just had to know how to use makeup. Ling had started wearing makeup in junior secondary, and since then there hadn't been a day when she didn't wear it. Some people said that makeup meant you weren't confident in your own bare face, and one day, when people saw your real face, it would be like exposing the lie of the century. However, she'd also heard that many Japanese women never let their husbands see them without makeup after they got married. As long as the lie wasn't exposed, it wasn't a lie.

But today, at the age of thirty-four, she felt that makeup was useless. Ling had gotten up at four in the morning, put on a face mask, splashed on some facial essence, applied subtle makeup that enlarged her eyes, then spent time in front of her wardrobe piecing together different combinations until she settled on today's outfit, a Céline polka-dot chiffon blouse paired with white slim-fit pants. Before heading out, she'd turned around in front of the full-length mirror, feeling pretty confident, but at this moment she felt that, even though she'd touched up her makeup, her haggard face still ruined her entire appearance, and no matter how nice her clothes were, they were in vain . . .

Was it because she'd seen the principal today?

Thinking of this, Ling felt hot all over again, so she stood up and pointed the fan at her so that the strong wind hit her face directly. She closed her eyes and took a deep breath.

Someone was standing behind her. "That's a nice outfit. What's the brand?"

Ling turned around. It was the head of the department. She leaned toward Ling, as though to avoid Wai's army of mirrors.

The head of the department was a Céline aficionado—how

could she not know Ling was wearing the same brand as her? Clearly, she was trying to find something to say. Ling casually said, "It's all Céline, bought during the big sale."

Ling sized up the department head. Today she was wearing a high-collar drop-shoulder blouse paired with a string of white pearls. While she still looked conservative and scholarly, there was a hint of sophistication as well. In the past, Ling had felt that the department head dressed like a fifty-year-old auntie, with a forty-plus-year-old face. No matter how many beauty treatments she underwent, she still wasn't as young as Ling. Today, however, Ling felt inferior to her.

"What were you thinking so intently about, standing over there by *that person's* seat?"

The fan was between Ling's and Wai's seats. Only then did Ling realize she was standing closer to Wai's side. She immediately picked up something from Wai's desk. "I just wanted to grab a folder . . ." She randomly picked up what turned out to be the folder full of Wai's Mandarin notes.

"Oh, you want to practice your Mandarin?"

"Oops . . . I grabbed the wrong thing. I was looking for a junior secondary worksheet." Ling quickly put back the folder.

The department head nodded, looking as if she wanted to smile but the tight skin on her face prevented her from doing so. "How was your meeting with the principal?"

"How do you know about that?"

"I saw you coming out of her office just now."

The head of the department was pretending to be relaxed as she was speaking, but in fact she was probing at the truth. Ling wanted to escape as soon as possible. At that moment, her mobile phone vibrated on her desk. "Nothing special. Excuse me, I have to take this call," Ling said, then returned to her seat.

She picked up her phone. It was her mom. Ling didn't press

the answer button, she just placed the phone close to her ear and pretended to talk, leaving her mom to disconnect the call. She hadn't wanted anyone to know about her meeting with the principal and, of all people, the department head had seen her. On top of that, she had also picked up Wai's Mandarin notes in front of the department head by mistake—why was she so careless? Was she possessed? She took out a wet wipe from her handbag and rubbed her hands vigorously until she calmed down a little.

Ling looked around. All of her colleagues from the Chinese department were in class, except for the head of the department. No one else should know she'd just come from the principal's office. The department head turned and stared at her. Ling trembled slightly, and suddenly caught a glimpse of the cosmetics strewn across her desk. *Click-clack*. She gathered the makeup and tucked it back in her bag, zipping it up with a screech, and returned to her blank desktop.

At first Ling thought Wai was competing to climb to the top, but after spending more time with her she didn't find her to be overly ambitious, just . . . weird. Ling still remembered how, during exam week in November, she'd received eight stacks of test papers that she had to administer to students during a one-week period. That week, she worked overtime until eight o'clock every night, and Wai likewise stayed after school, working in the cubicle beside her.

The crescent moon outside the transom window rose higher and higher. The sound of Ling dashing off checkmarks on the test papers was too loud, surprisingly in tune with Wai's click-clacking on the keyboard. Ling's phone kept buzzing, the screen flashing her mom's message urging her to go home. Her mom wasn't easy to please—if she went home too late, her mom would give her the cold shoulder. Ling wanted to finish grading the test papers as soon as possible and head home, but the rollerball of her red pen suddenly sputtered, and after getting stuck a few times, no ink would come out. Ling tried two other red pens, but they wouldn't write either. She and Wai were the only two people in the office. She had to look around and borrow a pen from Wai.

Wai was writing a test paper, her cheek almost touching the computer screen. Ling cleared her throat and gently called her name, afraid she'd startle her again. This time, Wai wasn't startled, but turned around slowly. "Sorry. I fell asleep . . . I worked till three in the morning yesterday." Rubbing her eyes, she handed Ling a red pen.

Ling had never seen Wai so worn out, the upside-down V of her eyebrows flattened from exhaustion, her slipped-down glasses overlapping with her eyes, making it impossible to see the whites of her eyes and her irises. For the past three months, Wai had kept her nose to the grindstone, and there were times she couldn't keep up. Ling thanked her, then rushed to bury her head in her desk. She'd grade five more test papers, then head home.

Before long, Wai swiveled her chair toward Ling and stretched. "How . . . how many test papers have you graded?"

"Most of them. Three to go."

"So fast. I still have more than ten left. What should I do? I'm dying, dying." Wai held her head in her hands, her voice like gossamer. "So then . . . how many essays have you graded?"

"I'm done."

"I still have half left to grade—I'm dying . . . so . . . did you collect all the *trav-traff-travel* notices?"

"No."

"I did." Wai sighed in relief.

Ling thought it was funny. She thought of students comparing their grades, but this wasn't a test, it wasn't a competition.

Wai continued talking. "Alas . . . the principal at my last school didn't renew my contract because my work *place-pace* was too slow, and I didn't pass the LPAT." The LPAT—the Language Proficiency Assessment for Teachers, used by the Education Bureau to assess Chinese language teachers' ability to teach in Mandarin. "This year, I'm sleeping less and working faster, but . . . my biggest problem is my poor Mandarin. I failed all four papers of the LPAT. I must've been born without a talent for *lane-lane-languages* . . ."

Did Wai want to vent her grievances again? Ling didn't raise her head to respond. She finished grading a page, then sighed and flipped to the next one.

"What do you think is the best way to learn Mandarin well? I asked the mainlanders in my class to privately teach me, but they just laughed."

"Huh?" Ling put down her pen.

"Mandarin is their mother tongue. If I talk to them more, I can speak like a mainlander. But some students make fun of me. 'Go back to school, don't be a teacher . . .' That Tsui Siu-Hin, he laughs loudly in every class, *dis-disrupting* the classroom order . . ."

Was she kidding? The teachers taught the students—no teachers asked the students for guidance. If you didn't respect yourself, how could your students respect you? How could you maintain order in the classroom like this?

"I told them, if you learn Mandarin well, then you can learn Chinese well, because Mandarin is the same as the standard written Chinese *lane-language*, but that Tsui Siu-Hin *re-feud-feud-futed* me, saying that the students with the best grades in the Chinese class aren't from the mainland, that learning Chinese well has nothing to do with learning Mandarin well . . . No matter what I say, he claims I'm partial to mainland students."

Ling felt that this student was more sensible than Wai. Rumor had it there had been a student at Sing Din Secondary School whose parents were Hong Kongers and whose mother tongue was Cantonese, but after he started primary school, his parents forced him to speak Mandarin at home and forbade him from watching Hong Kong TV programs, only allowing mainland TV. However, most subjects in school were taught in Cantonese. As a result, there were some words he only knew how to pronounce in Cantonese, some only in Mandarin.

Each time he submitted his homework, the Chinese he'd written was awkward—he couldn't differentiate between the vocabulary and grammar in the spoken and written languages. His grades in Chinese were much worse than those of his Cantonese-speaking classmates. Moreover, there were many everyday things he didn't know how to express in Cantonese—he referred to eggplant as "aubergine" and zucchini as "courgette." Everyone thought he was weird and made fun of him behind his back. As a result, after two years he couldn't take it anymore and switched schools.

However, Wai was so stubborn that, no matter how Ling explained it, she still wouldn't get it.

When Ling didn't say anything, Wai lowered her head and poked at the edge of her blouse. "Actually . . . am I unfit to be a teacher?"

Only you know whether you're suitable or not—no one can answer that for you. Ling raised her hand and glanced at her watch. "Wow, it's already eight p.m. . . ."

"Will I not be able to renew my contract this year?"

"Uh . . . there are many factors that determine whether a contract is renewed . . . Go home early and get some rest. I'm off. You've got this!" Ling quickly tidied up, setting aside the uncorrected exams, and hurried away, leaving Wai, who was on the verge of tears.

Wai was just too strange, and she oozed tension. However, after reflecting on what Wai had said, Ling felt that she was a simple person who spoke without thinking. Nowadays, the majority of teachers were on a contract basis, and it was commonplace for contracts not to be renewed. No one would've known if she hadn't said anything, but not only had Wai told Ling, she'd also disclosed the reason for her dismissal in great detail, as though she was worried that Ling didn't understand how much of a failure she was. As for the

LPAT, there was no need to deliberately emphasize that. The truth was, Ling was in the same boat as Wai—she hadn't passed any of the four papers—but she would never ask her students to teach her Mandarin, let alone discuss her LPAT scores with others. Silence was golden, wasn't it?

WHEN LING TOLD Wai, "You've got this," it was just a perfunctory saying. She'd never imagined that the next day when she got to school, before she'd even set down her handbag, she'd find a small card on her desk with a Sugus candy on it. The small card was a little yellowish, embossed with a red ribbon. The English word "Congratulations" was written on top, and inside was Wai's handwriting. *Ling, thank you for encouraging me. You're my only good friend in this school. We've both Got This!* Next to the words "got this," she'd drawn a strong arm.

Ling couldn't help but laugh. *I didn't do anything—why thank me? Besides, she doesn't even know how to buy a greeting card—shouldn't she have given me a thank-you card?* Did anyone even still eat Sugus candy? It was probably leftover stock from New Year's. She gave the candy to one of her students, and the card was soon lost.

From then on, however, Wai regarded Ling as a good friend. She talked to her about everything and tried her best to treat her well. Whenever she had time, she refilled her water and tea. If she saw Ling stumble, she rushed to help her. She bought breakfast for her in the morning and heat patches for her when the weather turned cold. Ling told her many times that she could do these small things by herself, without Wai's help, but Wai still insisted on "waiting on" her. Wai did a good job, but in many cases it was actually a disservice. On several occasions, she held her attendance list in her left hand and gave Ling coffee with her right hand, the coffee almost spilling on

Ling. Another time, Wai took it upon herself to accept a paper on Ling's behalf, but it turned out to be a school assignment handed out by another teacher, and Ling had to explain the situation to the teacher herself.

One morning, Wai bought Ling her least favorite breakfast, a Spam and egg sandwich, the layer of Spam so thick and greasy that it soaked the white square bread yellow. Ling picked up the sandwich, but didn't throw it away, offering it to her colleagues instead. None of them wanted it, so she had no choice but to place it back on Wai's desk. "Really, you really don't need to help me anymore . . ."

"No, you eat it, don't be polite . . ." Wai pushed the sandwich toward her.

"I can do a lot of things myself. You have to work and study Mandarin. I don't want to bother you."

"No, I'm not good enough. I want to do better."

Not sure what to do, Ling picked up the Spam and egg sandwich. When Wai wasn't paying attention, she took it to the kitchenette and threw it in the trash.

However, eyeing the Spam and egg sandwich in the trash, Ling thought to herself, *Since Wai likes to serve me, I might as well indulge her. As long as she can handle the trouble, having a personal servant wouldn't hurt.* While Wai washed her water glass or made her coffee, Ling stole time to read fashion magazines and sneak onto Facebook. After a while, the pleasant aroma of coffee would waft into her nostrils, and she didn't even need to glance up and say thank you. Her colleagues tsk-tsked in amazement to see Wai "serve" Ling so tirelessly. Smiling, Ling said, "I don't have to pay a worker to serve me. Don't be jealous."

However, no matter what Wai did for her, Ling couldn't tolerate her touching her desk. One day, she came to school to find that her desk was unusually neat. All of her files were stacked, all of her red pens were placed in the pen holder, and all of her notes were pinned on the partition board—suddenly, her desk had become much longer. Ling cried out, "Where are my price quotes? Student announcements? And the notebook I just bought?"

Wai's droopy eyes poked out over the partition. "I put your non-school-related papers in the small *dryer-drawer* . . . and your stationery in the big *draw-drawer* . . ."

"Who asked you to organize my desk?" Ling yelled.

Wai quickly replied, "*Suh-sorry*, I saw your desk was dirty . . . I was afraid there were *gems-germs*, and you'd get sick . . ."

"My mess is my business—what's it got to do with you?"

Ling had long been infamous in the teachers' office for her messy desk. Sometimes her colleagues made fun of her desk, but she didn't care at all, and even laughed at herself. A few years back, the teachers' office had been renovated and the entire Chinese department relocated. She'd had no choice but to clean up all the clutter. It took her a few days to get settled into her current seat. At first, the surface of her desk was clean—stationery was put in drawers, and documents were kept in marked folders; but Ling always felt she was coming up empty-handed—it took forever to find a red pen, and the important announcements, notebooks, and magazines she regularly read seemed to have disappeared into the clouds, so within a week she'd messed up her cubicle.

In the past, no matter how messy her desk was, Ling had never lost anything, but now the empty desktop was driving her crazy. However, what made her the most uneasy was not knowing whether Wai had read her confidential documents. *A person's desktop is always the most private place—why'd you have to meddle?*

Wai looked apologetic, seeming on the verge of tears. Ling felt it meaningless to scold her again, so she set down her handbag and rushed to search for the previous appraisal reports, credit card receipts, and tenant contracts she'd brought from home that were hidden below her desk. Whew. Fortunately, Ling's cubicle was so cluttered that Wai had only tidied up the desktop, without rummaging through the various items beneath it. Ling hurried to lock the confidential documents in a drawer.

After that, Wai no longer touched Ling's desk and just performed various chores for her. Ling assumed everything was fine. One morning, she showed up with a Chanel patent leather handbag. Wai's eyes were glued to it. "Your bag is so pretty..."

Taking in her appearance, Ling looked down on her. She was dressed like a schoolgirl, with a white blouse, black pleated skirt, and even bangs that were deliberately cut short so as not to obstruct her vision. Ling glanced at the handbag, then hung it over the back of the chair, casually saying "Thanks" in English.

"I've read about *chenille's-Chanel*'s history. She started out with a *hot-hot-hat* shop, then later *divined-designed* women's sportswear, becoming a modernist icon..."

Wai was like a student regurgitating the content of a Wikipedia page to her teacher, and she spoke too slowly. Ling lost her patience. "I had no idea. I just know how to wear the stuff."

"I thought you bought it because you identify with modernism..."

Buying a handbag because of modernism? That was a first for Ling! She clicked on her computer to check her emails, ignoring Wai.

After that, these "name-brand discussions" happened almost every day. Upon seeing the department head wearing Céline shoes and the principal carrying a Valentino handbag, Wai spouted information about Céline's chief designer and explained why Valentino was popular in Europe and the US, blathering on about its history, blathering on with some analysis, boring Ling to tears. Ling once asked her, "Do you think there's a difference between me and the head of the department?"

Wai gave a roundabout reply. "You're both alike. You both like *fringe-French* name brands. I heard the reason there are so many famous *fringe-French* name brands is . . ."

They weren't alike! The department head and other Chinese teachers stuck to one brand and had no individual personality at all. In contrast, on Ling's body alone she had four different brands, including a Guess ruffled blouse, an agnès b. floral pinafore dress, a Tiffany & Co. red diamond necklace around her neck—today, she was aiming to create a sense of breaking free.

Wai was spouting off nonsense. Ling turned away, letting her talk to herself.

Other than designer brands, Wai also liked chatting with Ling about cosmetic procedures. One day during her free period, Ling was talking to the head of the department and Miss Au about double eyelid surgery. Although the head of the department and Miss Au both had double eyelids, they often referred to them as "inner double eyelids," which weren't as deep and pronounced as those of Westerners. Recently, Ling had read about the latest South Korean double eyelid surgery technology in a fashion magazine. Supposedly, there were few side effects and you could go back to work after the procedure. Thinking that the head of the department and Miss Au would be interested, Ling cut out the article and shared it with them. Sure enough, Miss Au said that the three of them should check it out together and see if they could get a discount. Ling was a big talker, but the truth was, she was hesitant. Although she had single eyelids, she'd been using eyelid tape to enlarge her eyes. Undergoing double eyelid surgery could save her some time applying makeup, but this was plastic surgery, which she had always had reservations about. For women, plastic surgery was considered a crime—what female celebrity would admit to having it? When people asked them whether they'd messed with their faces, female celebrities always claimed it was just makeup tricks.

After she was done talking to the department head and Miss Au, Ling went back to her cubicle. Even before she sat down, Wai said, "You want to do *dabble-dabble-double* eyelid surgery?"

At the sound of Wai's voice, Ling felt disgusted. *Why is she always eavesdropping on me?*

"I just found a lot of *infarmation* about how people who get *dabble* eyelid surgery can't close their eyes. I'll send it to you."

In the blink of an eye, Ling received an email from Wai full of photos of botched plastic surgeries. The eyelids in the pictures were badly mutilated, the threads buried in the flesh blackened and rotten, the eyes filled with red veins. *Now you're cursing me to end up like this?*

"I always feel . . . it's not good to hurt yourself . . . Those plastic *search-surgeries* all . . ."

The last time I brought up HIFU to my colleagues, she scared them away by telling me not to hurt myself. Beauty is about self-improvement—why is she calling it self-abuse? Most cosmetic procedures are handled by doctors. Double eyelid surgery is a minor procedure, with little chance of causing complications.

Also, I haven't even decided whether to have any procedures.

When Wai started listing the various side effects, Ling couldn't take it any longer. "Actually, do you really like beauty and luxury brands?"

"I just thought since you like them, I—"

"You're the one who 'hurts yourself'!" Ling picked up her cup and walked to the kitchenette, leaving behind a stunned Wai.

WAI DIDN'T SEEM to understand how to get along with people. She wanted to be friends with Ling and always tried to please her. Every now and then, Ling expressed her annoyance, but Wai ignored it, continuing to "serve" and "care for" her.

Sometimes Ling wondered, was Wai genuinely being all that good to her? Or was it merely an act, and she was the type of person who'd smile to your face and stab you in the back? Ling wanted to test her limits. One day before work was over, she walked over to Wai. "A family member was recently admitted to the hospital. I have to go there every day to take care of her. I'm so busy. I haven't done anything for the Joint School Oral Exam. It's coming up in two months. Alas, being a teacher is really *horde lurk*."

"Is your family member okay?" Wai asked.

"Fortunately, it's just the early stages of cancer. She needs to stay there for observation . . ."

"That's so sad . . . Are you all right? How are you handling it?"

"Not so well . . . Do you think you can help me?"

"Of course! I'll help you prepare. Don't worry."

"I'm swamped. Do you really think you can help me finish all the work?" Ling emphasized "all the work."

Wai couldn't help but say "I can, I can," and urged Ling to get her the materials as quickly as possible. Ling hadn't thought she'd actually agree. Work was always a matter of personal responsibility, different from the usual tea-serving or water-pouring. Wai would be held accountable for any mistakes. Ling never interfered in anyone else's work so as not to be blamed for no reason but, surprisingly, Wai didn't mind at all. Ling located the folder containing materials pertaining to the Joint School Oral Exam on her desk. "I'm really sorry to trouble you . . ."

This was the first time Ling had been so friendly to Wai. Clearly feeling encouraged, Wai thumped her chest forcefully, producing a resounding thud that sounded like it was piercing her spine. "Relax, family matters come first! Don't stay at school—hurry and go visit your family member!"

When Wai said this, Ling felt a little guilty. Indeed, she did have a family member in the hospital. It was her cousin, who she didn't even see once a year, and it wasn't cancer but appendicitis. She'd just heard her mother say the day before that neither of them planned on visiting this family member in the hospital. She immediately returned to her seat and tidied up and, when she left, she took a piece of chocolate from the drawer and laid it gently on Wai's desk. "Thank you for helping me."

It was just an ordinary chocolate gold coin that didn't even taste like cocoa at all. Wai picked it up and put it in the palm of her hand. After a long time, she carefully tore open the imitation gold shell of the coin and placed the chocolate on the tip of her tongue. "It's *sweat-sweet*. I like it very much. Thank you."

After that, Ling often found excuses to ask Wai for help making worksheets and test papers, which Wai readily accepted. During that period, Wai had to handle the debate team, prepare for the Joint School Oral Exam, and attend to daily tasks. She worked overtime till 11 p.m. every night. She no longer had time to "serve" Ling, who enjoyed this rare "freedom." As the end of the day approached, Ling saw Wai with her head buried in work, so she quietly tidied up, tiptoeing around Wai's seat as she left, afraid that Wai would strike up a conversation if she caught sight of her. Sometimes she was lucky enough to escape, but often, as soon as she stood up, Wai noticed her because of the low partition that only covered half of her body. Wai would swing the swivel chair toward Ling and sigh: "Being a teacher is *horde lurk* . . . Last night, I didn't even have time to eat dinner. I suddenly realized why so many teachers jump off buildings and kill themselves."

Wai's eyes were like two leaden circles, dragging down her brows and eyes. Ling quietly set her handbag on the back of her seat. "I might as well do things myself."

"If a good friend needs help, I'll be there. Rest assured." Wai thumped her chest.

The resounding thud from Wai's heart encouraged her. *I've done nothing wrong. Wai volunteered to help me, and she was so adamant that if I refused, it would mean I didn't consider her a "good friend."* With this in mind, Ling no longer felt bad. She slung her handbag high on her shoulder, placed another chocolate coin on the desk, said good luck, and left the teachers' office.

Although Wai helped Ling with a lot of work, Ling still didn't like her. Wai was too weird, always wanting to finish grading homework the fastest and work the hardest, and even when it came to making friends, she had to be "the best." In the end, however, she achieved none of the three. Wai wasn't like a typical Hong Konger, who, after spending a little time out in the real world, wouldn't be as rigid and stubborn as her. Wai was more like the new immigrants in the school, dumb and isolated from the world, not caring about the jokes that Hong Kong students told or the pop culture they liked, thinking that doing their best was enough.

In Ling's eyes, new immigrant students fell into two categories: those who were rich, and those who were poor. The rich ones often walked around flaunting famous name brands, bragged about which overseas university they'd study at, and were dead set on refusing to learn Cantonese. The poor ones simply studied, studied, studied, knowing nothing except for books and exam papers. Ling always felt that, whether rich or poor, they all single-mindedly pursued "being good"—if it wasn't good grades, then it was more money. Ling preferred Hong Kong students. They were sharp, clever, and knew how to do the right thing at the right time. After years of being out in the real world, Ling understood that "being good" was secondary, while being savvy and knowing when to act and when to hold back were key. She frequently told her students that getting good grades wasn't about studying hard, but analyzing the questions and guessing what answers the teachers wanted. At school, Ling excelled in teaching exam-taking techniques. Many senior secondary students considered her to be competent and exceptionally accurate in predicting exam questions, even more impressive than the top tutors at cram schools. Under her guidance, the passing rate for Chinese in the DSE was over 90 percent. Every year, more than twenty students earned the highest grade of five stars. Rumor had it that one student who'd graduated even sold her notes on a discussion forum for the price of 1,000 HKD.

Many students in the school liked Ling. They felt she knew how to teach and could also get along well with them. Ling knew which celebrity trends the students were wild about, and she'd chat with them about gossip from the teachers' office— of course, she was careful not to reveal too much. She achieved a lot with little effort, striking a balance between maintaining the image of a teacher and keeping students hanging on her every word. Thus, whenever there were any disciplinary issues with students, or she met any difficulties, she only had to say one phrase, and the students understood: "Help me out— don't give me a hard time." However, some extremely earnest students would question whether she was actually teaching them or only teaching them how to take tests. In such encounters, she only responded with an indifferent "You'll understand in the future."

Learning wasn't about getting good grades? *Pfft!* Learning *was* about getting good grades. Be clever, understand the rules of the game, and you'll succeed in everything. In the past ten years, Ling hadn't passed the LPAT or pursued advanced studies, and neither the principal nor the department head dared utter a peep. Ling was likable, and her students maintained good scores on the DSE. They couldn't do without her. Ling deeply understood that as long as she was irreplaceable to others, she could keep her position. If the principal liked you, she'd keep you even if you didn't pass the LPAT. If she didn't like you, earning the highest grade was useless.

L ing didn't answer her mom's calls, but her phone kept on flashing. Her mom rented out more than twenty subdivided units in Mong Kok—had one of her tenants broken the lease, and she needed her to handle the aftermath? Or was she asking Ling to take someone to view one of the units? Regardless, at this very moment she didn't have the energy to deal with her mom. She just wanted to let her keep calling until she grew tired.

Ling hoped to finish her work before it was time to head home, but only two lines of words floated on the computer screen. The notice for her classroom observation in two days' time flickered beneath the fan. Beside it were the test papers for the Form 4 class and the essays for the Form 2 class, still tied with rubber bands. Ling glanced up. The head of the department was in her seat, reciting English vocabulary words. In recent years, the department head had made it widely known that she wanted to practice her English with her daughter, who was in primary school. "English is a world language. If your English is good, you can charge out of Hong Kong and go anywhere." It was as though she were persuading others to study English with her.

Looking at the department head's back, Ling felt envious and jealous. In her ten years at Sing Din Secondary School, she had never been so busy. In the past, she would chat with her colleagues during her free period. Every day, she finished work on time. Now, however, after Wai's passing, she didn't even have time to drink water, and she didn't leave school until eight or nine o'clock each night. When she arrived home, she had to grade homework, prepare her lessons, and record students' grades.

Among the eight Chinese-language teachers, only the head of the department, Miss Wu, and Miss Ip were Senior Graduate Mistresses, or SGMs. They had the most seniority and had countless time to do things other than work. The department head studied English, while Miss Ip and Miss Wu watched entertainment news and organized group shopping purchases. Since starting her job, Ling had never envied anyone with a higher position than her. She'd always been a contract teacher, but the principal had a conscience and paid her the salary of a regular teacher with a permanent post. Besides, the workload wasn't too heavy then, so she hadn't been too concerned with securing a permanent position. She knew that if she lived long enough, she'd be promoted one day, so what was there to envy?

But after seeing the principal just now, it was as though she'd stepped into an abyss. She couldn't sense how deep her feet were. She just kept sinking and sinking . . .

Right then, an ant crawled across the table with a small yellow cookie crumb in its mouth. As Ling watched, the ant took a few steps forward, fluttered its antennae, stopped, and walked in the other direction. Ling rushed to check that the desk was tidy and the bookcase showed no trace of insects. Where had the ant come from? She picked up a folder, swept away the ant, cleaned the border of the computer screen, and wiped the top of her desk.

Another call was patched through. She didn't want to answer any phone calls, but afraid it might be the principal, she hesitated for a moment, then picked up the phone.

"I'll be sure to let you proofread a draft of the interview, and I definitely won't reveal your name."

That reporter again. How annoying. "Why should I believe you?"

The reporter ignored Ling's question. "May I ask ... Has the principal ever mentioned switching to Mandarin as a medium of Chinese-language instruction?"

"I don't have time."

"Do you feel the school is showing signs of turning red?"

Bingo—she'd hit the nail on the head. Ling decided not to say anything, leaving the reporter with no choice but to carry on the conversation.

But noticing Ling's silence, the reporter continued her line of inquiry. "Has the principal raised the job requirements for switching to teaching in Mandarin?"

Ling's hand shook as she held the receiver. "Where did you hear that the school is switching to teaching in Mandarin?" She regretted the words as soon as they left her mouth—wasn't this more or less admitting it?

"I'm just speculating... Most schools now have switched to teaching in Mandarin." The reporter's voice was slightly awkward, but her tone was brisk. She asked again, "Did Miss Yu have any hobbies?"

"Studying."

She'd misspoken again. Why was she even bothering with the reporter when she clearly just wanted to hang up the phone?

The reporter didn't give her a moment to think. "Studying what?"

"I don't know."

"Wasn't it for the Mandarin LPAT?"

"I wasn't close to her."

"Do you think Chinese-language teachers need to take the LPAT?"

Wai's cubicle creaked. Ling stood up to see what was happening. It turned out that the fan was so strong that it had blown away the mirrors Wai had stuck to her desk, and the papers and pens on the desk had fallen to the floor as well. Ling's legs itched. A piece of paper floated in front of her feet. Picking it up, she saw it was Wai's lecture notes for the weekly assembly. Each sentence of the lecture notes was structurally complete, with a subject, predicate, and object. Every character was marked with pinyin, and even the tone marks were clearly noted. Each and every stroke was forceful, and when she turned it over and ran her hands over it, she could feel the bumpy texture.

This was consistent with Wai's personality, always being fully prepared and striving for perfection.

"Hello ... ? Hello ... ?"

Ling stared at the paper in a daze, leaving the reporter shouting on the other end of the line.

In the second semester of the previous year, the principal had suddenly convened a meeting with all the teachers in the school and announced that the school was moving toward internationalization and planned to switch to teaching in Mandarin after two years.

"Several parents have expressed to me that they'd like our students to have more exposure to Mandarin. Most students are already used to learning in Mandarin, having attended primary schools taught in Mandarin before moving up to secondary school."

There were no windows in the conference room. The principal sat at the front, two spotlights criss-crossing her body. All of the teachers in the school sat around the principal and listened quietly. Sing Din Secondary School was an English-language secondary school. Most of the instructors taught in English, and the switch to Mandarin as a medium of Chinese-language instruction had no impact on them. The head of the department and Miss Ko taught Mandarin. They both looked away. It had nothing to do with them. The other Chinese-language teachers stared at each other in disbelief. Wai's face turned pale with fear. Would they have to teach in Mandarin in the future? Were they capable of doing that? No one knew how to react. Ling, however, stood up and said in a loud voice: "Eighty percent of Sing Din Secondary School students are Hong Kong students. They can't understand spoken Mandarin."

"But twenty percent are mainland students. Sometimes as I walk through the hallway, I hear many students speaking in Mandarin. For students born in Hong Kong, creating an immersive language environment is necessary for learning Mandarin well." The principal smiled, as though she anticipated someone would challenge her.

"It's better to teach Classical Chinese in Cantonese than Mandarin. Many ancient Chinese words are Cantonese. For example, ancient Chinese and Cantonese use the same third-person pronoun."

"I understand, but—"

"I found a research report from Polytechnic University." Ling stepped forward and handed over a thick folder. "Research shows that teaching Chinese in Cantonese is more effective than teaching Chinese in Mandarin. The passing rate for the Chinese DSE at Sing Din Secondary School is ninety-five percent, with over thirty students achieving the highest score of Level 5 every year. I checked, and the Chinese-language results from the traditionally prestigious schools can't compare with ours. If we switch to teaching in Mandarin, the passing rate will definitely decrease, and even the university admission rate will be reduced." Ling didn't mention that three-quarters of those thirty-plus DSE Level 5 students were taught by her. Now was not the time to take credit.

The truth was, Ling had already heard that the principal was thinking of switching to Mandarin as a medium of Chinese-language instruction. She was close to the principal's secretary, Ivy. When she started her job, the first person she made friends with wasn't one of her colleagues in the Chinese department, but Ivy. On her first day of work, on her way to the principal's office, she had passed by Ivy and glimpsed her watching a makeup tutorial on YouTube. When Ivy noticed Ling approaching, she immediately closed the window, straightening her body as she told her that the principal wasn't in. Ivy had a doll-like face, double eyelids as thick as a foreigner's, and a deeply contoured high-bridged nose, and looked 60 percent similar to the Taiwanese model Lin Chi-ling. She was dressed like a Korean girl, her long crystal nails inlaid with glittering stones. Ling thought, *Ivy must be a plastic surgery beauty.*

Ling didn't know much about cosmetic surgery, and besides, it was too awkward to bring up as a topic of conversation, so she tried talking about facials instead. "I was watching YouTube in the teachers' office just now. Fortunately, no one caught me. I know a salon that's offering a fifty percent discount on Vital Injector treatment, only four hundred dollars a pop. I have a coupon. Are you interested?"

It was the result she'd hoped for. The principal was away and, seeing that Ling was a fellow beauty aficionado, Ivy dropped her guard, becoming more and more enthusiastic as they chatted, which is how she and Ling started talking. From then on, whenever Ivy saw Ling approaching, she no longer pretended to be working, and instead boldly looked at beauty magazines and watched YouTube videos. Ling often gave Ivy samples of different skincare products, some of which were gifts, and some that Ling had specifically bought to give to her colleagues.

Ivy had clued Ling in on that meeting early on. That day when the principal was away, Ling had sought out Ivy for afternoon tea. As they chatted about Link Real Estate Investment Trust acquiring the public-housing-estate shopping mall near the school, Ivy picked up a fried chicken leg, talking as she ate. "After the mall's been renovated, I heard they're opening up a large Chinese restaurant. From then on, the principal will switch to eating at the Chinese restaurant instead of eating Western food. Now she's decided to switch to teaching in Mandarin . . ." Realizing she'd slipped up, Ivy quickly swallowed the food in her mouth. "I . . . um, I don't know—pretend you never heard that."

Ling was shocked that the principal had such an idea. She still remembered when two years ago at the parent–teacher association dinner, the principal had brought a wireless microphone and spoken to hundreds of parents about the school's vision. When it came to the medium of instruction, the principal reiterated, Sing Din Secondary School attached great importance to students' English proficiency, and that except for Chinese language and Chinese history all subjects were taught in English. In order to highlight the school's distinguishing features, the principal also incorporated current events into her speech. "In recent years, many schools have switched to teaching in Mandarin. Sing Din Secondary School absolutely will not use Mandarin to teach Chinese language and Chinese history. We will defend Cantonese, as it's the most important part of Hong Kong culture."

The teachers sitting in the front row had no reaction. The school had always taught Chinese in Cantonese. The principal's use of the words "defend" and "culture" sounded even more impassioned. Earlier, when the principal mentioned things such as increasing teaching resources and foreign exchanges, the parents couldn't stop applauding, but when she brought up defending Cantonese, there was only sporadic applause. Ling turned to look around. Some parents were even frowning.

Over dinner, Ling took the initiative to chat with parents. Many of them expressed to Ling their hope that teachers would teach Chinese in Mandarin. They believed that learning Mandarin was the general trend now that mainlanders were everywhere. Ling wanted to say that the school already had Mandarin classes, and if the students studied seriously, they could learn it well without the school switching to teaching all Chinese classes in Mandarin, but she didn't want to argue with the parents, so she just made a perfunctory statement that it was up to the principal. However, the parents were pushier than she imagined. A few days after the dinner, one parent kept calling to persuade Ling to tutor her son in Mandarin after school, even offering to pay her 1,000 HKD per hour. Ling thought to herself, *There are so many monster parents! Since you all love Mandarin so much, why don't you send your kids off to the mainland? Wouldn't it be more competitive to study on the mainland and get to know mainlanders from a young age?*

Of course, there were also parents who supported Cantonese education, and some of them were even fervent anti-establishment "yellow ribbons." They shared the principal's words on Facebook, garnering more than 5,000 comments and 20,000 likes, and attracting media attention, with several newspapers vying to interview the principal. The school suddenly became famous, its enrollment much better than in previous years, drawing numerous students with good grades. She still recalled how last September everyone had gathered to read the newspaper interview with the principal, discussing whether it was her propaganda strategy. Laughing, Ling quoted Deng Xiaoping, saying, "It doesn't matter if a cat is black or white, as long as it catches mice it's a good cat."

Several reports of the principal's interview were still pinned to the bulletin board in the teachers' office. Ling had never imagined at that moment that the principal would completely overturn her remarks. The principal glanced up at her colleagues, seeming to understand everyone's meaning. "Recently, the school has become increasingly famous, and many mainland students have been applying for admission. They already meet the requirements for Mandarin education. What do you think?"

The conference room was as silent as the grave, except for the whir of the air conditioner.

"We'll table this discussion. Now I'd like to discuss the arrangements for the weekly assembly for next semester. Last semester's weekly assemblies were led by guest speakers, while the upcoming semester's will be led by our teachers. I hope that the weekly assemblies for the upcoming semester will only be conducted in English or Mandarin, so as to establish a good language environment." The principal placed a form on the table beside the executive chair. "Everyone, pick a date."

When the principal first threw out the topic of switching to Mandarin, everyone was shocked, but now that she had requested that the weekly assemblies be held in English or Mandarin, they weren't that surprised. However, when the teachers picked up the form and looked at it, they hesitated. The form was passed from teacher to teacher, and finally set back on the table in its original form, as though just filling in one's name would open Pandora's box. Seeing that no one was responding, the principal squinted and swept her gaze over the teachers present. After a while, she fixed her eyes on Ling. "Ling, you speak. You're the best at speaking, and students like you. You won't bore them to sleep."

"I can't. I have to take students to compete on Tuesdays." In fact, the competition dates weren't yet confirmed, but there was no guarantee they wouldn't fall on Tuesdays, so it didn't hurt to say this.

The principal thought for a moment, then said, "Anyone else?"

Still no one spoke up, and the silent air suddenly became very noisy. Finally, the head of the department broke the silence. "It's better for English and Mandarin teachers to give the talks. Their pronunciation is the most authentic, and it will benefit students." Upon saying this, she wrote down her own name.

The principal eyed the department head appreciatively, and all the colleagues in the other departments unanimously agreed with her suggestion. The English teacher was forced to write down her name, and Miss Ko, who also taught Mandarin, had no choice but to follow suit. Everyone filled in a slot, but there was still one left, which was the last weekly assembly of the semester.

Everyone avoided the principal's gaze. Ling pretended to be sorting through files. Wai lowered her head, her face red as a tomato, and kept rubbing her fingers. The shyer Wai was, the more she attracted attention. Ling had a hunch that the principal would choose her. Sure enough, the principal said, "Wai, you speak. This is a good opportunity to improve your Mandarin."

"No, no . . . My Mandarin is worse than the students." This was one of the rare moments when Wai spoke in Cantonese.

Wai admitted she was even worse than the students. *So then, why is the principal paying you money?* Ling sneaked a glance at the principal, who kept staring at Wai, her face expressionless. The head of the department chimed in, "There's no way an instructor in the Chinese department would have poor Mandarin. Wai, it's you."

Nodding, the principal wrote Wai's name in the blank.

Wai waved her hands again like she'd done during the first academic affairs meeting at the start of the semester, umming and aahing, unsure of what to say.

But no one paid attention to her. Upon seeing the principal put away the form filled with names, the teachers breathed sighs of relief. After the principal left the conference room, Ling walked over to Wai. "In the future, of course you'll be better than the students. You've got this!" Ling's hand trembled slightly on Wai's shoulder. Other colleagues looked at Ling, but no one said a word.

CLUTCHING WAI'S LECTURE notes from that weekly assembly, Ling felt Wai's handwriting dart off the paper like a snake, crawling up her hand and onto her face, causing a burning sensation.

"I'm more concerned about your career . . ."

When did the principal decide to make the switch to Mandarin? Why did the principal seem to have . . . changed?

Since the start of the previous year, when the principal had dined with the Chinese department, she often brought up the mainland property market and mainland stock market. Ling assumed the principal just wanted to make money. So-called businesspeople had no "motherland"; they invested wherever they could make money—mainland China, the UK, the US, Africa . . . Back then, the principal had still liked her. When Ling brought up the insider investment information she'd learned from her mother, the principal had kept asking her about it. At the time, how could Ling have imagined that not only would the principal invest in the mainland, but she was also moving closer to the mainland education industry?

I realized it too late.

In the past, the principal had never undertaken such major endeavors as she was now. In the six years of her tenure, she had never carried out any major reforms. Instead, she continuously reduced her workload. Previously, assignment checks had been carried out three times a year, but once she became principal she changed it to two. The school magazine used to be published every year, but after she became principal she eliminated the project, citing a lack of resources. Staff meetings with the entire faculty were only held twice a year, and she handed over teachers' proposals to Ivy to stamp without even taking a look. To put it mildly, she governed without action, but in reality, she was just lazy. Ling had never heard of a school principal lazier than this one. She was absent from school three days a week, and often left work after lunch. Students rarely caught a trace of her. The most visible sign of her existence was her signature on official notices.

How Ling missed this version of the principal. The principal had been lazy, but not without standards—the public examination results couldn't be too poor, and the enrollment level had to be maintained above Band 2. The principal didn't discuss educational ideals, nor did she interfere with the teachers' instructional methods. Each appraisal, the teachers were only evaluated based on student performance. Ling's classes achieved good results in the public examinations every year, and she could please the principal, so she never worried about her career. The year before, she'd asked for a month of sick leave at the end of May to secretly travel to northern Europe. Although the department head was unhappy, her students still came out on top in the final exam, so no one could find fault with her.

Ling often mused on how it was good to have a lazy principal. As long as the requirements were met, the teachers could do whatever they wanted, which in turn gave them more room for creativity. Some teachers held Egyptian cultural festivals in their spare time, and others led their students to participate in robot competitions, winning first prize. Of course, there were also teachers like Ling who only cared about students' grades, but so what? Wasn't it great that every teacher found their own place?

Everyone believed that the principal's laziness stemmed from her predecessor. The former principal was a British man who could only communicate in English. As he didn't speak Cantonese, all the affairs were handled by the vice-principal—who was the current principal. He had only come to work one day a week, and the rest of the time he was rumored to have been playing golf. When he came to school, he didn't look as if he were going to work. Loose-fitting sportswear and sneakers were his trademark, as though the school were another golf club. The British principal had been installed by the St. David's Society to indicate that Sing Din Secondary School was indeed an English-language secondary school and to advertise its English education as superior to other schools when recruiting students. It did the trick. Most parents were as stupid as pigs. They assumed that since there was a foreign principal, the students would need to speak English all the time, and their English would naturally be good. The parents didn't realize that the principal had never been determined to turn Sing Din Secondary School into a second Diocesan or La Salle, two elite schools that placed special emphasis on English. These more prestigious schools had at least two foreign teachers, whereas Sing Din only had one. The prestigious schools offered courses in English literature, while Sing Din only had general English classes. The prestigious schools admitted foreign students, while Sing Din only recruited students who lived in nearby housing estates.

For Ling's first two years at Sing Din, the school was run by the British principal. During those two years, she met him fewer than ten times, but there was one scene that particularly left a deep impression on her. That year, the school had to undergo an external evaluation, and the Education Bureau sent personnel to inspect the school. The principal had to lead the Education Bureau personnel to observe classes and tour the school after hours. The vice-principal and higher-level staff weren't free after school (they'd gone home early to rest), so they instructed Ling and a female English teacher to accompany the principal to greet the personnel from the Education Bureau. That day, the principal was dressed in a crisp suit, his beard cleanly shaven, a faint smell of cologne emanating from under his suit. Seeing the principal dressed in such formal attire was truly a rare sight to behold. The wide shoulder pads made him look so tall that both Ling and the English teacher were a head shorter when standing next to him. That day, the principal was extremely clever. Each time he walked through a particular room, he was able to describe its use in great detail. The personnel from the Education Bureau kept checking off items in their files. However, when the principal led them to the English corner, they weren't very satisfied. The area was as tiny as a bird's nest, with dirty rubber mats covering the floor and a pile of English books haphazardly placed on the bookshelf, creating the impression that students could come here and study English at any time, but the design was too rudimentary, and it didn't seem like something the students would necessarily use. Before that, Ling hadn't even known there was such a facility. The Education Bureau personnel asked in English, "How do you improve the English level of students with this area?" The principal kept smiling, politely explaining that they held English-language gatherings every week. He also showed the proposal for the design of the English corner and the students' attendance records, thus dispelling the doubts of the Education Bureau personnel. (Later, Ling found out it was all fake. The vice-principal had instructed the English teacher to set up the English corner the day before, and the proposal and attendance records were also fabricated. The principal's familiarity with each special area was all due to the vice-principal preparing a memo for him the day before.)

The Education Bureau personnel didn't leave till 5 p.m. The principal saw them out the door and watched them enter the MTR station, then loosened his tie. Although Ling didn't hear the sound, she knew from the shape of his mouth that he was saying *fuck*. Realizing that Ling was looking at him, he blinked and said, "Let's have a drink."

The principal took Ling and the English teacher to the Western restaurant (the one the current principal loved) for afternoon tea. She remembered that the principal ordered a bottle of red wine and a cheese plate and, after pouring each of them a glass of wine, started drinking in large gulps. After drinking half a glass, his face turned purple. Ling and the English teacher sat across from the principal. Although they were sitting down, Ling still found him tall, and had to look up to meet his gaze. The English teacher smiled demurely and respectfully chatted in English with the principal, showing off. Ling didn't teach English, so there was no need to compete with her, so she politely smiled and nodded. When the English teacher mentioned the personnel from the Education Bureau inspecting the English corner, the principal, who'd been drinking his wine, raised his glass high and drained it in one gulp. "Well, I never bother with the English level of Hong Kong students. They can never be good, no matter how hard they try."

For the principal to say that, he must've been drunk. The English teacher was slightly embarrassed. Ling smiled at her to show her support. The principal didn't seem to notice and poured himself another glass of wine. "Hong Kongers always think that their English is up to standard. Hahaha . . . lawyers, doctors, teachers . . . But as you can see, they only use the language. They never own it."

The principal had probably forgotten that Ling and the English teacher were both Hong Kongers. Ling didn't feel offended, but the English teacher's face reddened. The principal glanced at the English teacher, poured more wine for her and for Ling, and laughed. "It doesn't matter. *You* are always an expert at using language. It's not easy to use it in different ways, is it?"

The English teacher lowered her head and didn't say anything else, nor did she take a sip of the wine on the table.

In fact, what was the problem in "using" it? Did people have to "own" everything? If Ling were that English teacher, she would've retorted in English, "We know how to USE both English and Cantonese, but you only have one." In life, who doesn't use something? Wasn't the principal also using the school? How would he have the money and time to play golf without the school? If he had "owned the school," he'd be too busy.

The British principal retired and returned to his home country, and the vice-principal was promoted. Previously, she'd shielded the British principal from trouble, but now that she was in charge shouldn't she take a good rest? Although the principal was higher in rank than everyone else, she was still just a salaried worker. In the six years since she assumed office, the principal had kept the existing policies. Everyone felt that the school was still the same, it was just that the principal had changed in nationality and skin color. It was only in recent years that the school had undergone some changes. Due to the declining birth rate during the SARS period, although the principal's remarks about protecting Cantonese provoked a lot of reactions that improved admissions, still the enrollments actually continued to decrease, and so the principal held several seminars with primary school parents and also sent teachers to the North District to conduct a publicity campaign that brought in a lot of new immigrant students. At the time, Ling found this understandable. The school didn't have enough students, and the new immigrant students needed to attend school, thus killing two birds with one stone. But . . . why did the principal now want to switch to using Mandarin as a medium of instruction?

Recalling the past, Ling stroked the forceful handwriting of Wai's lecture notes for the weekly assembly and sighed. *I was too stupid to realize the change last year and only looked for topics to chat about with the principal. Wai was one step ahead of me . . .*

No no no . . . Wai was so stupid—how could she compare with me?

Ling wadded Wai's notes into a paper ball and threw it in the trash can.

THE REPORTER STILL hadn't hung up on her office phone. Meanwhile, Ling's mobile phone rang again. The reporter wouldn't let her go, and her mom wouldn't let her go.

Ling didn't want to answer anyone's calls, but the school year had been too busy, and she couldn't help handle her mom's rental affairs or spend much time with her, and she felt she owed her. Her mom kept calling—was she ill and in the hospital? Had she had an accident on the street? If something happened to her mom, and she still ignored her, that really wouldn't be right. Taking a breath, she picked up the phone from the desk and slid the answer button.

"I told you to track down that mainland woman. Many tenants have complained. Do you think I'm dead?" Her mom was screaming at the top of her lungs.

Sure enough, it wasn't an emergency. She was just calling to vent. *Mainland* woman. When she heard the word "mainland," Ling remembered that the school was switching to Mandarin. She pinched the space between her eyebrows. "I'm so busy. I'll help you after school."

"Busy my ass! You just don't want to help your ma!"

Holding her breath, Ling whispered, "I've really been so much busier this year . . ."

"Isn't there a dim-witted colleague who helps you out all the time?"

Heart twitching, Ling took a deep breath. "Wai is . . . dead. I already told you."

Ling inadvertently glanced over at Wai's seat, hoping that Wai would still be there, helping her finish her huge pile of work and diverting the principal's attention, but there was only a boundless sea of mirrors before her eyes, directly reflecting the sunlight. Ling shut her eyes, leaving a pile of white shadows underneath them.

Her mom was silent for a bit, then cursed again. "I warned you not to become a teacher. Mrs. Cheng's daughter makes a lot of money doing business. In Hong Kong, it's best to go into business . . ."

Knowing her mom would keep on chewing her out, Ling repeated, "I'm really busy," then hung up and powered off her phone.

After more than ten years of selling knock-off handbags, Ling's mom had earned enough money to buy a flat. She'd always hoped that Ling too would go into business after graduation, feeling that as Hong Kong had a low tax rate there was a bright future in doing business. In Form 7, Ling had also wanted to study business when she went to university, but unfortunately she didn't do well in the college entrance exam. She only earned a good score in Chinese, and the rest of the subjects were merely at the C-level. Choosing the Chinese department was a safe bet—she was afraid she couldn't make it in business. When she was filling out her university application, she kept explaining to her mom that she had no choice but to select the Chinese department, but her mom didn't understand, and repeatedly snatched her course selection form, trying to change her selection. Ling had to fight to snatch it back.

"I've told you time and again. Studying such garbage subjects, do you want to end up begging for food? You'll definitely be eliminated. So stupid."

Ling didn't particularly like the Chinese department. Her good grades in Chinese were only because the teacher's notes closely resembled the exam questions, and they often did practice tests in class, so she easily earned an A. In fact, Ling had no idea what she wanted to study, but upon hearing her mom chastise her for wanting to study garbage, she was indignant. "It's precisely because I'm smart that I'm choosing the Chinese department. I'll become a teacher and can have summers off, and I'll be a professional. I'll get a raise every year and won't have to worry about losing money in business." As soon as she heard "become a teacher," her mom sneered and derided her as "incurably foolish."

Ling didn't know if being a teacher was better than going into business, but since the Chinese department was her sole option, she could only stand on her own two feet and keep on going. The Chinese department was a teacher-producing factory—80 percent of its graduates became Chinese teachers. After only a few interviews, Ling easily got a teaching job. As she had advanced along this path, she had never regretted it; teaching was the most lucrative and accessible career for her.

Her turned-off mobile phone was on the corner of her desk, but the reporter still called out *Hello? Hello?* from the office phone. Ling remembered the reporter's words about "trying to make a living"—was her mom right that being a teacher was the most foolish idea? Should she not have become a teacher in the first place?

Ling didn't want to keep talking to the reporter, and she wasn't in the mood to work. Her head drooped like lead, and she just wanted to keep spacing out. Right then, a black speck appeared in her field of vision, shining in the sun. It was that ant, still carrying food crumbs in its mouth. It had been swept to the ground but still hadn't died. Its vitality was truly tenacious. The ant's legs scurried, as though it were fleeing or searching for something. Suddenly, an idea occurred to her. Unconcerned whether it was dirty, she removed a transparent lid from the drawer to cover the ant. Wherever the ant went, the lid followed. Whenever Ling lifted up the lid, the ant thought it could escape. Ling covered the ant again. After several rounds, the ant was so worn out that, even if she lifted the lid, it just stopped in its tracks and looked at her. Ling covered the ant again.

The ant walked along the edge of the transparent lid, but no matter what, it couldn't get out. Ling saw that under the ant's feet was the strip of paper on which she'd just written the reporter's name. Why not look her up online? She resolutely closed the window for her writing lesson plan and typed "Wong Wai-Yee" into Google. Several political news articles popped up on the screen, the most recent being a report on the election of the chief executive. Wong Wai-Yee started writing in 2016. She really was such a novice; but she was a Hong Kong news reporter. Ling wondered, shouldn't an education reporter be interviewing her instead? Was she tricking her? The ant paced up and down the characters for "Wong Wai-Yee" as though it were eyeing the body of a juicy insect corpse. The *Hello? Hello? Hello?* from the office phone kept urging her. Ling took a breath—how she longed to hang up.

"If you're a reporter with the Hong Kong press, why are you interviewing me? You're obviously making up fake news. I have nothing to say. Bye . . ."

"Don't hang up. There's been such a huge response to Miss Yu's death because it reminds people of the absurdity of the educational system. If you'll let me interview you, you could at least raise the issue and put pressure on the government . . ."

The reporter's tone was sincere. Ling didn't put down the phone. "After Miss Yu's suicide, many people online criticized the government for not having enough resources to hire permanent teachers. Some also criticized the government for not promoting small classes and forcing the switch to teaching in Mandarin, which makes teachers' work more and more stressful. It's really hard to be a Chinese teacher in Hong Kong, but not many in the community know about the plight of teachers. *Mango Daily* is Hong Kong's bestselling paper. If my article is published, it'll certainly make a difference."

The reporter was like a saleswoman. Ling sneered. "Interviewing me can really have such a big effect?"

"Of course it can! Previously, the teachers of Ming Dak Secondary School reported their principal's negligence to us. It was published on *Mango Online News* and shared many times on Facebook. People protested at the school gate, and finally the principal was forced to resign. The truth is, the power of the internet is so great that if you speak out it'll definitely make a difference."

Force the principal to resign? What qualifications and abilities do I have? "Being a teacher is inevitably hard work. Since I'm bringing home a paycheck, I should suck it up and face the consequences . . ."

"You really think so?"

"What can I do? I'm only a staff member."

"Do you think it's inevitable for schools to switch to teaching in Mandarin? Do you think it's inevitable for teachers to be on a contract basis?"

If it's not inevitable, what can I do? Can writing a news story change society? Pfft! Do you think I'm one of those activists? I'm not a yellow ribbon, or a blue ribbon, or any ribbon.

Usually when Ling looked at the news, she found the protesters uninteresting. Those people took to the streets and blocked traffic, making it impossible to get to work and do business. *If you don't need to make a living, that's your business. Why are you so selfish, forcing everyone to do the same?* She was a member of the Hong Kong Professional Teachers' Union, and when she received their emails asking her to sign petitions and join demonstrations, she threw them all into the trash can. In recent eras, some students in the school had become politically active. They were too naïve, thinking that writing a few words and pressing "share" could turn the world upside-down. She never liked or responded. Young people had never experienced storms and often wanted to be heroes, but the reality was cruel. After entering the workforce, they'd understand how hard it was to make a living.

Noticing her silence, the reporter continued, "May I ask, are most of the teachers permanent employees, or are they contracted?"

"I'm very busy."

"It's really my last question."

Ling didn't know why she was still indulging her, losing her usual shrewdness and determination. The reporter seemed to have a magical hold over her. Ling said, "Some are permanent, some are contractual. This is common sense. You can find the answer online. You don't need to ask me."

The reporter didn't lose her cool. "And Miss Yu?"

"I don't know."

"Did Miss Yu renew her contract last year?"

"I never said she was a contract teacher. Why are you asking me this question?"

"Did Miss Yu ever express that she was worried about her contract not being renewed?" The reporter seemed to understand something, and her tone lightened, no longer the deferential attitude of a newcomer to the workplace.

"I don't know."

"Miss Ng, are you a contract teacher?"

"What business is it of yours?"

The reporter scoffed. "Did you renew your contract this year?"

Sure enough, she was up to no good. At first, she'd sympathized with Ling to win her trust, then she'd become hostile as soon as she achieved her goal. Humiliated, Ling snapped, "Eat shit," then repeatedly pressed the disconnect button and slammed down the receiver, letting the phone beep continuously.

After a while, she regained her senses and scanned her surroundings. Fortunately, she was alone. The head of the department had just left, and no one had heard her swear.

WOULD HER CONTRACT be renewed? Of course it would. For the last ten years, Ling had never worried about her contract renewal. Previously, when the principal conducted performance appraisals with her, it had been just like chatting with a friend. She noticed that the principal often went to the kitchenette to make coffee. During the appraisal meeting the year before last, she had brewed the principal a cup of Kopi Luwak specially bought from Indonesia. The principal fell in love at first sip, and they ended up chatting about coffee beans and coffee machines for half an hour before Ling finally handed over the appraisal form for the principal to sign.

Seeing that the principal was such a coffee aficionado, last summer she had found a type of coffee online called Geisha coffee that was even more precious than Kopi Luwak. There was a café in Taipei that sold it, so she flew to Taipei specifically to buy several bags for the principal and her colleagues, spending more than 10,000 HKD. Although the annual appraisal was held in June, it was best to prepare as early as possible for peace of mind. If the principal summoned her in

March, she'd be safe. Ling thought, *Geisha coffee tastes more delicate, and is more fragrant. If I offer it to the principal this year, she'll definitely prefer it.*

But Ling's wishful thinking was wrong. After the New Year holiday, one day Ivy dragged Ling away to the bottom of the staircase located toward the back of the school, frantic. Ling and Ivy loved gossiping on the back stairs, where year-round there was no sunlight. Students didn't know about this place, and the custodian rarely came to clean it. That day, Ling and Ivy were the only ones on the stairs, but Ivy still turned her head several times to make sure there was really no one else around before whispering in Ling's ear, "I heard that the principal is considering choosing between you and Wai for contract renewal."

Ivy's voice echoed throughout the back stairs. Ling couldn't believe her ears. "Are you joking around or telling the truth?"

"I went into the office today and heard the principal on the phone—"

"Who was she talking to?"

"I just vaguely heard her say she's thinking of firing some-one . . ."

"Did the principal say why she wasn't going to renew my contract?"

Ivy shook her head, adding, "Don't say anything. If the principal finds out, I'll be in trouble."

Ling gestured okay, and Ivy rushed back to the principal's office. Still in shock, Ling leaned on the back stairs and took a deep breath, the heat from Ivy's words swelling in her ears. *Is this true? Is it really true? I maintained the students' DSE scores, but the principal doesn't want to renew my contract? Every day I have a good chat with the principal over lunch—what did I do wrong?*

After that, Ling was in low spirits the entire morning, and

told her students in all of her classes to study by themselves. At noon, she still asked everyone in the WhatsApp group if they'd like to grab lunch, and she still responded to the principal with two thumbs up and the heart-eyes emoji. They all went to the Western restaurant to drink red wine and eat foie gras. Ling opened the door for the principal as usual, ordered food for her, refilled her wine, and chatted about the secrets of the real estate market. As Ling joked with everyone, her smile was glued on, her mouth busily opening and closing. She only took one bite of the German pork knuckle on the plate. While everyone chatted and laughed, the head of the department raised her glass and took a sip of wine, then suddenly stared at Ling. "Your face is so pale. Are you sick?"

Ling's heart tightened. Did the head of the department know? She laughed loudly. "Huh? Do I look sick?"

"I saw you with Ivy just now. When you came back, your complexion looked awful." The head of the department eyed Ling with concern.

Everyone was silent, fixing their gazes on Ling. At that moment, time stopped. Ling could only hear the sound of her heart thumping. She glanced at the head of the department, feeling hostile. "I just did a micro-injection foundation treatment to lighten my skin. How does it look?"

The truth was, she hadn't undergone any sort of treatment; she was just spouting off bullshit. Everyone's focus turned to beauty. Ling babbled on and on about which salons had the best techniques, and which were the cheapest. While talking, she intentionally or unintentionally added a sentence: "If I tell Wai I went for a beauty treatment, she'll definitely say I'm hurting myself again—she's too stubborn, completely different from Hong Kongers."

"Wai is like a mainlander, always speaking in Mandarin," Miss Au agreed, and the other teachers nodded. The topic followed whatever Ling said. She couldn't help but feel a sense of achievement.

"What do you think makes someone a Hong Konger?" Ling seized the opportunity to change the subject.

"At the very least, being born in Hong Kong," Miss So said.

"What about those who were born on the mainland but later immigrated to Hong Kong? Would they count as Hong Kongers?" Miss Au countered.

"Whether someone is a Hong Konger is simple—if you speak Cantonese, you're a Hong Konger," Miss Ko said.

"People in Guangdong province and overseas Chinese in Indonesia also speak Cantonese," Miss Ip interjected.

"It's about identifying with Hong Kong culture and speaking Hong Kong–style Cantonese," Ling said.

"What about foreigners living in Hong Kong who don't speak Cantonese? Are they Hong Kongers?" Miss Ip asked.

"Hmmm . . . Hong Kongers are hard to define, but Wai isn't like a Hong Konger. Obviously, Cantonese is her mother tongue, but she speaks in Mandarin all the time—does she want to become a mainlander?"

After Ling said this, everyone burst out laughing. Ling just wanted to belittle Wai, and calling her a mainlander was simply the most effective way. Although many mainlanders were knowledgeable about books and etiquette, and the admission rate of new immigrant students had also increased, most teachers still had a poor impression of new immigrant parents. On Parents' Day, some said they couldn't understand and kept clamoring for a translation. "Hong Kong is part of China—why not speak Mandarin?" This was totally overbearing. They felt that, since they sent their children to study, the teachers should automatically accommodate them. Ling had encountered a couple of parents like this. She'd insist on speaking Cantonese, telling them to switch to

English if they didn't understand, citing school policy, and saying that there was no Mandarin interpretation service. There were also some new immigrant parents who didn't understand Hong Kong culture, which caused a lot of trouble. Ling once heard that a cross-border student was punished for using a mobile phone in class. The head of the department called the parents to inform them, and the parents said that students on the mainland could use mobile phones during class. They were dissatisfied with the strict punishment of the head of the department, and called the principal to complain . . .

Imitating Wai's manner of speaking, Ling cracked several jokes that left everyone laughing so hard they were out of breath, making her forget about the earlier "greeting" from the head of the department. However, Ling noticed that the principal lifted her wine glass, studying the red wine inside and occasionally nodding at it, as though she weren't listening, making Ling feel uneasy.

When she arrived back at school after lunch, Ling quickly walked over to Wai. Wai was preparing materials for her class, the desk strewn with notes, the lunchbox she hadn't yet cleaned casually set aside. Ling stretched out her hand and swept it in front of Wai's eyes, smiling as she said, "Relax, there's no need to be nervous . . . I only want to say, I just received a call. My family member is out of the hospital. Thank you so much for your help. I can resume my work. Can you send me my materials?"

Wai looked slightly taken aback, staring up at Ling's smiling face, before coming back to her senses and grabbing Ling's hand. "Really? That's great. How's your family member?"

"The cancer index is zero, and they've already recovered."

"It's okay. I can keep helping you."

"Hurry up and study for the LPAT. You're taking it soon.

Thank you very much for helping me earlier. I really can resume my work, really."

Seeing Ling so anxious, Wai was surprised. Just then the bell rang, signaling the end of lunch. As she cleared off her desk, Wai said, "I've only written half of the Form 4 test paper. I'm so sorry—I'll email it to you after class. Take a look and see whether it's useful . . ."

"Send it to me now. I want to finish it as soon as possible."

The teachers' office filled with the sound of chairs being pushed back as teachers left one after another. Wai grasped her textbook, clearly wanting to leave, but seeing the distraught expression on Ling's face, she had no choice but to turn on her computer and send Ling the file.

"Actually, I really can help you—if you need anything, come find me again . . ." After pressing the transfer key, Wai grabbed the book and rushed out of the teachers' office.

Smiling, Ling waved goodbye. After Wai had left, she returned to her seat to check if she'd received the email. When she did, she immediately sent it to the trash. She peered over Wai's side of the partition, noticing that her computer was still on. Most of the nearby teachers were gone. Ling sneaked over to Wai's seat, hoping to retrieve all the materials she'd given her.

Ling propped up her phone on Wai's desk so that if anyone passed by, she'd see their reflection on the screen. She stared at the computer screen, her heart racing, her hand sweating as she gripped the mouse. After a while, she found her file in the sub-folder of a folder. Steadying her trembling hands, she simultaneously pressed the control, shift, and delete keys to completely erase the data.

Behind her, she heard footsteps click-clacking. In the glowing screen of her phone, a pair of legs walked toward her. The figure grew larger and larger, the screen filled with clothing wrinkles. Turning her head, Ling saw it was the head of the department. She didn't have time to get back to her seat. She pretended as though nothing had happened, remaining calm and collected as she moved the mouse.

"Hey, why are you in Wai's seat?" When the head of the department spoke, her mouth was the only thing moving; the rest of her facial features remained frozen, giving off a cold and detached air.

Glimpsing a folder called "The Oil Peddler" on Wai's computer, Ling said, "Earlier, Wai asked me to search for something on her computer to help her make a worksheet on 'The Oil Peddler.'"

The head of the department tilted her head, frowning slightly. Ling added, "She said she has to study for the LPAT and has no time to do it."

The department head walked away without saying anything, returning to her seat and propping up her IELTS book, glancing at Ling every now and then. She seemed to be everywhere—was she the principal's eye? But at that moment, Ling couldn't think that much. After deleting all of the information, she heaved a sigh of relief and went back to her cubicle.

When school finished, Wai returned with a big pile of homework and slammed it onto her desk. Ling, who was beside the partition, also felt the vibration on her desk. Gasping for air, Wai fanned her hand. Ling decided the timing was right and swiveled her chair toward Wai. "Wow, you really *lurk horde*."

Wai smiled sheepishly.

"You want to make a worksheet on 'The Oil Peddler'?"

"How do you know?"

"Miss Au mentioned it to me. You helped me earlier. I'd like to repay the favor."

Wai quickly said, "No no no, it's just something small . . . I didn't help you at all . . ."

Ling thought, *Of course you didn't help me. I don't need your help—just don't hurt me.* However, instead she said, "I'll help you. You're taking the LPAT this week. You need to concentrate on studying."

At the mention of the LPAT, Wai sighed, eyeing the partition covered with notes in pinyin, a dazed look on her face.

Ling patted Wai on the shoulder, causing her whole body to shake. "You've got this! Study hard. I'll help you for sure. We're good friends, after all." After she finished speaking, she took the exercise books from Wai's desk.

Wai stared at Ling for a while. "Do you really consider me a good friend?"

"Of course! You're too good to me."

"Thank you . . ." Wai was moved to tears.

That week, every day after completing her teaching duties, Wai stayed at school to review pinyin, while Ling silently worked amid the hiss of what sounded like Wai reciting sutras. Previously, Wai had helped Ling with making test papers, creating worksheets, and chairing meetings for extracurricular activities. Now it was Ling's turn to help Wai. Ling had to take care of her own work as well as Wai's, so she finished work later than Wai every night. She began to understand Wai's earlier hardships, but she didn't feel guilty. Now they were even.

Around 9 p.m., Wai finished working. Before leaving, she placed a cup of Nescafé and a Sugus candy on Ling's desk. "I have no way to repay you." Then she bowed at a ninety-degree angle.

Ling wanted to laugh, but she didn't. She popped the candy in her mouth, oohing and aahing about how delicious it was. She also smiled as she watched Wai leave.

As soon as the door to the teachers' office closed, Ling spat out a *pfft* of contempt. Seeing the desk full of pinyin notes, she felt all the more like spitting. Forget it—Wai was gone, and the teachers' office had finally quieted down. Ling continued working hard on Wai's behalf. Whatever Wai hadn't given her, she picked up from Wai's desk, returning it to its place when she was finished.

At 10 p.m., all the lights in the school had been shut off, leaving only Ling's desk lamp. Standing up, she peered out the transom window, making sure there weren't any moving shadows on campus, and even turned off her desk lamp. She sat in Wai's seat, logged into her computer, and replied to emails on her behalf, taking the opportunity to peek at the files on the computer. The blue glow from the screen in the pitch-black room was glaring, causing Ling's eyes to well up with tears, but what could be more exhilarating than monitoring Wai's every move? What if Wai was a "wolf in sheep's clothing," secretly plotting with someone against her? She couldn't let her guard down.

Ling never thought that Wai would actually hand over her intranet account password. A few days earlier she had said, whether intentionally or unintentionally, that by logging into Wai's computer, processing documents for her, and replying to her emails, she could really reduce her workload. At the time, Ling had carefully said, "After you take the LPAT, I'll destroy the password. If you're uneasy, you can ask a technician to reset the login."

Much to her surprise, Wai scribbled her password down on a slip of paper without giving it a second thought. "You're so kind to help me. Of course I can trust you!"

How stupid!

However, Ling didn't find anything. She only saw numerous Mandarin-learning pages bookmarked in her browser. She turned off the computer and exhaled. How could someone so stupid beat her?

Meanwhile, Ling specifically chose Friday afternoon to secretly meet with the principal. She learned from Ivy that the principal would stay after school that day; and moreover, on Friday her colleagues would leave work early. No one would notice her in the principal's office except for Ivy—it was an ideal time to seek out the principal. Also, the following day, Wai would take the LPAT. Regardless of how she scored, Ling needed to strike first. Armed with liqueur-filled chocolates bought at YATA Department Store, before entering the principal's office she took one out of the box and gave it to Ivy, then put her finger to her lips. Ivy smiled knowingly. Ling was going to give the principal the paperwork for the Joint School Oral Exam to sign, and talk about her job while she happened to be there.

As the principal scribbled her signature on the paper, Ling said, "Actually, do you think you can hire another TA? I see how busy Wai is. Not only does she have to study Mandarin, but also teach and handle administrative affairs. This week, I helped her make a worksheet for Form 1 and helped teach her classes, staying at school till around ten o'clock every night. If you hire one more TA, we could share Wai's workload."

The storage cabinet behind the principal was filled with snacks from Ling, such as Kopi Luwak, Japanese mixed dried fruits, and Italian cookies . . . but at that moment, the principal stroked her water glass without touching the chocolates that Ling had placed on her desk. A mist obscured the principal's face, and Ling couldn't see her expression clearly. After a while, the principal spoke. "What do you think of Wai's ability to do her job?"

"She's very diligent, but she works rather slowly, and doesn't react quickly enough. I have to help her often."

The principal nodded, picked up her glass of water, and took a sip.

Ling continued, "In fact, I excel in training people, and I work efficiently. I have plenty of spare time to handle administrative work. If you need any help, you can come to me."

The principal glanced at Ling, then lowered her head in thought. The atmosphere was a little stiff, so Ling held up the box of chocolates as a reminder that she'd brought a gift. "These are delicious."

The principal took the chocolates and smiled, but didn't continue the conversation.

Ling hadn't expected the principal to be so uninterested in the snacks she'd given her. When she came out of the office, Ivy asked how it went. She shrugged her shoulders noncommittally. At the time, Ling didn't think it was anything out of the ordinary, simply assuming that the principal was swamped with work, or an investment had failed, thus souring her mood.

The Monday after she'd met the principal, Ivy showed up with a summons paper for Wai. Ivy winked at Ling, who covered her mouth and snickered. Wai pinched the summons paper, both hands shaking so much that the paper rattled. Pretending not to notice, Ling picked up her cup and went to the kitchenette so that Wai wouldn't complain to her.

When the bell rang, Ling was in the kitchenette holding her coffee. In the distance, she saw Wai walking out of the teachers' office, trembling as she held the summons paper. Ling was a little uneasy. On the one hand, she wanted to know the principal's reaction. On the other, she was afraid that the principal would tell Wai what she'd said. But then she thought, *I didn't smear Wai's name—can I help what colleagues have said? Moreover, Wai herself said she was slow at work. I just phrased it bluntly.*

Fifteen minutes later, Wai weakly pushed open the door to the teachers' office, returned to her seat, and plopped down, panting heavily. Ling picked up a chocolate coin from her drawer and quietly placed it on Wai's desk.

Wai turned to look at her. The lower half of her face sank into the shadow of the desk lamp. Ling's heart shivered with fear—she wanted to turn away. Taking a deep breath, Wai spoke at great length. "The principal asked about Saturday's LPAT. I said that, except for pinyin, I did poorly on all the other papers. I made a lot of mistakes on the listening paper, and my individual short speech was terrible . . ."

Fortunately, the principal didn't say anything. Ling had expected that Wai would bomb the exam and that she'd reveal everything when reporting to the principal. That's how stupid people were.

"Then the principal asked if I was busy and wanted you to help me. I said that you're my best friend. Not only do you listen to my complaints, you also do many things for me . . . The principal asked me if my job was such *horde lurk* that I had to complain . . . I was shocked. I didn't expect the principal to ask me this question. I said, 'No, no,' then the principal looked at me sternly, and I wondered if she hated me . . ."

AFTER SHE FAILED the LPAT again, Wai became even weirder. That day, the head of the department came up to Wai and gave instructions about her work. Wai's face reddened and her ears burned, her hands tightly clenched. The head of the department stared at her. "Do you have any other questions?"

"Is it about . . . the *work-work-worksheet* for 'Hong-Hong-Hong* Kong . . . Story' ?" Wai's mouth and hands shook.

The head of the department glared at her impatiently, and Wai nodded abruptly. "No—no questions . . ." Before Wai had finished speaking, the department head was gone. Wai leaned over the table, shrugged her shoulders, and began sobbing.

Wai's cries sounded like a thin needle drilling into her ears, neither painful nor itchy. Ling didn't want to pay attention to her, she just wanted to quickly finish writing the announcement as soon as possible and send it to students in the afternoon. However, the head of the department looked at Ling when she left, and Miss Au behind her also turned to see what was happening. Ling felt everyone's eyes on her. Since she was sitting next to Wai, it'd be impolite to ignore her. Reluctantly, Ling leaned over and asked, "You've been crying a long time—is everything all right?"

When Ling said this, Wai began to cry even more intensely, so choked up that her nostrils shook like hooks. "Why is it the more . . . the more . . . I speak, the *worst-worse* I am? Will I *puh-puh-pass* the next LPAT?"

Wai cried and cried and cried. There was nothing Ling could do. She'd already fulfilled her duty and tried to console her to the best of her ability. This was an office, not a home; you came here to work, not seek sympathy and comfort.

After an unknown amount of time, the sound of Wai's crying stopped. "Thank . . . you . . ."

Ling was formatting an announcement and didn't want to be distracted by her.

"Thank you . . . for *core-caring* about me . . ."

"No need to thank me. Hurry up and get ready for your class."

Wai blew her nose vigorously and said nothing. Ling thought she was continuing to work, but after a while she poked her head over again. "My mom also wants to thank you and invite you to eat a—a—*mule-meal*. Do you have time?"

"You're really . . . polite . . ." In shock, Ling typed a different character than what she'd meant.

"Just an *ornery-ordinary*—meal."

"But soon I'll have to give exams." Ling gave an offhand excuse.

Wai's eyes welled up with tears, and she lowered her head. Afraid that she would cry again, Ling said, "When . . . were you thinking?"

Wai immediately wiped away her tears and spoke quickly. "Thank you. Is tonight okay?"

Was she wanting to strike while the iron was hot? Ling had promised her mother she'd go home for dinner that night. Her mom would be upset if she canceled last minute—but after thinking it over, she decided it would be good to learn more about Wai's background, so she said, "I have to finish grading essays before I can go."

"No problem! I'll wait for you."

AT SEVEN THAT evening, Ling and Wai left the school and walked onto Nathan Road. The sky between the buildings was suffused with the glow of the sunset, the neon signs on either side like fences, blocking the blood flowing from the sky. The road was jam-packed. Wai and Ling started out walking side by side, but soon Wai ended up in front, with Ling following behind. Ling silently thanked the other pedestrians. Before long, they left Nathan Road and turned onto Reclamation Street, where a series of red fluorescent lights illuminated the entrances of tong lau tenement buildings, emitting a blinding glow.

"You . . . live here?" Ling asked awkwardly.

Wai nodded, embarrassed.

Reclamation Street was full of shops selling tools and machinery. After dark, the shops closed, and there weren't many people on the street, only a few women waiting by the roadside, along with two or three men loitering about. They seemed like prostitutes and pimps, but they didn't appear to have any affiliation with one another. Ling's mom had several flats on Dundas Street that were subdivided into rental units. Ling handled the rentals for her mom and frequented the area, but she avoided entering Reclamation Street and Portland Street at night. Although Dundas Street was also lined with nightclub signs, it was still a main thoroughfare directly connected to Nathan Road, and was more respectable than the narrow side streets and alleys.

Wai led Ling into one of the tong lau tenement buildings. At the doorway, there was a fluorescent light box with green characters on a red background spelling out the phrase DREAM GARDEN. Fluorescent pink paper was stuck to the entrance, advertising STUDENT GIRL 300, MALAY GIRL 350, JAPANESE GIRL 400. Even though she had spent so much time in this area, it was the first time Ling had entered a building with one of these light boxes at the door.

Wai climbed the stairs, Ling behind her. The stairway was dark, with only one tube of light illuminating each corner, and was full of trash, giving off an acrid stench. Ling had on a full-length dress. With each step, she had to hoist it up to avoid dirtying it. There were three households on each floor, fluorescent paper pasted on the doors with various prices and services. After a while, they arrived on the fourth floor, and Wai stopped in front of the door of one of the units, the iron gate also pasted with fluorescent paper displaying PEACE AND SAFETY FOR THE WHOLE FAMILY.

"I've never dared invite friends to my house, but my mom and I really wanted to *ex-express* our thanks, so I *un-un-invited* you. I hope you don't *muh-mind* . . ."

Ling smiled wryly. They were already here—could she still mind? Wai pushed open the door, revealing an ordinary residential unit, about two hundred square feet. The paint on the walls was peeling, and there was a dilapidated sofa against the wall, a mismatched landscape painting hanging over it. A circular drying rack full of underwear was hooked on the window frame. Nearby was a wooden dining table, one of its legs conspicuously reattached. The table was covered with a plastic tablecloth, a few dishes, and three bowls of rice placed on top, emitting the strong aroma of food.

The kitchen clanged with the sounds of stir-frying. Wai invited Ling to sit down. Soon, Wai's mom appeared with another dish. Wai's mom was wearing a shirt that had been practically torn to pieces by washing. Her shoulders were wide, but her neck was unusually short, and her head was so small that it seemed as though her head and neck retracted into her shoulders. Her eyes were dull—when she looked at you, it looked like she was looking elsewhere. The most striking thing was that, like Wai, her eyebrows drooped into an upside-down V shape.

Without removing her apron, Wai's mom picked up a rice bowl and chopsticks and began serving Ling, plucking a generous amount of each dish and stuffing it into the bowl. Ling kept saying, "No need, no need," but Wai's mom insisted, piling up the bowl like a small mountain. After serving Ling, Wai's mom served herself and Wai.

"Help yourself. Don't be polite." Wai's mom spoke slowly, spitting out each word.

After serving the food, Wai's mom sat down and began eating. Ling observed that Wai's mom's fingers were short, and her movements were clumsy as she shoveled food into her mouth.

"I heard from Ah Wai that you worked overtime every day to help her." With the food in her mouth, Wai's mom spoke even more slowly. After she finished, she gave Ling more food.

"You don't have to serve me . . ." Ling moved her bowl closer to her.

"Ah Wai's like me—we're not smart, but we're diligent! I worked hard every day to make money and raise Ah Wai, and now Wai's a teacher, very impressive!" Vegetable shreds were stuck between Wai's mom's front teeth. When she spoke, bits of food sprayed onto Wai's face. Wai wiped the residue from her face, then wiped her mom's mouth.

"My mom is *mantelly handy-clapped*. I hope you don't *muh-mind* . . ." Wai spoke haltingly. Ling had never imagined that Wai would still speak Mandarin at home.

Wai's mother stared at Wai wide-eyed.

"I said you're '*mantelly handy-clapped*,'" Wai shouted in her mother's ears.

"Don't speak Mandarin. I don't understand!" Wai's mom threw her bamboo chopsticks on the table with a snap.

"Wai said . . . you're mentally handicapped," Ling said, embarrassed.

Wai's mom broke into a grin. "Many people mock me for being an idiot. You're a good person—don't laugh at me." After she said that, another piece of food flew toward Ling's bowl. Feeling full, Ling stretched out her hand to block it.

"Give it to me. Ling doesn't want it." Wai handed over her bowl to take the food from her mom.

"I won't listen to Mandarin." Wai's mom threw the food on the table.

"Mom, be good. I have to learn Mandarin well. Otherwise, I can't be a teacher." Wai put the food on the table into her own bowl.

Watching Wai and her mom, Ling felt like they were protagonists in a comedy, and tried not to laugh out loud.

After dinner, while Wai's mom washed dishes in the kitchen, Wai took Ling to her room. There was no window in the room. The ceiling light tube emitted a dim white light. The walls were covered with notes in pinyin, which were stuck everywhere but the bed, looking from afar like dense fish scales. Beside the bed there was a desk full of notes in Mandarin, and the full-length mirror next to it was covered with words. Upon closer inspection, these were also Mandarin pinyin. Against the wall, there was a large bookcase filled with books such as *Essential Selections of Tang and Song Poetry*, *Duan Yucai's Annotations on Explanations of Graphs and Interpretations of Characters*, *Miscellaneous Annotations on Mencius*, and many books on literary history, all of which were assigned reading for university Chinese majors. Ling hadn't read a single one.

Ling looked up at the bookcase. Wai asked her in the mirror, "I don't want any of these books—do you?"

Ling chuckled. "What would I do with them? I sold all mine after I graduated."

"Sometimes I wonder, what's the point of studying? Even if you study hard, you may not be able to become a teacher."

Glancing at the books on Wai's bookcase, Ling changed the subject. "Hey, you have Sirena Cheng's new novel—how is it? I like Ong Yi-Hing's books."

Wai didn't answer, fixing her gaze on Ling in the mirror. "Why did you decide to become a teacher?"

"Graduating from the Chinese department, what else can I do besides being a teacher?" Wai's question was so boring—wasn't the point of being a teacher to make money?

"My grades weren't good, but my mom really wanted me to become a teacher. She frequently says that the teachers at the special school were very kind to her. They taught her to read, taught her to take care of herself, and even found her a job so she could raise me. I think being a teacher is meaningful, as what I've learned can *con-continue* on. My college entrance examination results only allowed me to enroll in the Education University Department of Chinese Studies. At that time, I thought I'd become a Chinese teacher, but it turns out that being a teacher isn't as easy as I thought. If I can't renew my contract, I won't be able to *con-continue* on."

Hearing Wai complain again, Ling could only smile helplessly.

"Is my Mandarin terrible?"

"No. Right now, you're speaking so fluently." Ling was telling the truth. In her room, Wai relaxed and spoke more naturally than usual; but in the mirror, her eyes gradually turned red.

"You're lying to me . . ."

"Your Mandarin isn't bad. Sometimes you're too nervous, so you can't speak well."

"I know my pronunciation is substandard."

"Language is for communication. As long as other people can understand you, it's okay."

"But I can't be a teacher if I don't speak standard Mandarin."

Wai occupied most of the full-length mirror. Ling stood beside her, her dress slipping into the frame. The hem of the dress in the mirror swished with two stains—she must've stepped on something dirty while climbing the stairs. She rushed to wipe them in the mirror. At that moment, she happened to meet Wai's gaze. Her eyes were full of inexplicable paranoia. Ling turned away.

"I feel I'm becoming more and more like my mom. Do you think so too?"

"The spitting image," Ling quipped. The Wai in the mirror not only looked like her, even the expression in her eyes was the same, her eyes seeming to look at you but without any focus.

"People say I inherited my mom's stupidity. Even if I'm not *mantelly handy-clapped*, I'm not smart, either . . ."

Another difficult question to answer. The corners of Ling's mouth twitched. Wai seemed to see through her mind. "I often think that the body is like a frame that can't be broken through no matter what. If I'd been born a mainlander, and grown up speaking Mandarin, I could be a Chinese teacher. If I'd been born a British person, I could be an English teacher. Not being able to speak Mandarin or English in Hong Kong is a *duh-deficiency*, another kind of *dis-dis-disability*." Speaking the last two phrases, Wai stuttered again.

"Don't make it sound so serious . . . If speaking improperly is a disability, then most people in Hong Kong are disabled."

"Only by speaking properly will others respect you. In Hong Kong, if you speak English like a foreigner you're superior to others. The same is true for speaking Mandarin. This is the reality. Moreover, I'm a teacher . . . Mandarin-language education is the general *tend-trend* . . ." The Wai in the mirror didn't lift her head.

"Teachers used to all teach in Cantonese, but now they're required to speak Mandarin. It's only that society has changed, it's not a disability."

"What's the use of Cantonese? Except for in Hong Kong and *Gang-Guangdong*, English and Mandarin are spoken all over the world. If you say in your résumé that you know how to speak Cantonese, will that get you an interview? Will the principal renew your contract because you understand Cantonese?"

Ling didn't know what to say.

"If you don't speak standardly, you're inferior to others. It's a *duh-deficiency*, a disability. My mom and I are both language idiots. She also studied Mandarin at the *spuh-spuh-special* school, but still couldn't grasp it. Genetics can't be changed— no matter how hard you try, it's useless."

After speaking, Wai grew quiet again. Ling chatted about Sirena Cheng's novels, the latest movies, SK-II's newest anti-wrinkle day cream, but Wai wasn't interested. She only stared at herself in the mirror, as if Ling no longer existed.

IT WAS AFTER 10 p.m. when Ling left Wai's home, and the fluorescent paper at the entrance of the tong lau tenement building looked even more alluring under the reflection of the light box. There weren't any cars on the road. Reclamation Street, Soy Street, and Portland Street stretched endlessly in the darkness, cut off from the bustling city noise of Nathan Road. Hidden among the horizontal signs on either side of the building, the sparse streetlamps revealed a fuzzy light that made Ling uncomfortable. Ling stood in the middle of the road. She had to walk along this street to return to Nathan Road. After taking a few steps, she spotted a woman standing against a nearby wall, hands crossed, looking around. The fluorescent tube above her head dyed her whole body bright red. Ling couldn't make out her age. She could only see that she was wearing a low-cut vest specially folded to reveal her cleavage, and an umbrella skirt that was so short it only covered her buttocks. On the other side, two men were heading toward the woman, one fat, one thin, both smoking cigarettes. Ling couldn't get a clear view of their appearances, but felt their eyes locked on her.

Ling bowed her head and walked quickly. As she passed the woman, she lowered her head even more. A strong, choking scent of perfume assailed her nostrils. The two men came closer and closer. Ling concentrated on the silk bows of the high-heeled shoes protruding and retracting from the hem of her dress, but she still felt their needle-like gaze. She sped up, and when she passed them, one of the men blew a puff of smoke at her. "How much for an hour?"

Without answering, Ling ran. The woman behind her giggled and called out "Little sister" in Cantonese with a mixed accent.

Ankles wobbling in her high heels, Ling managed to run all the way to Nathan Road. At 11 p.m., the streets were jammed with traffic, neon lights were still flashing, long lines snaked outside the restaurants, and there were just as many cars as during the day. Heaving a sigh of relief, Ling bought a skewer of fish balls from a small food stall. Eating as she walked along Nathan Road, she suddenly felt ridiculous. She should've told that man off for being a worthless scumbag and a clueless idiot, showing him who was boss; and that whore, dressed so cheaply, doing that kind of work, how could she ever compare to Ling? She was a teacher, a professional.

Wai was also quite pitiful. Her mother was mentally handicapped, and she lived in this kind of environment where she was no doubt treated like a prostitute every day. A teacher's salary was good—why didn't she move out? Could it be that her mother was a . . . ? Yes, there was fluorescent paper pasted outside their door, just like their neighbors'. On second thought, Wai was also somewhat like a prostitute, always eager to please others, the only difference being she didn't take off her clothes.

After that evening, Ling always wanted to ask Wai, but she didn't dare open her mouth. While having lunch with the Chinese department one day, Ling ate her favorite black truffle spaghetti and deliberately lowered her voice as she described the place where Wai lived and Wai's mom's appearance in vivid detail. Everyone listened intently, holding their breath. The principal held her wine glass, but had no time to take a sip. At the end, Ling leaned forward, placed her palm over her lips, and softly added, "Wai's mom is mentally handicapped."

The principal set down her glass and mixed her Caesar salad on the table.

"Her mom must be 'in the business.' Otherwise, how would a mentally handicapped person be able to make money?" Miss Wu said.

"Maybe even Wai is . . ." Ling said.

Everyone became quiet.

After a while, Miss Ip broke the silence. "No wonder Wai's so stupid—might she have below-average intelligence? I have a student with below-average intelligence in my class. It drives me crazy, they're even dumber than a pig . . ."

"Such students, if they work hard, can still go to university. There was a student who studied diligently and ended up being admitted to Lingnan University. However, his reaction time was too slow—will he be able to find a job in the future?" Miss Wu said.

"If not, then . . ."

Everyone looked at each other and smiled. The principal picked out the croutons from her Caesar salad one by one, carefully chewing them and saying nothing.

The office phone beeped and beeped. The ant continued to pace back and forth inside the lid. It seemed to have a particular fondness for walking toward Ling, shaking its tiny head at her. Ling observed it closely—was it begging for mercy? Or expressing hatred toward her?

Why climb up here to die? It served it right. Ling moved the lid quickly, and the ant couldn't keep up with the speed. After crawling and rolling around, it soon lay still, letting the lid drag it along. But the lid stopped, and the ant got back up again, walking faster than before, as though it couldn't be killed.

Watching the ant walk around aimlessly, for some reason Ling thought of Wai again. Her mother's words from just now sounded in her ears. *Isn't there a dim-witted colleague who helps you out all the time?*

She still remembered opening the door that night and trying to be as quiet as possible. At the time, her mom was lying on the sofa, watching TV with a toothpick in her mouth. Ling wanted to sneak into her room, but how was she supposed to get by? Her mom spat out the toothpick and scolded her for not coming home for dinner, scolded her and scolded her. She exhaled, placing both hands behind her, until her mom had finished yelling at her, before saying, "I went to Wai's tonight."

Her mom sat with her arms crossed, watching TV without

looking at her. A National Geographic program was play-ing on the TV. An anteater on dried-out grassland stuck its crescent-shaped nose into an ant-hole, drilling twice with its whip-like tongue, then rolling up bunches of ants into its mouth. After a while, her mom said, "Other moms cook better than I do, so you don't come back to eat . . ."

"Her mom is mentally handicapped, like a young child."

Ling's mom sneered, "No wonder your colleague is so stupid." Then she raised the remote control to lower the volume of the TV, waiting for Ling to continue. Her mom enjoyed hearing gossip, especially when it came to criticizing Ling's colleagues—who was the bootlicker, who was the old fox—and she was even more scathing than Ling. Whenever the topic turned to Wai, her mom rocked back and forth with laughter, saying there was no cure for stupidity.

"They live on Reclamation Street, next to ladies of the night. Maybe . . ."

Her mom waved her hand in the air. "Of course! If you're mentally challenged, don't have kids and pass the genes on to your daughter, having to resort to turning tricks to make money. Serves them right."

Her mom no longer seemed annoyed with her. Ling breathed a sigh of relief. "You're lucky I was born clever—the student has surpassed the master."

"Your clever mom gave birth to a clever daughter. If you'd been mentally handicapped, I'd have sent you to the Po Leung Kuk orphanage."

Ling remembered how she just giggled at the time, and her mom looked at her. "That's the way the world is. Those who are useless should leave as soon as possible." After she'd finished speaking, her mom turned up the volume of the TV and stopped talking to her.

Even though she knew her mom spouted off her mouth as

she pleased, Ling still felt hurt. That night, she had a dream that she was running barefoot on the grassland, an anteater chasing her from behind. She ran for her life, over uneven stone paths and scorching-hot asphalt, the soles of her feet bleeding, but the anteater had a long tongue and no matter how fast she ran, she was at risk of its tongue sweeping her up. Soon, she had no strength to keep on running, and fell to the ground. The anteater captured her and wrapped its tongue around her neck. She was unable to breathe, her whole body trembling with fear . . .

Ling woke up to the sound of screaming. The dream was so realistic. She sat up, hugged her knees, and pinched each toe. Fortunately, it was only a dream . . .

The ant on the desk approached Ling again, stopping before the edge of the lid, and looked at her, as though preparing to declare war on the enemy. Recalling the dream from that night, Ling resolutely lifted the transparent lid, then crushed the ant to death with her fingers. The ant's corpse looked like a speck of dandruff. Ling brushed it away with a flick of her thumb.

June was sweltering, the courtyard of Sing Din Secondary School brimming with morning sunshine. The male students played basketball on the sports field, while the female students wore gray jackets they thought were pretty, sitting side by side at the snack bar eating breakfast. When the teachers got to school, they discussed where to travel in August. The campus was filled with the joyful atmosphere of anticipating summer vacation. The head of the department said she'd go to the UK to study English. Miss Ip and Miss Wu were traveling to Malaysia and Singapore respectively. Ling held the latest issue of a travel magazine, sharing which attractions were must-see and which restaurants were must-try. It was as though everyone had already left Hong Kong and was lying on a beach, sipping sweet lemon specialty drinks.

In the Chinese department, the only one who was busy was Wai. When Ling saw Wai holding two sheets of paper filled with words and muttering to herself, the desk lamp's reflection giving her black-framed glasses a silvery sheen, she remembered that this was the day of Wai's presentation at the weekly assembly. Wai had carefully prepared for this assembly, redrafting her lecture three times. After the lecture was finalized, she marked each character with pinyin, the symbols and tones marked in different colors. Several times during lunch, when Ling passed Wai's seat, she saw her reading her speech while eating, accidentally spitting out food.

It was just a weekly assembly. No one had ever taken it as seriously as Wai. Compared with other academic matters, the weekly assemblies were completely irrelevant. Usually during these assemblies, the students were either in a daydream or fell asleep; starting from the next semester, all weekly assemblies would be conducted only in English and Mandarin, and the auditorium would be even more silent. When the teacher on the stage asked questions, no students would dare to raise their hands to respond. Everyone was afraid of speaking English and Mandarin.

More importantly, the principal never inquired about the quality of the weekly assembly. Although she required teachers to give lectures in English or Mandarin, like the students she dozed off or played games on her phone, not caring about the teachers' performances. Ling recalled one time that an English teacher with nasal allergies accidentally mixed up "excuse me" and "execute me." None of the students noticed, but the teachers couldn't stop laughing. The principal used to teach English, but she didn't react in the slightest, eyes glued to her phone, focusing on getting through the game.

And so, for the weekly assemblies the following semester, the first couple of times, the teachers, unaware of the situation, would still prepare diligently. However, for subsequent assemblies, the teachers would speak their minds freely since, no matter what they said, the principal wouldn't care. On days when the principal was away on business, they were even more unrestrained. The head of the department once played a movie during the weekly assembly, and only made a few remarks at the beginning and the end. It was so relaxed.

The weekly assembly started at 8.30 a.m. Wai set off for the auditorium around eight o'clock. As she walked, she recited the lecture notes in her hands, knocking over the exercise books on her colleagues' desks several times, and nearly tripping over the garbage can at the front of the teachers' office. Watching the back of Wai's stumbling figure, Ling quietly mouthed, "Looking forward to it." Everyone covered their mouths and snickered.

Soon after Wai left, they all arrived at the auditorium with great fanfare, fifteen minutes earlier than usual. The custodian was still arranging the seats, the sunlight shining through the organ-like transom windows onto rows of empty benches, like an army holding weapons. Wai stood on the stage, mumbling at the turned-off microphone, as if addressing an army preparing to attack.

"Does she really need to work that hard?" Miss Au, who was sitting next to Ling, remarked.

Ling rolled her eyes and smiled.

Before long the class bell rang, and students entered the auditorium one after another. Teachers followed the students, walking to the front row from the narrow aisle, on the side of the auditorium. The principal walked along the aisle, between the two rows of chairs, to the first seat in the first row. Only the principal could walk down the middle aisle—this was an unwritten rule. When the bell rang again, Wai slowly returned to the stage. She wore a suit jacket and black corduroy pants. As she climbed up the stairs off to the side, with each step her pants were pulled up to reveal the white edges of her socks. Ling peeked at the principal's reaction. The principal gazed straight ahead, the sun gleaming on her raven-black hair, the side of her face suffused with a fluffy glow.

Walking up to the podium, Wai clutched the microphone and solemnly asked everyone to stand up, leading the students in singing the school song. After finishing singing, she instructed the students to sit down, cleared her throat, and spoke into the microphone. "Today's topic is 'always strive for improvement, even when you have reached the pinnacle.' How can we strive for improvement? As the idiom says, 'advance against the current, or you'll fall behind.' Society is changing rapidly—if we don't equip ourselves early enough, we'll be eliminated . . ." Wai's lecture topic was dull, but it suited her "positive and progressive" personality. Her Mandarin was also much more pleasing to the ears, without her usual stuttering; she'd obviously rehearsed repeatedly. While her pronunciation was standard, her voice had no intonation, like a computer-generated voice, completely lifeless.

Beside her, Miss Au had long been emitting even breathing sounds. Looking behind her, Ling could see that many students had fallen asleep. Ling glanced at the principal. Her side profile was bathed in white light. Apart from the light, there was no visible expression on her face, which was slightly disappointing. Before long, Ling also nodded off amid Wai's cotton-like voice.

After an unknown amount of time, the auditorium roared with laughter. Ling woke up and saw Wai on stage, her face turning red, then white. Ling asked Miss Au beside her what had happened.

"Tsui Siu-Hin from the 1D class suddenly raised his hand and said loudly in Mandarin, 'Teacher, I have a question.' Tsui Siu-Hin has ADHD and has repeated two grades. He's naughty and a troublemaker. Wai teaches the 1D Chinese class, and he likes to bully her. The truth is, everyone knows Tsui Siu-Hin has problems. Wai could've just ignored him, or asked the discipline teacher to deal with him, but Wai actually asked him what his question was. He naturally took the opportunity to act out, loudly saying, 'We aren't studying crap.' Then in Mandarin he said, 'We should *hit* the books, not *shit* the books.'"

Laughter continued to erupt. All order had been completely lost. Face ashen, Wai stood on the stage, glancing in every direction. The discipline teacher, Miss Ho, saw things were going south and stood up, loudly ordering everyone to be quiet. Miss Ho's voice was louder than Wai's even without the microphone. Intimidated by Miss Ho's authority, the students finally quieted down.

Wai continued her lecture, but she began stuttering again, to the point that she was unable to convey her ideas. Obviously, "to learn and constantly review what one has learned" came from Confucius, but she mistakenly attributed it to Mencius. Or, she clearly meant to say Liu Shan in reference to the last ruler of the Shu-Han Dynasty, but mispronounced his name as Liu Dan. Some students heard Wai's mistakes and secretly made fun of her. Others who couldn't understand her had already fallen asleep. The only sound left in the auditorium was Wai's voice trembling like a bouncing marble. Ling turned to glance at the principal. The principal was squinting at the podium, her eyebrows arched like two mountains in the sun. After a while, she left her seat and returned to her office through the aisle in the middle of the auditorium.

As soon as the bell rang, the students filed out of the auditorium, and the teachers dispersed with the crowd, everyone having forgotten what Wai had just said. Ling observed Wai still standing on the stage, staring blankly at the sunshine-filled seats, her face buried in the shadow of the stage, her drooping upside-down-V-shaped eyebrows looking hideous. Ling was overjoyed.

Back in the teachers' office, everyone quickly gulped down their water, grabbed their textbooks and writing materials, and rushed off to class. No one noticed that Wai wasn't there.

When it was lunchtime, Ling's class finished late. By the time she returned to the teachers' office, the head of the department and her colleagues had already packed up, standing in front of the office and waving their handbags to urge her on. In a hurry, Ling set down her textbooks, picked up her wallet, and prepared to set out. As she passed by Wai, she patted her on the shoulders, wanting to say hi to her, but Wai ignored her, staring at the pinyin notes on the partition without blinking, entirely frozen.

Ling looked around, but Wai didn't respond, so she didn't bother her and kept on walking.

Smack! Suddenly, Wai picked up her Mandarin textbook and slapped it on the table. Several red pens crashed to the ground, startling Ling. She only saw Wai forcefully breathing in and out, then slowly turning the swivel chair, glancing up at Ling, eyes blazing with a resentment that Ling had never seen before. After a while, Wai said, "I—can't—renew—my—contract." It was rare for Wai to speak Cantonese, and she enunciated each word deliberately, every one of them seeming to land on the floor with a lingering echo.

"Oh . . ." Ling avoided Wai's gaze. The head of the department again called out from the door. Ling turned to leave without saying goodbye to Wai. When she got back from lunch, she discovered that Wai had left work. Ivy said she'd taken sick leave.

Ling still remembered that afternoon. The afternoon sun shining down on her body, the pores of her entire body greedily absorbing the prickly heat. She stretched, gazing out the window at the cloudless blue sky, planning to buy a coffee from IFC Mall after school. At lunch just now, the principal had mentioned wanting to buy a coffee machine. Ling was delighted to hear that. Certainly, the Kopi Luwak she'd given the principal would taste better brewed in a coffee machine. Ling did her best to recommend her preferred model, and taught the principal how to brew high-quality coffee. She'd already crawled through the discussion boards, so she knew which brand worked best and the tricks of making coffee. As she spoke, the principal frequently nodded her head. Ling thought, why not buy one today as a celebration—it's only 3,000 HKD.

The following two days, Wai also took a leave of absence. With no one beside her to attend to her, no one complaining, no one silently reciting pinyin, it was much quieter. Ling could freely check Facebook, read magazines, and chat with her colleagues. With Wai gone, Ling saved a lot of time that she'd usually have spent dealing with her, and she finished work early.

But the happy time was short-lived. Two days later, when the bell was about to ring to signal the start of school, Wai pushed open the door to the teachers' office with a bang. When she entered, everyone was scared silly—her once-long hair had been cut down to the roots, her uneven, ultra-short bangs skimming her forehead, which now seemed too wide, her upside-down-V-shaped eyebrows hanging mid-air, unable to find a landing point. She strode forward, eyes blazing ahead, as though she were a different person.

Wai plopped down, tossing her handbag on the desk. Even Ling's seat shook. Usually she'd take the initiative to greet Wai, but at that moment she stared at the pinyin sea of the partition, speechless.

Everyone looked at Ling, trying to discern clues from her expression, but Ling was also at a loss. Wai used to annoy Ling, but now Wai ignored her, and the ever-sinking silence weighed heavily on her heart. All eyes on her, Ling approached Wai, tentatively saying, "Wow, you cut your hair."

Wai said nothing, motionlessly staring at the pinyin notes.

"Are . . . are you better?"

Wai remained silent. After a while, she stood up, ripped off the pinyin notes one by one, crumpled them into balls, and threw them in the trash can, but she didn't seem as though she

113

actually wanted to toss them in the trash; she was just throwing them in that direction. The paper balls that missed the trash can were scattered all over the place. Usually, Wai loved being neat and tidy and couldn't stand the slightest mess, but now she turned a blind eye to the balls of paper all over the floor and just sat there staring straight ahead. Soon, the class bell rang, and Wai strode out of the teachers' office holding her attendance book, slamming the door behind her.

Looking at the door shut tight, Ling felt rather uneasy. Why did Wai seem like a ghost? Colleagues from the Chinese department gathered around her to sound out what was going on. Eyeing them, Ling softly said, "Wai's contract wasn't renewed."

Everyone said, "Oh."

"But . . . I feel like she's pissed at you," Miss Au whispered.

Ling shrugged. Everyone smiled and walked away.

For the whole day, Wai didn't talk to anyone. When she returned to the teachers' office after class, she randomly cast aside homework and worksheets, then sat down in a daze. Ling seemed to see the sun cross her face, then fall to the ground. Usually, she diligently studied Mandarin—was she discouraged because of the LPAT? Wai always liked chatting with her about name brands and beauty. Today, Ling had on new shoes and was carrying a new handbag, but Wai didn't react at all. She went to class as usual, and after class, while she was still at school, it was as though she were on strike, not against anyone else in particular, but against herself.

What on earth had happened to Wai? Was the principal not renewing her contract really that big a blow? Previously, Ling had been able to guess Wai's next move, but now Ling seemed to be constantly flailing her arms yet unable to swat the fly swirling around her.

Just before she left work, Ling walked over to Wai and set down a piece of Godiva chocolate. "Are you unhappy because your contract wasn't renewed?"

Wai stared ahead, not looking at Ling.

"Try another school. Now a lot of schools are hiring." Ling passed her a newspaper. "Some schools don't state that they require passing the LPAT."

Ling circled in red ink the job ads in the newspaper, placing asterisks on the ads for positions that didn't require the LPAT. Wai looked at the newspaper, licking her dry, peeling lips. She suddenly beat the newspaper hysterically, the paper instantly ripping. "Teacher, teacher, haha—can I really be a teacher?"

Ling was taken aback. "Why not? You graduated from the Chinese department. Next time if you work hard enough, certainly you'll succeed . . ."

Wai threw back her head and laughed loudly. Her laughter grew louder and louder and then, after a while, stopped. She tore the newspaper into pieces, then picked up the shreds and threw them at Ling. Like carnival ribbons, the pieces of paper slowly floated to Ling's feet. Wai fixed her eyes on Ling. "No matter how hard I try, I can't change."

Ling's heart shuddered. "Instead of a teacher, you can be something else . . ."

"According to the principal, I'm not as clever as you, so she chose you and not me. I'm not smart by nature . . ." Wai kept maniacally laughing.

Had she gone mad? Ling stepped back, turned around, and walked away. Wai continued to laugh at Ling's retreating figure. As Ling walked out of the teachers' office, her colleagues exchanged looks with her. Ling twirled her finger near her temple and her colleagues' eyes filled with fear.

Was Wai devastated by the principal telling her what I said?

Why did the principal tell her? Doesn't she know my relationship with Wai? Regardless, I was just telling the truth. There's no point in Wai being upset with me. I'm not the principal—it's not up to me to decide whether to renew her contract. The principal doesn't want her because she's incompetent—what does that have to do with me? I've been helping her. She should be grateful to me . . .

From then on, Ling no longer greeted Wai, but just kept her distance from her. June was exam season. Teachers could leave work early after supervising exams and go home to grade them. Every day, Ling left school as early as possible, and she didn't return to her cubicle unless it was necessary. Other colleagues also avoided Wai. Normally, the Chinese department would chat around Ling's cubicle, but now no one dared to go there; when they saw Wai in the kitchenette, they waited for her to come out before sneaking in. When Wai left the teachers' office to go to class, everyone waited until she was far away before they went out, so as not to run into her in the hallway.

However, Ling gradually came to discover that, aside from cutting her hair super short and that time she cackled in the teachers' office, Wai no longer acted differently; she just stared ahead all day long without talking. She resumed her habit of tidying up her desk, disposing of trash properly, arranging her stationery neatly, and tearing most of the pinyin notes off the partition, so her cubicle appeared neater than before. She no longer stayed at school to study, but left work as soon as the bell rang after the last class. She was much more "normal" than before, but she often muttered, "How can I change myself?"

There was nothing new going on with Wai, so everyone stopped paying attention to her. Ling silently waited for the day when the semester would end—from then on, she'd part ways with this weird colleague.

ONE DAY AT the end of June, Wai returned to school at the last minute before the bell rang. Ling was drinking coffee in the head of the department's cubicle, discussing the Milan fashion show with everyone, when suddenly there was a bang. The door of the teachers' office slammed against the wall, then slowly bounced back. Wai, carrying a black fake Dior backpack, shot to her seat like an arrow, then threw the backpack on the desk with a cracking sound. The entire teachers' office immediately quieted down. Wai looked around at them, smiling, and unzipped her bag with a creak. A pile of white light reflected on her face, her eyes and nostrils hidden in the shadows, just like a ghost. Wai reached into the light, pulling out mirror after mirror—large and small, oval, rectangular and square—and placed them all around her cubicle in a dense row: on the bookcase, on the desktop; even the computer screen was covered with mirrors, reducing the screen to a narrow rectangle.

Wai wanted to swap out her pinyin notes for mirrors?

Not long after the class bell rang, Wai left the teachers' office. As soon as she left, everyone came over. The countless mirrors formed a sea, reflecting a circle of curious eyes.

"It's like a dance studio—does Wai want to learn to dance? Or is it performance art?" Miss Wu said, smiling at her colleagues in the mirrors.

Miss Au's eyes in the mirrors turned to Ling. "What's Wai up to?"

Ling threw up her hands at her reflection in the mirrors. She was also puzzled.

The head of the department came over and glared. "When I pass by, I see many 'mes.' It's so uncomfortable. Can you tell Wai to remove the mirrors?"

Everyone looked at Ling in the mirrors. She felt embarrassed. "I'll try my best, but lately Wai's been ignoring me."

During her break, Wai returned to the teachers' office, threw down her textbooks and sat down, randomly picking up a mirror, moving it closer to her face, carefully looking up, down, left and right, muttering to herself, her voice so low that no one could hear her.

The teachers in the Chinese department signaled to Ling one after another, so Ling had no choice but to bite the bullet and venture into Wai's sea of mirrors. She saw countless selves talking as she spoke. "Wow . . . Your mirrors are so pretty. Where'd you buy them?"

Wai ignored Ling, and brought the mirror closer to her cheeks. There was nothing in it other than Wai's facial features. "Why is this me? Why is this me?"

Ling swallowed a mouthful of saliva. "Can—can you take these mirrors away? Everyone feels . . ."

Wai moved the mirror in her hand to reflect Ling, then swung it back to herself over and over, the mirror continually switching between Ling and Wai. "In fact, what's the difference between me and you?" Soon, Wai fixed the mirror on Ling. "You."

"Me? What about me?" Ling was terrified.

Wai stopped talking, and concentrated on studying herself in the mirror.

FROM THAT DAY forward, Wai constantly looked in the mirror. She often went to the bathroom to look in the mirror and didn't come out for a long time. She even brought a mirror to class. According to Miss Au, Wai didn't face the students in class, but turned her back to them, speaking to them through the mirror she held. The news that Wai suffered from mental illness circulated on the school's secret page. Whenever students saw Wai passing by, they all stayed far away. Even the teachers tried their best not to have any contact with her.

When Ling saw Wai walking in the hallway holding a mirror, she pretended not to see her, lowering her head and walking faster, fearing those eyes that might suddenly pop out of the mirror and fix on her tightly.

You—

It has nothing to do with me that you can't renew your contract, nothing to do with me . . .

BEFORE LONG, it was the last day of classes. Students were looking forward to summer vacation. The campus was abuzz with people. Many students had called in sick so they could take an early flight out with their families. The head of the department had dragged her suitcase to school that morning, saying that after school she had to rush to the airport to catch a 3 p.m. flight. Everyone gathered around her, clamoring for souvenirs.

When Ling arrived at school, she kept chatting with her colleagues, afraid that if she walked half a step closer to her cubicle she'd fall into Wai's circle of mirrors, greeting never-ending versions of Wai, or never-ending versions of herself; when the bell rang, however, she had to go over to grab her attendance book before class. Holding her breath, she tiptoed to her seat and carefully fetched her roll-call book; fortunately, Wai didn't notice. Ling exhaled, peeking at what Wai was doing, only to find that she wasn't looking in the mirror but staring intently at the computer screen. The screen glowed pink. It was a pile of unknown internal organs with throbbing blood vessels, and countless rubber tubes transporting blood. People in purple surgical scrubs stood nearby, turning flesh over and over with pliers—did Wai want to kill someone because her contract wasn't renewed? Ling's hair stood on end. She walked away immediately. At that moment, Wai turned her head and stared at her. The air was filled with a fishy, sweet smell. Wai slowly said, "I finally understand."

Wai stood up and walked over to Ling, leaning in close, the tips of their noses almost touching, her turbid breath giving Ling chills from head to toe. Ling wanted to step back and run away, but for some reason her legs felt weak, as though they were shackled, unable to move.

"I just need to change my brain, just need to change . . ."

"I'm . . . heading out." Ling stepped forward with all her strength and walked toward the door, but Wai followed right behind, toes clinging to Ling's heels. Terrified, Ling walked faster and faster, until she was out of the teachers' office, then turned back, relieved that Wai was no longer following her.

On the first day of summer vacation, the headline in the *Mango Daily* had read: FEMALE TEACHER UNDER PRESSURE FILMS SUICIDE BY DRILL. The online news broadcast a clip of Wai's suicide. In the video, Wai sat in a windowless room, to her left a mirror covered in pinyin, to her right an electric drill perched atop a red plastic chair. Wai set up the camera, straightened up her clothes in front of the camera, took a deep breath, and said, "I was born too stupid. I need to change my brain." Her voice was quiet, but firm. Wai held the electric drill and turned it on, the drill swirling in a puff of smoke, then looked at the full-length mirror and pointed the drill bit at her temple. Immediately, there was a whirring noise. Blood spurted out and the camera lens was covered with a red filter. Wai fell into the thick red liquid, the rumbling of the electric drill not stopping but becoming louder and louder, screwing into the depths of bone . . .

Now, the sun reflected off Wai's mirrored wall, the exercise books on the desk bathed in golden light, only three lines of a lesson plan written on the computer screen, a turned-off mobile phone placed next to the desk, the office phone still disconnected, the corpse of the ant thought to have been swept away still in front of her, lying quietly on the junior secondary-school test papers. Ling had accomplished nothing in these two free periods except for repeatedly answering phone calls from the reporter and her mom. It was as though they'd raised an electric drill to her temple, her headache splitting...

Before long, the bell rang to signal the end of class. Stuffing the test papers into her handbag, Ling darted out of the teachers' office.

PART 2
LING AND WAI

At night, IFC Mall's floor-to-ceiling windows reflected the twinkling lights of Victoria Harbour, the halo of the spotlights scattering on the marble floor tiles, the brightness dizzying. IFC was Ling's favorite shopping mall, as it was elegant and spacious. The school was close to Langham Place, which was half an hour away, but she seldom went there. Langham Place was located on Portland Street—every time she passed by she saw numerous nightclub signs, and middle-aged women standing on the side of the road, flaunting their ample assets. It was a modern building towering amid dens of iniquity, akin to a woman in an evening gown walking into a street market, the hem of her dress sucking up all the filth from the ground. Moreover, the shopping mall was full of suitcases, packed shoulder to shoulder with people prattling in Mandarin, knock-off dresses and high heels everywhere, the stench of perfume mixing with body odor, pungent despite the strong air conditioning. IFC was still the most pleasing, as there was no need to squeeze through crowds. The shoppers were rich, and the highest-end name brands were concentrated here: Céline, Fendi, Valentino . . . These specialty stores weren't found in every mall, and the salespeople had a better attitude than those elsewhere.

Ling spent a long time browsing at Céline and Valentino. She bought a red crocodile-skin handbag at Valentino, and a high-waisted skirt and patterned chiffon shirt at Céline.

When she passed by Fendi, she also bought a wallet. In one evening, she spent a whopping 60,000 HKD, her hands loaded with so many paper shopping bags that they pushed against her legs, making it hard to walk. Around eight o'clock, Ling walked into the café on the first floor, casually piled her shopping bags on the empty seat next to her and, without looking at the menu, ordered a two-person set meal from the waiter: two plates of lobster carbonara, two cappuccinos adorned with latte art, and two mango puddings. She picked up a fork and started eating the lobster. She felt full after eating less than half of it, but she kept on eating, wanting to focus her attention on chewing. She continued eating until she was about to burst, then finally stopped, rubbing her stomach and belching.

With a belly bloated twice its size, Ling strolled to the carnival amusement park outside IFC, where a small temporary roller rink had been set up. On the rink, a girl in a small umbrella skirt kicked, jumped, spun around, and pushed back with her legs, her movements graceful. Feeling a sudden urge to skate, Ling went in, paid the fee, and crammed all her shopping bags into a storage locker, then picked out a pair of size nine red roller skates from the shoe rack. With the skates on, Ling instantly became taller, as though she'd had another growth spurt; but when she went in, before she'd even taken a step she lost her balance and fell to the ground, the pain piercing her heart. She propped herself up with both hands and stood up, taking a step forward, but her front foot slid too fast, and her back foot couldn't catch up. She fell again, scraping the skin on her palms.

Ling wanted to forget everything about her meeting with the principal that day, but she couldn't forget the pain. Her palm started bleeding, and the food she'd just eaten rushed back up, the acid burning and stinging her throat. The girl in the little umbrella skirt whooshed past her, rainbow-like marks glinting on the rink.

WHEN SHE GOT home, the living room light was off. Her mom lay on the sofa watching TV, her legs lightly shaking on the cushion. Outside the floor-to-ceiling window, Victoria Harbour glimmered with neon lights, reflecting on the walls like colorful cellophane. When her mom had worked as a hawker, pushing a cart to the Ladies' Market every day to sell counterfeit handbags, she had slowly saved up a nest egg—she had wanted to buy property and, after looking at units for a few months, had chosen this one with a sea view. At that time, the view of Victoria Harbour was vast, the scenery from the Bank of China Building to Heng Fa Chuen unobstructed, and for that sea view her mom argued with the owner until she was red in the face. The owner asked for two million, and her mom haggled for two months before the cost dropped to 1.5 million and she sealed the deal. Ling still remembered the day that they moved in; her mom opened her arms wide, facing the sea. "Our home has a sea view—awesome!"

Ling used to think that living in a place with a sea view was a sign of superiority, but as the years passed there were more and more buildings outside the window, like teeth that were constantly growing, leaving only a small strip of blue between the gaps—what was so "awesome" about that?

Her mom's favorite National Geographic program was playing on TV. A hairy spider rubbed its legs and feet in its web, poised to take a bite out of an unknown large insect. Ling crept back to her room with her shopping bags. When she passed her mom, her mom said, "I've been sitting at home waiting for you so we can eat dinner. It's ten o'clock."

"I left you a message saying I wouldn't be home for dinner."

Before Ling had finished speaking, her mom raised the

remote control and turned up the volume to drown out her words. Keeping her cool, Ling tossed the Fendi wallet she'd just bought at her mom. Her mom turned. "You scared the hell out of me!" She clearly wanted to chew Ling out, but catching sight of the wallet at her feet, she said, "If you couldn't call, you could've at least sent a WhatsApp message."

Ling didn't answer.

Her mom fished her phone out of her pocket and glanced at Ling. "Anyway . . . when I called you this afternoon and you didn't take my call, I thought you were ignoring me."

Ling wanted to say, *You usually don't answer my calls or WhatsApp messages*, but she swallowed the words on the tip of her tongue and, thinking that her mom must be hungry, said, "Let's grab a midnight snack."

Her mom cast a sideways glance at her, then went to her room to change. Before they set out, she reminded her over and over, "Don't call me 'Mom' out there."

Having donned a full-length knitted dress, and with a colorful silk scarf tied around her waist, Ling's mom clutched the Fendi wallet Ling had just given her. Ling followed behind her, finding it funny—her mom was fifty-eight, but still pretended to be a girl.

Ling and her mom passed from Ferry Street to Dundas Street, then turned in to the Ladies' Market. Over the past twenty years, the market had changed a lot, but it felt like it hadn't. Countless shops had quietly closed and opened, like waves ebbing and flowing; there was the same deluge of neon lights, the garbage constantly overflowing, the stalls still buzzing. In the past, every afternoon, her mom would wait for Ling to come home from school, then push her sofa-shaped cart covered with patent leather to Ladies' Street, select an eye-catching location, put up a few metal rods, then hang fake LV and Dior handbags on them, and hawk them to passersby.

Her mom preferred doing business with foreigners. "Have a look . . . four hundred. Five hundred fifty . . ." she'd say in English. Ling would carry a small LV waist bag to collect money, keeping an eye out for police or hawker control teams in the area. At the time, she was still little. When foreigners saw her, they liked to touch her head and praise her as "cute," "lovely," and "good girl." She pleased them by replying "Thank you so much" in English in a childish voice. Her mom used this as an opportunity to chat with customers and sweet-talk them into buying something.

Before long, her mom led Ling into a cha chaan teng. It was hidden behind a food stall, and Ling recalled that it used to be a replica shop. Her mom chose the innermost booth and sat down. A big-bellied server handed them two cups of tea and removed a notepad from the chest pocket of his shirt. "Is Sister Maggie collecting the rent tonight?" he asked, addressing her mom in familiar terms.

"I collected it this morning."

"Your new tenant brings men to eat here every day, a different man each time. She's decked out head to toe in luxury brands. She looks loaded."

"Do you mean that mainland woman with the daughter?"

The server nodded. Her mom thought for a while, then said, "She signed the lease last week. She seems perfectly normal, and she lives with her daughter. There shouldn't be any problem."

The server said, "Never mind that. The most important thing is that she pays the rent." He waited, pen in hand, to write down their order on the notepad.

"Music to my ears," her mom said, and laughed.

The server glanced at Ling. "Your younger sister?"

"Yes. She often helps me chase after rent. She's a teacher and a professional, sharp as a tack." Her mom loved bragging about her, praising Ling to the skies to anyone she met, quite the opposite to how she usually scolded her to her face.

"Sister Maggie is really talented in two areas—one is a knack for real estate investment, the other is being a professional."

"Of course! How can Hong Kong people make money if we're not resourceful?" The server's playful banter made her mom grin from ear to ear. Ling gave her a sidelong glance and forced a smile.

Her mom took pride in her subdivided flat business. The year when Ling was in Form 6, SARS broke out, and Ling stayed home to prepare for her A level entrance exams the following year. At dusk, her mom put away her hawker cart, returned home, and set down two boxed meals, casually opening a box of scallion-oil chicken rice, reading the real estate section of the newspaper while chewing and mumbling to herself, "Good timing, good timing . . ." For the next month, her mom led her through the Yau Tsim Mong district, the core urban area of Kowloon, viewing units with different realtors. At the time, there were very few people on Nathan Road, and the realtors all wore face masks when they showed them the units. Ling didn't know whether they were smiling. They didn't have masks at home, and her mom set up her stall bare-handed. She couldn't help but worry about her mom when looking at the flats, but her mom spat out, "It's not that easy to die." She went to a convenience store to buy herself a mask, and her mom looked at her with disdain.

Of course, her mom didn't die. That year, she bought several units in one go. A year later, the property prices doubled. Her mom divided the units into more than twenty rental flats, earning a monthly income of more than 100,000 HKD. From then on, she ceased to be a hawker, and dealing with brokers became her interest.

No matter how big or small the matter was, usually her mom asked for Ling's help with everything, such as collecting rent, attending to maintenance issues, and taking back a vacated rental unit. But this semester, Ling was too busy and didn't have much time to help her. Today, too many things happened. Her mom kept calling, but she ignored her. It wasn't until 8 p.m. that Ling turned on her phone and saw fifteen missed calls and twenty WhatsApp messages. Thinking of this, Ling felt guilty, and picked up the greasy menu. "Mom, go ahead and order."

It was only after she'd spoken that she realized she'd slipped up and called her "Mom." Ling was too exhausted. She seldom misspoke. The server scratched his head awkwardly, and Ling winked at him. "My mom takes good care of herself. She's more youthful than me." The server hastily replied, "Yes, yes." Her mom gave Ling a dirty look. "I'll have the wonton noodles."

It was 11 p.m. They were the only two diners left in the cha chaan teng. The server was cleaning up, and the sound of her mom slurping her noodles could be clearly heard. Ling rested her cheek on her hand, gazing out the glass door. The street vendors were packing up their stalls. After the canvas awnings were taken down, the long and slender iron poles were exposed, and the streetlights once again shone into the cha chaan teng. Her mom glanced up at her from the rim of her bowl of wonton noodles. "Mrs. Cheng's daughter is doing business. She often takes her mom on cruises, dining on Kobe beef in Japan. You? You just bring your ma to eat at a cha chaan teng. I keep telling you to go into business, but you won't do it."

Ling wanted to say, *Last month I took you to the buffet at the Peninsula Hotel*, but she didn't say it out loud. "Today I was just too busy ... What's up with that mainland woman?"

"Suddenly you care about me. I had dim sum with Mrs. Cheng today. Tenants keep calling to complain, saying that the mainland woman is too noisy. It made me feel uneasy the whole time we had lunch. After, I went to talk to the mainland woman and told her that if there were any more complaints I'd throw them out without mercy."

"That woman really might be—"

"I handled it. There's no need to keep talking about it." Her mom shoveled a bunch of noodles into her mouth.

Early on, Ling had tried to persuade her mom not to rent to that mainland woman, sensing she wasn't on the up and up, but her mom had ignored her. "Why are mainlanders inferior to Hong Kongers? Your ma is also from the mainland."

Now Ling's prediction had come true. She felt something accumulating inside her. She was so tired, so tired.

After her mom was finished, Ling paid the bill and they left the cha chaan teng. Ling and her mom walked down Dundas Street, climbed up the Ferry Street footbridge and walked toward the residential area ahead. The rumbling sound of cars beneath the footbridge was like flowing water, separating them from the neon-lit Yau Ma Tei neighborhood on the other side. As Ling followed her mom, she saw a cockroach pop out from left to right, trying to scuttle between them. After a few steps, her mom stomped on the cockroach with one foot, leaving behind a puddle of liquid mixed with its remains. Feeling she'd stepped on something, her mom twisted her foot to clean the sole of her shoe. "I asked you to buy a handbag, and you bought a wallet instead. You're such a cheapskate!" Her voice was faint, blending into the insect-scented night.

AT THREE IN the morning, the roar of cars racing downstairs pierced her ears like needles. Though the curtains were drawn, the light outside the window still penetrated her eyelids, leaving a whiteness patterned with tiny blood vessels. Scenes from her meeting with the principal that afternoon looped in Ling's mind, and the more she thought about it, the more she couldn't fall asleep.

After lunch, Ivy had come to give Ling the message that the principal wanted to see her. She asked why the principal was looking for her, but Ivy merely shook her head. With no choice, Ling needed to be fully prepared. She picked up her work report, research materials on Mandarin education, and a bag of taro chips from YATA Department Store, then walked into the principal's office with Ivy. Ivy said, "Maybe the principal wants to promote you."

She wished it were a promotion. In the past, the principal had rarely summoned staff one on one; she usually only met them when a big mistake had been made. Ling had a bad feeling.

When the door opened, the aroma of coffee hit her nostrils immediately, but Ling could smell it wasn't the Kopi Luwak. The principal sat in an executive chair, hands clasped together. On the left side of the pine table, there was a white file rack and a cup of coffee. On the right side was the principal's beloved Valentino handbag, white with a V-shaped flap cover and a metal clasp that looked like a lucky cat statuette. The large bookcase behind her was filled with folders, and one shelf was devoted to snacks, neatly arranged in transparent and airtight containers, including the Kopi Luwak and mixed dried fruits that Ling had gifted to her. After coming in so many times, only now did Ling notice how tidy the principal's office was.

"Did you enjoy the coffee I gave you before?"

Previously, when she brought up food or investments, the principal would talk non-stop, but now the principal picked up her cup and sipped her coffee. "It's good, but sometimes I just feel like drinking regular coffee."

The principal was hinting at something. Ling didn't know how to respond. The principal smiled faintly. "How many years have you been teaching at Sing Din Secondary School?"

"Ten."

"Earlier, I mentioned planning to switch to using Mandarin to teach Chinese. Do you remember?"

"If we switch to teaching in Mandarin, we'll definitely sacrifice our public exam scores. Sing Din's scores in Chinese have always been very good. In contrast, schools that teach in Mandarin have lower scores." Ling handed over a research report on teaching in Mandarin and a record of the Chinese department's past scores. Last year, upon learning that the principal planned on switching to teaching in Mandarin, she had begun conducting research, compiling a lot of data, just to be safe, but she hadn't really expected the principal to bring up the issue of switching to Mandarin again.

Halfway through Ling's speech, the principal's gaze shifted from the research report to Ling. "You're worthy of your name, which means 'clever.' You're well prepared. You're the smartest in the Chinese department."

Ling quickly said, "Only a good principal can lead to good colleagues."

"The success of a school depends on many factors besides public tests . . . Ling, you've been teaching for ten years but still haven't taken the LPAT. This actually puts you at a disadvantage."

Ling's smile froze.

"You've been a contract teacher for ten years. If you pass the LPAT, I'll consider promoting you to a regular teacher. I see a lot of schools now indicate on their websites that all of their Chinese teachers have passed the LPAT. Sometimes, parents ask whether we can use Mandarin to teach Chinese, and I don't know what to say. I hope you understand my quandary."

"But if the school switches to teaching in Mandarin, I guarantee we won't get a 90 percent pass rate on the public exam. If the results of the exam aren't good, it will affect admissions. What about trying one or two classes at each level to see how the results are, and then deciding whether to switch the whole school to teaching in Mandarin?"

The principal took another sip of coffee, her laryngeal bone calmly pulsing, then said, "Think long term. Did you know registration for the LPAT is now available?"

"Yes." Underneath the table, Ling's hands tightly held the aluminum bag of taro chips.

Smiling, the principal closed the folder on her desk. "I care more about your career. Even if you don't teach at Sing Din Secondary School, the principals at other schools will require you to pass the LPAT. Now there are many mainlanders coming to Hong Kong to work as teachers. Competition is fierce. Ling, you're smart. You understand what I'm getting at."

Coming out of the principal's office, the sunlight glared so brightly that Ling felt like the rays were about to pierce her body. The package of taro chips hidden in her arms was crumpled, suddenly transformed into warehouse stock. She tossed the chips on Ivy's desk.

Ivy didn't mind at all. She tore open the bag, pouring a handful of taro chips into her mouth. "Did everything go okay just now?"

Ignoring Ivy, Ling walked down the back stairs outside the teachers' office. The stairs kept spiraling, filtering out the sunlight, until she reached the almost pitch-black corner at the bottom. Ling leaned against the wall and slumped onto the stairs. The principal had seemed to be chatting amiably with her, but in fact had been scheming against her all along. All these years, she'd been signing contracts only with her—that's what she was implying. All her contributions to the school had been in vain. Without her, who could guarantee good DSE Chinese-language scores?

The dampness from the back stairs seeped through Ling's skirt, scratching at her buttocks. Ling closed her eyes, taking a deep breath. There was no problem that couldn't be solved. Over the last ten years, what had been difficult for her? Just then, a dark shadow crept up from behind. She stood up at once. *Is it Ivy coming to comfort me? Is it the head of the department coming to interrogate me?* A hand rested on Ling's shoulder, light as a feather. She didn't know why, but her entire body shivered. Not daring to turn around, she hurried up the stairs, the shadow trailing behind, as if trying to invade her body through her damp skirt. Ling faintly heard someone say:

You—

Ling awoke with a start, her body drenched in sweat. The orange streetlights reflected off the window frame like a lock, the shrill drone of racing cars unable to pierce through. She could no longer sleep.

After Wai passed away, the principal posted a job ad in the newspaper. According to Ivy, there were many applications, but no one came in for an interview. It seemed that the principal wasn't in a hurry to hire someone. Without a new teacher, Wai's classes had to be taught by someone else. During the academic affairs meeting in mid-August, the head of the department wrote the classes from all grade levels on the whiteboard and asked everyone to choose their preferences. No one wanted to make any major changes; everyone selected the same classes they'd taught the previous year. Soon, most of the blanks were filled, with only classes 2C and 2D left unclaimed.

The head of the department looked as if she had probably had Botox recently, but it wasn't done evenly, with one side of her face larger, the other side smaller. Tugging at the swollen side of her face, the department head said, "Last year, *that teacher* taught two Form 1 classes, along with Chinese history. I'll leave the arrangement for the Chinese history class to the head of the Chinese history department, but someone here needs to take over her two Chinese classes."

"I teach two senior secondary classes and am in charge of tutoring. My hands are full." Miss Wu was the first to raise her hand.

"I teach two senior secondary classes, and I'm also in charge of the school development committee," Miss Ip piped up.

"I have to manage the whole Chinese department, and also teach Form 2 Mandarin," the head of the department added.

Miss Wu, Miss Ip, and the head of the department were the first to draw a clear line with everyone. Miss Wu was in her fifties. She'd worked at Sing Din Secondary School for more than thirty years, and her daughter had also graduated from here. Miss Ip was close to retirement and often showed her colleagues pictures of her grandchildren on her phone. The head of the department had recently declared that she wanted to study English with her daughter and was busy taking IELTS practice test papers in her free time. They were the first teachers in the Chinese department to finish work, leaving school when the students went home.

The head of the department glanced at the four other colleagues. Everyone pretended to be busy copying the materials. Ling's gaze drifted over to the department head's Céline suit. The department head wore a new belt around her waist with a diamond-shaped butterfly buckle in the middle. Ling hadn't realized Céline had launched a new product this season.

"Miss Ko, you've been teaching junior secondary. Can you take on one more class?" the head of the department asked.

"One more class? I'm already teaching four junior secondary classes, plus Mandarin classes for all of Form 1." Miss Ko had been here for four years. Like the head of the department, she taught Mandarin, but she also taught Chinese studies, so she had a heavy workload.

"Miss So?"

"I'm teaching Chinese to two classes of Form 1, and also teach Form 3 Chinese history and Liberal Studies. I'm responsible for three subjects." Miss So was only in her second year of teaching. She held a double degree and, when the principal hired her, it was made clear that she would teach both Liberal

Studies and Chinese history. Teaching three subjects at the same time was indeed extremely demanding.

They were new teachers so, being "fresh blood," it was normal for them to have a heavier workload.

The only two yet to be named were Ling and Miss Au.

"Miss Au? You don't have to teach multiple subjects, so you can teach an additional class of Form 2."

"This year I have to teach two Form 3 classes and two Form 2 classes. I have no time." Miss Au kept waving her hand. Miss Au had joined the school two years after Ling. She was an experienced teacher who specialized in teaching junior secondary school. Ling had been teaching senior secondary school. Though she had a relatively light workload, classes 2C and 2D were junior secondary classes, and should go to Miss Au. But after Miss Au had spoken, the head of the department looked at Ling. "Ling, it's you. You don't have to take care of administrative matters, and you don't have any extra teaching duties."

"But I have to teach four classes of senior secondary, and the DSE will be restructured in the future. Plus, I've never taught junior secondary," Ling said.

The head of the department looked at Ling, then at Miss Au. After a while, she wrote Ling's name on the whiteboard. Ling was stunned. This was clearly a case of using strong-arm tactics. She started to refuse, but the department head interrupted her. "I've thought it over. Your workload is lighter than Miss Au's. I've factored that into my consideration."

"Other than workload, you should consider experience. Miss Au's been teaching junior secondary—"

"What about *your* experience? You've been teaching for ten years."

The head of the department was aggressive, different from her usual self. Ling was at a loss for words.

"Actually, the principal suggested you teach Wai's two classes."

The principal suggested it?

"If you force me to teach them, I'm afraid the quality of teaching will suffer—"

Before Ling finished speaking, Miss Wu spoke up next to her. "If you have trouble with your senior secondary classes, Miss Ip and I can help you."

Miss Ip nodded.

Turning to Miss Au, the head of the department said, "You're most familiar with the junior secondary curriculum. If you have time, you can help Ling, sharing the materials for junior secondary with her."

Miss Au nodded indifferently, and the head of the department packed up her stationery. Seeing the head of the department packing up, Miss So and Miss Ko placed the documents back in the folder.

"Will you suggest hiring a replacement teacher to the principal?" Ling asked.

"I received word that the principal will increase staff after the start of the semester, and after a couple of months of hard work, things will be much easier. All right, the meeting is adjourned."

No one wanted to pick up the two extra classes, so they made her the scapegoat. What did this mean? There had been no time for Ling to refute it. The door of the teachers' office opened, and everyone quickly disappeared into the scorching daylight. All that was left in the conference room was the squeak of the swivel chairs.

MISS AU SAT behind and to the left of Ling. She was short, with a round baby face, bangs slanting across her forehead. She looked like she'd just graduated, but in fact she was only two years younger than Ling. She and Ling weren't close, but they exchanged a few words during their free periods, joking around and making casual conversation. Miss Au taught junior secondary, and they'd rarely worked together in the past. For Ling, Miss Au posed no threat and held no utilitarian value, so she never really gave her much thought.

During the first week of school, Miss Au gave Ling the Form 2 worksheets, presentation materials, and supplementary extracurricular exercises for writing test papers without any reservation. The two junior secondary classes should've been hers, but now Ling shouldered both of them. Miss Au's help was simply a small gesture.

"Last year, 1C and 1D were taught by *that person*. Class C's grades were poor, but there was no problem keeping order. The most troublesome class is D, and in class D, Tsui Siu-Hin is the biggest troublemaker. Tsui Siu-Hin is very smart, with an IQ of 150, but he likes to challenge authority. He often makes trouble in class and never turns in his homework. He's been held back twice, and so far has two major demerits on record." Miss Au handed the student files for the two classes to Ling.

Ling nodded. Miss Au leaned over to Ling's ear and whispered, "When *that person* was the class teacher for 1D, she often tried to practice her Mandarin with mainland students. Tsui Siu-Hin took great delight in bullying her, making her cry in front of the class."

"Of course, *that person* was too stupid." Ling chuckled.

No one mentioned Wai's actual name in the teachers' office now. The head of the department was the one who had first referred to her as *that person*, and now, whenever anyone needed to bring up Wai, they also referred to her as *that person*.

Wai had died by suicide on the first day of summer vacation. At the time, the school had set up a crisis management team, with the head of the department, Miss Wu, and Miss Ip as its members. After releasing a press statement to the media, the head of the department refused to answer any questions from reporters. When school resumed in September, the principal instructed all teachers not to mention Wai to the students, and announced at the weekly assembly that students weren't allowed to accept interviews from the media, or they'd be punished. On the first day of the semester, Ling entered the 2C and 2D classrooms. When Wai's former students saw Ling come in with her textbook, they were abnormally silent, and some even had tears in their eyes. Even the infamous troublemaker Tsui Siu-Hin sat in a daze. Ling pretended not to notice, and started teaching as usual. Supposedly, the principal had arranged for the head of counseling and a social worker to lead a class on emotional management for Wai's former students, but there was no follow-up afterwards.

But since the start of school, the video of Wai's suicide was still circulating widely online. There were still students using anonymous accounts to post comments on the school's secret page, and also students who nestled in a corner, sneaking peeks at the video and screaming. When a teacher passed by, they'd put away the phone and, as though nothing had happened, stand up and return to their classroom. Recently, it was rumored among students that every night at three in the morning, a woman dressed in gray wandered around the school carrying textbooks, knocking on the door of each classroom, then entering the teachers' office and sitting grading papers until dawn. When the students mentioned this ghost story to Ling, they spoke in hushed tones. "The school janitor who lives on campus says there really is a woman in gray who comes back to the school every night. Ask the janitor yourself, he won't lie to you." She knew the students were joking, but fear crept up her legs like a vine, gripping her heart, though she still kept a smile on her face.

No teacher ever checked with the janitor, but everyone believed it. Whenever Miss Au came to take something from Wai's cubicle, she'd grab the broom, sweep what she wanted to the floor, bend down to pick it up, then walk away in a hurry. Ling happened to catch Miss Au chuckling awkwardly. "I used to work with *that person* and wanted to get back some documents. Obviously there's no one sitting there, but it always seems as if someone has been moving things around . . ."

In fact, there was no need for Miss Au to explain—everyone understood. Seeing Miss Au's flustered face, Ling thought of herself. After taking over Wai's classes, she'd go over to Wai's seat to grab things every now and then.

"Are you telling ghost stories to the students?" Ling tried to lighten the mood.

"The head of the department said that right after school started, her computer broke. Miss Wu said one of her students has cancer . . ."

"It's just psychological."

Miss Au shrugged and walked away. As Ling watched Miss Au's retreating figure, her gaze accidentally landed on Wai's configuration of mirrors. In the blink of an eye, it was as though her face had been shattered by an electric drill. She gasped, and turned away immediately.

THE CLASSES WAI had taught the previous year all fell onto Ling. Except for when she taught junior secondary during her first year, Ling had been teaching senior secondary school. The junior secondary-school curriculum had changed a lot over the past few years, and the previous teaching materials were no longer in use, so Ling had to redo her lesson preparations. At the same time, she had to prepare senior secondary test papers, revise senior secondary essays, and practice oral exams with senior secondary students after school. She'd never been so busy. Every time she opened a classroom door, she felt an unusual heaviness on her shoulders, as though she couldn't catch her breath.

There was nothing easy about teaching junior secondary. Miss Au generously shared her own teaching materials with her, but it didn't reduce Ling's workload. Ling distributed Miss Au's notes to the students in classes 2C and 2D. Within ten minutes, the students were either looking down and twiddling their fingers or resting their heads and dozing off, a pool of saliva wrinkling the mimeograph paper. Ling slammed a book down on the desk. "Do you sleep or study in class?"

The students woke up, rubbed their eyes, and stretched.

When class 2C saw Ling losing her temper, they remained hesitant, propping up their chins and pretending to listen. As for class 2D, as soon as Ling began reprimanding them, Tsui Siu-Hin stood up. "This homework isn't suitable for Form 2 students. It requires answering long questions and writing comments." The other students followed suit, shouting *Yes, yes, yes.*

Sing Din Secondary School adhered to an elite class system: Class A was the best, followed by Class B, and classes C and D were the worst. Miss Au's assigned topics were too difficult for these two classes; as a result, all of the papers Ling collected were filled with random answers and even doodles. She had to prepare another set of questions for them, changing the long-answer questions to fill-in-the-blanks, and preparing an additional answer key for them to memorize before the test.

This was Ling's consistent practice—have the students memorize answers; not because she was lazy, but because students didn't want to review the materials yet wanted to get high marks. Who wouldn't want to reap big rewards with little effort, playing smart to avoid doing extra work? In her notes for senior secondary school, Ling would provide detailed notes on types of exam questions over the years, analyzing various ways to answer them, so that students didn't have to organize things themselves and could just spend time memorizing things by heart so they could hit the mark. All that talk about heuristic learning or guided learning—in the end, didn't it all come down to grades? If Ling taught these two new classes the same way she taught senior secondary school, maybe their grades would improve, and then, even if she didn't do well on the LPAT, she might still be able to bluff her way through.

In the second week of September, Ivy's crystal nails flashed in front of Ling's eyes, setting down a notice—the principal wanted to do an assignment check. She had chosen class 2D, and wanted Ling to send the homework to her desk two days later. Embarrassed, Ivy giggled, as though she were the one who'd given these orders. The principal usually did an assignment check once a year, in May. Ling asked Ivy what was the matter, but Ivy just shook her head. The principal had always paid little attention to assignment checks; each time, Ling only submitted ten homework assignments, and the principal never followed up. Was the Education Bureau sending someone to check, so they had to make a show of it? Ling randomly grabbed a few worksheets from class 2D and handed them to Ivy. Ivy bit her lip. "Don't rush it . . . You have two days to prepare."

"I'm up to my ears in work." Ling stared at the screen and resumed her work, waving her hand to indicate that Ivy should take the papers to the principal. With the extra two Form 2 classes, her workload had doubled, and she really had no time to prepare.

Unexpectedly, two days later, just as Ling was coming back from the kitchenette, she saw Ivy from afar, tiptoeing over to Ling's cubicle. She had obviously wanted to set something down while Ling was away. Ivy smiled awkwardly and left. It was another notice from the principal, stating that Ling had failed the assignment check—not all homework had been submitted, and there were too few blanks for the students to fill in, so she'd do a recheck the following week. Ling was perplexed. Her performance in past assignment checks hadn't been ideal, but she'd still passed—why did she fail this time? Picking up the notice, she set off in search of the principal, but when she arrived at the door of the principal's office Ivy saw her and stood up. "The principal said she won't communicate with you about the assignment check issue until you pass . . ."

What? Was the principal targeting her? Ling tried to reach past Ivy to knock on the principal's door, but Ivy blocked her. "C'mon, don't be like this . . ." she said.

Ling sighed. Forget it—Ivy was just doing her job. There was no point in sacrificing her relationship with her. What on earth was going on?

A few days later, Ling noticed that except for the head of the department, Miss Wu, and Miss Ip, her other colleagues in the Chinese department frequently organized student assignments, and behind her, Miss Au even took out a folder she had bought herself to properly categorize the homework. It seemed that the principal had made the same request to other colleagues, and everyone had known she was serious this time. Ling was the only one who'd taken it lightly.

Ever since Ling had left a bad impression on the principal, the principal regularly sent Ivy to relay messages about the assignment checks throughout September, always for class 2D. Class 2D was a disaster in terms of homework. Tsui Siu-Hin never handed any in, and influenced by him, many students followed his lead and didn't turn theirs in either. In order to satisfy the principal's demands, Ling had to punish students by making them stay at school and do homework almost every day. Ling wrote six large words on the blackboard: *Do not leave until you finish.* Nevertheless, Tsui Siu-Hin still didn't take his homework seriously. He pretended to write with a pen in one hand, the other hand in his desk drawer playing a game on his phone, whispering to his classmates, "Mouse Ng often punishes us with detention. In comparison, Mouse Yu was a lot more fun."

"Go bring back the ghost of Mouse Yu," another student said, and laughed.

The deliberate mispronunciation of the word "Miss" kept circling in Ling's ears, annoying her more and more. If she weren't forced to stay in the classroom keeping watch over them, she wouldn't have to work overtime every night, and now they were still insulting her. She walked over to Tsui Siu-Hin's desk. The entire class quieted down at once. He raised his face and stared at her. "I don't feel like doing my homework."

Tsui Siu-Hin hadn't yet gone through puberty; his face was full of baby fat and his voice was high-pitched like a girl's. Ling gave the brat a sidelong glance. "Do your homework, or stay after school. Your choice. I'll stay with you till midnight if I have to."

Ling wasn't trying to scare the students, but she had to receive their homework. Tsui Siu-Hin rolled his eyes and supported his head with his hand, muttering over and over, "This is no choice at all," stomping his feet to vent his anger. Other students lowered their heads to write amid Tsui Siu-Hin's rumblings. Under Ling's strict supervision, she didn't collect all the homework until 7 p.m., and there were still many tasks awaiting her when she returned to the teachers' office. It was nearly nine o'clock when she finished work each day.

However, Ling soon discovered that the assignment check was the least of her worries. One morning at the end of September, Ivy once again tried to sneak over to Ling's seat while she was away, but Ling happened to be returning from class and caught her quickly. Like a child caught with her hand in the cookie jar, Ivy twirled her bangs. "This time, the principal is going to do a class observation . . ."

A surprise class observation? And would it be class 2D? Seeing Ivy's bewildered expression, rather than asking to see the principal, she smiled, and said, "Why is the principal doing a surprise class observation?"

"She seems to be . . . dissatisfied with your assignment check performance . . ."

Ling glanced at Ivy doubtfully. Ivy comforted her. "I'm sure it's nothing . . ."

Ling had never been afraid of a class observation. Previously, she had had at least one week to prepare. Moreover, she had a good relationship with the senior secondary school students. They were sensible, and paid special attention during class, taking the initiative to raise their hands to answer questions. But this time, she had been notified in the morning, and the class observation would take place that afternoon. There was no chance to tell students, and Tsui Siu-Hin in 2D was out of control. What could she do?

During lunch, while Ivy was away, Ling went to the principal's office. When the principal opened the door and saw it was Ling, she grabbed the doorknob. "I'm busy. We'll talk after today's class observation." Then she shut the door, almost bumping Ling's nose.

She had no choice but to accept it, and there was no room for turning back.

Ling prayed that Tsui Siu-Hin would be absent that day, but of course he was there. The principal and a middle-aged woman entered the classroom. When the students saw the principal bringing in an outsider, they grew quiet immediately.

Ling glimpsed Tsui Siu-Hin casually propping up his legs, showing no fear of the principal. It gave her an ominous feeling in her heart. Without introducing the middle-aged woman, the principal simply moved two empty benches to the farthest corner of the classroom and sat down beside her. Ling had never seen the woman before. Was she an inspector sent by the Education Bureau? But she hadn't heard there was going to be an external review this year. Forget it. It didn't matter who she was; Ling just needed to do a good job handling the class. She instructed the students to open their textbook and began teaching Lu Xun's "An Incident." Since she'd had no time to prepare, Ling just explained the text as usual. Intimidated by the principal's authority, the students watched Ling attentively, not daring to do anything wrong. Tsui Siu-Hin just lowered his head and dreamed, not spouting off any nonsense. Ling silently willed the class to continue like this. She managed to make it through most of the class, and with only ten minutes remaining was writing the characteristics of Lu Xun and the rickshaw driver on the blackboard. She described Lu Xun as selfish and lacking compassion, whereas the driver was upright and responsible. Tsui Siu-Hin suddenly stood up, pointed to the blackboard and shouted, "How come you teachers teach us to be upright, when you yourselves are not upright at all?"

The whole class looked at Tsui Siu-Hin. Ling saw the middle-aged woman standing with her hands on her hips, leaning forward, while the principal was expressionless. Ling's scalp went numb. She snapped, "Sit down! Please raise your hand when you speak in class . . ." But before she could finish speaking, Tsui Siu-Hin pushed his hands forward, and his desk fell over with a bang. He pointed at Ling. "Mouse Yu is dead. Mice watch over the whole class and won't let us talk to reporters—you're only afraid of your wrongdoings being exposed. Lu Xun reflected on himself, but do any of you reflect on yourselves?" He turned and pointed at the principal without lowering his hands, as though he were holding a gun. The students looked at Ling, then the principal. The classroom filled with an eerie silence. Ling had no choice but to reprimand Tsui Siu-Hin in order to save her own hide, but she'd only gotten out a couple of sentences when the bell rang, signaling the end of class. Without waiting for the students to salute, the principal and the middle-aged woman left the classroom without turning back.

The result was a terrible class observation. The next day, Ivy sent over the evaluation for it. The word FAILED immediately caught her eye. The comments included that the teacher had lazy pronunciation, students didn't raise their hands to answer questions, and students yawned during class. At the end, there was a sentence stating that another class observation would take place the following week.

In her ten years of teaching, Ling had never failed a class observation. She wanted to rip up the evaluation. The principal was too harsh. She couldn't control students not raising their hands to answer questions, or yawning. Was it because there was an outsider beside her, so she evaluated Ling more harshly? Even more problematic, she was coming again next week. Teaching two additional classes was already more than Ling could handle. A class observation on top of that was adding insult to injury.

What bothered Ling most, however, wasn't the increased workload, but the principal's nitpicking. One day Ling was buried in work and didn't notice anyone was behind her. Suddenly, she smelled the scent of perfume, and when she turned around, she saw the large profile of the principal. Beside the principal was another person she didn't know. This time, it was a middle-aged man with a half-bald head, holding a folder, writing something from time to time. After a while, the principal straightened up and said, "Your desk is so messy." Then she whispered something in the man's ear, and solemnly ordered Ling to tidy her desk.

Ling wanted to defend herself to the principal, but shortly after she escorted the middle-aged man away, ignoring Ling. When she looked around, all of her colleagues were working, with their backs stick-straight. The snack box on Miss Au's table was gone, her *ELLE* magazines were also tucked away, and the head of the department's IELTS textbooks were hidden somewhere. *When they saw the principal inspecting my desktop, did they all clean up immediately?*

Ling slumped down with a sigh, accidentally glancing in Wai's mirrors again. The principal's countless eyes stared back at her. She took a breath, then turned away.

After that, the principal did assignment checks every now and then, and sometimes came with unknown people to observe classes and inspect the teachers' office. Ling didn't know who they were, and she didn't have time to figure it out. She was worn out from meeting the principal's demands— she spent two nights cleaning up her desk, she prepared each lesson before class, collected every single assignment, and paid attention to the formatting and line spacing when making worksheets.

For the past ten years, Ling had never encountered such a situation. She considered herself good at her job. She'd always been able to figure out what the principal wanted and tried her best to satisfy her. Yes, there were some areas where she could've done better, but no one had ever paid attention to them before. Why were they being so nitpicky now?

EVER SINCE THE principal's style had changed, so had the atmosphere in the teachers' office. The snacks, magazines, newspapers, and the like on teachers' desks had all disappeared, and if they wanted to display some decorations, they swapped out the previous cartoon models for small potted plants. All the clutter in the walkway was cleared away. As soon as someone found the slightest mess on their desk, they cleaned it up at once. It was as though everyone had developed OCD.

Moreover, whenever Ling passed her colleagues' cubicles, she always noticed that the partitions were covered with announcements about assignment checks and class observations. In the past, everyone used to gather around and chat; now, whenever they returned to the teachers' office, they glued their rear ends to their seats, not moving an inch, other than to go to the kitchenette or bathroom. The whole Chinese department had fallen silent. Teaching two extra classes, Ling was even more overworked than her colleagues. It was only October, and during her free periods she had to prepare her classes, correct homework, handle students' problems, and spend extra time cleaning her desktop. The pressure was unprecedented.

Although everyone was busy, Ling never heard a single complaint. Even in private chats, people still prattled on about name brands, travel, and restaurants as though nothing had happened.

In the Chinese department, only Miss Wu, Miss Ip, and the head of the department were not affected. During their free periods, the department head often practiced conversing in English with Miss Ip and Miss Wu, deliberately putting on an American accent, those "R" sounds all tangled up like balls of thread. Sometimes she hung out with the English department and openly asked them for advice, as though she wasn't there to work but to learn English.

One day Ling came back from class and saw the three of

them chatting in English and laughing together. When she looked more closely, she realized they were on Skype. On the screen was the former British principal. Five years later, he looked the same, still robust but pudgier, his belly protruding beneath a loose tracksuit, grinning like Santa Claus. The head of the department smiled at the computer. "We miss you. We are so regret not to talk with you when you are here . . ."

Miss Wu pointed at the department head beside her. "Wrong grammar, isn't it?"

The British principal burst out laughing.

So, in order to improve her English, the head of the department did everything she could, even seeking out the British principal. Ling wished she could be as free as they were. She stayed at work until eight thirty every night, and she had to handle school affairs when she got home. She used to go to bed at 10 p.m. to ensure a full eight hours of sleep, and after work she'd go to the beauty salon, afraid that if she didn't take care of her skin now, it would get worse, and the circles underneath her eyes would darken; but now she didn't have time to sit in front of her vanity and apply layer after layer of skincare products until 1 a.m., let alone go to the salon. The toner, facial essence, and anti-wrinkle cream she rubbed on her face quickly turned from cold to warm and evaporated. It was only the beginning of the school year, but in the mirror, she saw that the dark circles under her eyes had become permanent bags, the flesh around her mouth was pulled into marionette lines, and even her eyebrows were drooping rapidly . . . She couldn't help but think of Wai, no, no, not only her eyebrows but also how Wai's whole body drooped, as though it was about to melt away. *Looking so old at such a young age was* her *thing—I'm only thirty-four.*

Skincare products weren't strong enough, so it was time to start applying masks. Ling put a super strong anti-aging mask on her face, hoping that after her skin absorbed the essence, the outermost layer would fall off and it would be rejuvenated; but only five minutes after application, Ling felt countless needles pricking her face, and she had to tear off the mask. Walking over to the mirror, she found her cheeks covered in red rashes, and hurried to the bathroom to wash her face. After a while, the rashes disappeared. Ling breathed a sigh of relief; but her skin returned to its original shape: wrinkled, dull, and sagging . . .

Forget it. Ling dried her face, sat on the bed, opened her pinyin textbook, and tried to recite pinyin while keeping her eyelids open as best she could. Her bed was cluttered with skincare products, used wads of tissue, bras she'd worn, back issues of magazines . . . It was a sea of trash, the never-ending initials and finals of Mandarin exuding a sour smell. She'd take the LPAT exam in February next year—could she really pass it? Just then, Wai's cubicle covered in pinyin notes appeared before her eyes. Ling felt her skull being opened, and there was nothing inside except blood. She woke up screaming.

The light of the streetlamps streaming through the curtain, Ling opened her bloodshot eyes, lying in bed and staring in a daze, her pinyin textbook still on her lap. Wai's intentions began to make sense. Wai wasn't stupid at all. Being a teacher was really *horde lurk*, *horde lurk*.

But she wasn't like Wai, who raced against the clock to study Mandarin, completely ignoring how others saw her. She tried to find time for Mandarin lessons. The LPAT had four papers: listening and recognition, pinyin, speaking, and classroom language assessment. The pinyin paper could be solved by memorization, and her listening ability could be improved by taking more practice tests, but Ling wasn't very confident about the speaking and classroom language assessment papers. Her pronunciation was substandard, and she always got stuck whenever she wanted to express complicated meanings. She specifically sought out a teacher with a Beijing accent, an elderly woman who was fond of wearing red—red hair accessories, red dresses, and red shoes that, when put together, resembled a festive Lunar New Year banner. This teacher had obtained the highest possible grade on the PSC, Level 1-A. Even among Beijing locals, not many spoke as perfectly as she did; moreover, she taught with a methodical approach, and could meet the exam requirements. Being a teacher herself, Ling could tell at first glance who was good at teaching.

However, she was too strict. Every lesson, she made Ling give a short speech. If Ling mispronounced something, she'd walk up to her and loudly say, "No! Say it one more time." If after several tries Ling couldn't get it right, the teacher would write down the pinyin on the whiteboard, tapping it with a marker. "How do you pronounce it?" She wasn't allowed to continue until she said it correctly. Ling was usually good at talking, but she became tongue-tied by the sound of the dry-erase marker, just like how her students were too shy and afraid to speak up when she called on them to answer questions during class.

In her most recent lesson, the teacher had kept tapping the whiteboard full of pinyin. When she turned around, her skirt transformed into a red umbrella. "Look at you—with so many mistakes, how can you pass the exam? You can't pronounce 'g' and 'h' sounds correctly, and you keep messing up the first tone and fourth tone. You're not trying hard enough."

Every class, the teacher accused her of being lazy. Ling knew she needed to study but she couldn't muster the energy to do so the entire day and could only read a few pages before bed each night. Her job was exhausting. After grading homework on Saturday and Sunday, if she had time, she slept or went shopping. She had some free time during her commute, but she just wanted to play games on her phone, the Mandarin notes crumpled at the bottom of her bag like a ball of tissue she'd forgotten to throw away. She couldn't be like Wai, who always squeezed in time to study no matter how busy and tired she was. It was only a job—why did she have to sell her soul? It reminded her of the discomfort she had felt when she had braces back in secondary school. Braces were external objects, but you had to keep them in your mouth at all times; now, it was as though her whole body were covered in braces, and she couldn't move.

"I've been really busy lately—is there any way to learn faster?" Ling whispered.

"You Hong Kongers just love to be fast. There's no short-cut to learning a language. It takes time."

"But . . . some people learn fast and pass the exam after half a year."

"People who learn fast might have frequent exposure to Mandarin and be imperceptibly influenced by it. But you— first of all, you don't work hard enough, and what's more, your efforts are in the wrong direction. Most Hong Kongers have this problem." The teacher pondered how to express what she meant. After a while, she pointed her finger at Ling. "You need to change your mentality."

Mentality?

"Your Hong Kong accent is too strong. You need to think of yourself as a Beijinger."

"How? I'm a born Hong Konger . . ."

"You Hong Kongers are so self-important and think it's beneath you to be a Chinese person. I've taught many students, and those with this mentality can't learn Mandarin well. I once had a student who fought with me every class, saying they were a Hong Konger, so why couldn't they keep their Hong Kong accent? Some students call me a commie—if they hate mainlanders so much, why study Mandarin? I won't keep these students. They're too prejudiced. The students who do well on the exam are the ones who don't constantly think of themselves as Hong Kongers, giving themselves any excuse to speak with a Hong Kong accent." The teacher's fingernails almost scraped the tip of Ling's nose.

Ling moved back. "I didn't think it was that complicated. I just really don't have time to study."

"Then, forget you're a Hong Konger, and speak Mandarin as though you're a Beijinger."

"But . . ."

"From here on out, don't speak Cantonese anymore, just speak Mandarin, think in Mandarin, even dream in Mandarin if you can." The teacher paced around the classroom, her red skirt swishing from side to side, like a splash of blood on a whiteboard full of pinyin. Ling seemed to see Wai's entire body wrapped in gauze, eyes wide open, stepping closer to her holding an electric drill dripping with blood . . .

Ling kneaded her hands, pinching them so she left crescent moons on the backs, red like birthmarks. The teacher glanced at her, and Ling touched the backs of her hands. "At my current level, do you think I can pass the exam next February?"

"You don't have a good foundation. Have you thought about taking it next year instead?"

"Is it really impossible?"

"If you're only taking the pinyin test and are willing to put in the effort, it shouldn't be a big problem, but if you want to talk like us Beijing locals within a short period of time, it's not just about being able to speak, right?"

THE PRESSURE OF the school transitioning to teaching in Mandarin fell not only on Ling but also on all of her Chinese department colleagues. At the faculty meeting in late October, the principal leaned back in her chair, stretched out her hand, and tossed a blank form in the middle of the conference table. "Just like last year, teachers will be responsible for leading the weekly assemblies next semester. Lectures will be in Mandarin or English. Fill in your names."

In the same windowless conference room, more than forty teachers surrounded the principal, who rested her hands on the arms of the chair, raised her legs, and shook the high-heeled shoes hanging on her toes. The row closest to the principal was made up entirely of Chinese teachers. Ling had had to collect homework from class 2D, so she arrived two minutes late and was forced to sit in the back row. When discussing candidates for the weekly assembly the previous year, everyone had looked around to see who'd take the lead, but this time, as soon as the form fell on the table, the head of the department grabbed it to fill in her name, then passed it to Miss Wu; while Miss Wu was writing, beside her, Miss Ip, Miss So, and Miss Ko held out their hands, waiting to receive the form. Ling sat behind Miss Au. When the form was handed to Miss Au, Ling saw that the head of the department had filled in three boxes, Miss Wu and Miss Ip had filled in two boxes, and the other teachers had filled in one box each. There was just one box left. Ling called out softly, but Miss Au seemed unable to hear her, and filled in the last box with her own name and then placed it back on the table.

In less than three minutes, the form was filled out completely, much to the relief of the other teachers. The principal picked up the form, removed her reading glasses, and studied it. "Wow, Chinese teachers reign supreme—all the weekly assemblies next semester will be in Mandarin."

Ling raised her hand, wanting to tell the principal that she still needed to add her name to the form. She tried to ask the head of the department if she could give her one of her slots, but the department head pretended not to notice, instead standing up and clapping her hands. "I believe that Sing Din Secondary School is absolutely capable of making a seamless transition to teaching in Mandarin. All colleagues are working hard together. Are there any questions?"

Everyone in the Chinese department avoided Ling's gaze.

In the past, Ling would've stood up for herself if she'd been treated coldly, but at this moment she was timid. Had all the teachers passed the LPAT? *If I fight back, and the principal publicly announces I haven't passed the LPAT and am not qualified to speak at the weekly assembly, wouldn't I be making a fool of myself?*

Ling quietly lowered her hand.

No one voiced any objections. The principal surveyed the room, then nodded in satisfaction. "All right. The meeting is adjourned."

On the way back to the teachers' office, the head of the department, Miss Wu, and Miss Ip chatted and laughed as they walked side by side. Other colleagues formed a circle to discuss the meeting. Only Ling was left behind. The afternoon sun was hooked on the fence of the corridor, as though it could be blown away by the wind at any time. Walking in the sunlight, Ling felt completely worn out.

From then on, everyone began to keep their distance from Ling. Once upon a time, they had all loved gathering around her to chat. Now, unless there was something important, no one came near her. Behind her back, people murmured that she sat too close to Wai's cubicle, and was trapped in her configuration of mirrors all day long, so she fell out of favor. If a group of colleagues had been chatting in the kitchenette and noticed Ling approaching, they immediately quieted down, dispersed, and went back to their seats.

SINCE THE BEGINNING of the school year, Ling had been eager to do some shopping.

In the past, she would only go on a shopping spree during major sales or outlet clearance events. Now she was like an addict, her phone full of brand catalogues, constantly worrying about buying things. After finishing work around eight o'clock, Ling left the school and took the subway to Hong Kong Station. As soon as she arrived at IFC Mall, she ran up the long escalator, making a beeline for Céline and Valentino. Ling liked to flick the hangers in the shops with her soft fingers, like a small fish cherishing the soft hair of a piece of coral, selecting a few pieces of clothing at random, then putting them together and holding them up to her body to see how they looked, the sales clerk attentively standing by, saying the clothes looked beautiful no matter what. Most of the time she didn't even bother trying them on, picking things out and then handing them to the sales clerk, feeling a peculiar sense of pleasure at the sight of the clothes piling up around the other woman's neck, the clerk managing to squeeze out a smile while struggling to hold them.

She followed the sales clerk to check out. The sales clerk neatly folded her clothes and straightened out the shopping bags after placing the clothing inside, careful not to wrinkle the paper bags. All of this cheered her up. Ling handed over her credit card and signed her name on the bill for 10,000 HKD.

Each morning, Ling woke up in an ocean of shopping bags, with many clothes she'd yet to unpack and put in her closet. Although she was busy and only slept four hours a night, she insisted on waking up at 5 a.m. to put on makeup. As soon as the alarm rang, she climbed out of bed, walked over to the full-length mirror, and took off her pajamas. The first things she noticed were her breasts that sagged to her belly, and the two love handles that were a result of having no time to exercise.

Ling hurriedly picked out a few pieces of clothing from the paper shopping bags and stood in front of the mirror putting various pieces together. When she was done, she sat down to do her makeup. She considered makeup an important ritual to start the day. Ling first applied an oil-control foundation to even out her skin tone, then dabbed several layers of concealer on her drooping eye bags and acne scars. Soon, all the blemishes disappeared, and before her very eyes she had the skin of a newborn baby. But new skin wasn't enough— the eyes were the soul of makeup. Ling tilted up her head and inserted colored contact lenses, tugged at her eyes to draw on eyeliner, stuck on eyelid tape and false lashes, and brushed on eyeshadow; in twenty minutes, her single eyelids doubled in size, as though they had been replaced by double eyelids. Ling also contoured the bridge of her nose and her forehead, which immediately raised her nose and made her forehead fuller, then used a lip pencil to draw a fuller shape for her too-thin lips. An hour later, she looked left and right in the mirror to make sure the contouring wasn't uneven, and that her lashes weren't drooping. After ensuring everything was in place, she dusted on loose powder to set her makeup.

At school, female students cast envious glances her way, and male colleagues peeked at her when they passed by. Of course, she was decked out in designer brands from head to toe, dressed impeccably. She felt like a model, constantly walking under the spotlight. Some students with whom she was familiar joked, "Miss Ng, you look so pretty—are you dating someone special?"

Laughing, Ling replied, "I'm dating myself."

When she returned to the teachers' office, she noticed that the head of the department had on the same Céline suit that she had been wearing for the past ten years, and that her handbag was a style from two years ago. Despite how little she'd slept the night before, Ling still perked up at the sight. She placed the latest Valentino, worth 40,000 HKD, upright on her desk, the side with the metallic plate facing outward, shining brightly in the sunlight. The teachers acted nonchalantly, but sneaked glances when they passed by. The head of the department even searched for information about the handbag on her mobile phone, turning off the screen when Ling walked past her. When the principal came to see the head of the department, she couldn't help but size up Ling's handbag.

Dressing well was a fundamental of life. Even when facing enemies, one should do so in a splendid manner, even if that splendor was only fleeting.

"ALL YOU CARE about is shopping till you drop. What about your poor ma?"

Since September, Ling had frantically been working overtime, then going shopping after work. She hadn't had a meal with her mom in an entire month. When she returned home at 11 p.m., she opened the door and found no lights on in the living room, only the TV. Her mom was lying on the couch, snoring steadily and deeply. Ling picked up the remote control and turned off the TV.

Mom is punishing me by skipping dinner again. Without waking her up, Ling put her shopping bags in her room, then grabbed a blanket and draped it over her mom.

Lately, her mom had been dissatisfied with her. Each day after class when she returned to the teachers' office, as soon as she turned on her phone, more than ten missed calls and WhatsApp messages popped up. In your eyes, you don't have a mom. I raised you, and you won't help me. If there was trouble with one of the tenants, her mom would bother her even more. This semester, Ling had five or six classes a day, and couldn't keep up with her mom's work orders, only leaving them on read; she didn't dare reply, fearing that her mom would assume she was available and keep calling her. Usually when her mom noticed Ling ignoring her, she'd send her a barrage of bitter messages. "Which is more important: your work or your ma?" "If your ma were to die, you wouldn't care." From her mom's tone, Ling would know the issue at hand had been resolved, and would continue to grade homework without replying.

Previously, if a tenant had any problems, she had dealt with them during work hours. If she didn't have class in the afternoon, she'd leave work early to show rental properties to clients and collect rent for her mom. But this school year was too busy, and she couldn't be on call anymore. However, whenever she had time, she tried her best to take her mom's calls. Even if she went shopping at IFC Mall after work, she'd still take the time to collect rent for her mom.

Earlier, when Ling returned to the teachers' office after class, she had listened to a message from her mom saying she heard a dog barking when she was collecting rent. She knew her mom didn't care for dogs, so during her free period she helped her mom mediate. The tenant was a Nepali man who'd always kept a dog, but Ling hadn't told her mom, and she hadn't expected her to find out. The dog was a small chow chow that never disturbed anyone, and the unit had no peculiar smell. The man was also very careful when he took the dog in and out, never letting other tenants or her mom see it. He paid the rent on time without needing Ling to remind him. Sometimes, he even repaired the plumbing and electrical appliances for her for free. On several occasions her mom had asked Ling to find someone to repair the air conditioner, but Ling had meetings after school and was too busy, so she texted the man, and he quickly took care of it for her. So even though she had known early on that the man had a dog, she didn't tell her mom because she didn't want to lose a good tenant. Now that her mom knew, she had no choice but to call him and warn him to be careful and not to let her mom see the dog. She also urged him to give the dog away, but the man was very hesitant. "I won't let him make any noise, okay?" he said in English.

She didn't want upset on either side. After talking to the man, she told her mom she'd convinced him to give the dog up for adoption. Her mom was silent on the phone. Ling said, "The Nepali man is easy to get along with. I did try my best to persuade him—"

"If you're trying your best, you won't ignore my calls." Her mom hung up the phone.

Two weeks later, she received a text message from her mom. I'm in the emergency room. Shocked, she called her mom, but she didn't answer. Ling had five classes in a row that day, and a meeting after school. She couldn't leave; but her mom was still her mom, and if something unfortunate happened to her it would be unforgivable. Ling had no choice but to ask the head of the department for personal leave. At the time, the head of the department was practicing her conversation skills with an English teacher. Upon hearing Ling's request, she looked displeased. "Can you go to the hospital after school? We can't find a substitute on such short notice." Ling had expected the department head to refuse and had found a picture of a traffic accident online. There was so much blood that you couldn't make out who was in the picture. Ling pointed to the picture, her face filled with emotion, and said her mom had been seriously injured. The head of the department eyed her dubiously. "Remember to fill out the form requesting leave."

As she was leaving, she overheard the head of the department say, "I need to find someone to cover the classes and have to reschedule the meeting . . ."

After she left school, her mom finally picked up the phone. Ling asked her which hospital she was at. Her mom didn't answer, so she asked again. Her mom finally said, "Come to the fifth floor of the Wing Ming Building on Dundas Street at once."

It was her mom's unit—what was she up to? Ling rushed to Dundas Street, walked up to the fifth floor, and saw her mom and the Nepali man in the crowded passageway of the subdivided unit. Her mom was wearing the Céline dress that Ling had recently given her and didn't look one bit sick. The man had on a white vest and black shorts and leaned against the door frame, explaining something to her mom. As soon as her mom saw her, she said, "You said he gave the dog up for adoption." Then she turned to the man and spoke in English. "The contract, no dog no dog."

The man walked over to Ling, telling her in English, "You said I can have dog. You've promised me."

Ling wanted to speak. Her mom pointed at the man, telling him in English, "Dog dirty noisy get out get out."

"My dog is not dirty and noisy. You see." The man quickly brought out the dog. Oblivious to the danger, the dog stuck out its tongue at Ling, wagging its tail, without a single bark. "You see. So quiet and clean. The woman next door always brings men to home. She is dirtier. Why don't you get her out?"

The man lived next door to the mainland woman with the daughter. He'd complained to Ling several times that the woman was noisy. Ling could only appease him by promising to warn the woman. Now there was no sound coming from the woman's room—she'd likely gone out. Her mom continued in English, "No sound. You hear! You which eye see her bring men home?"

"You don't always come here."

Ling rushed to interject in Cantonese, "Actually he helps us out a lot, and never asks for money . . ."

"Shut up! These are all my units—whatever I say goes. In short—" Her mom pointed at the man and again switched to English. "People live house not dog. Dog live in street. You get out."

Ling was a little angry. "You tricked me into coming here so you could evict the tenant in front of me? Don't you know how busy I am?"

"Have you been paying attention to me lately? All you do after work is shop for clothes." After shouting at her, her mom left the unit. Ling felt wronged. She'd explained to her mom over and over that this was a busy semester, and she went shopping after work because she wanted to have a little rest, but her mom felt she was just making excuses. "You've been at that school for ten years and are in the middle of the pecking order—you have subordinates who can help you."

Middle of the pecking order? How could it be so easy to be promoted to the middle? Did her mom know that in the future, the head of the department might hold it against her for taking this leave in the middle of class?

The clatter of her mom descending the stairs gradually faded away. The man looked helpless. The dog still wagged its tail happily. Ling looked at it, as though she were looking at herself, and sighed. "My mom is like this. I have tried my best. We have no choice . . ." From then on, Ling went shopping even more after school, waiting till her mom was asleep before she came home.

But after not seeing her mom for many days, Ling felt guilty again, and had no choice but to make it up to her with material things. Her mom had texted her that she wanted to eat American oysters, so Ling went to the supermarket after work to buy a few boxes. Her mom said she wanted the latest

Prada makeup bag, so Ling went to a specialty store to buy it for her. But no matter what Ling did, her mom was never satisfied. Last month, her mom had said she wanted La Mer face cream, which cost at least 1,000 HKD a bottle. Ling thought it wasn't worth it, but since her mom liked it, she bought it. However, when her mom opened the shopping bag, she said, "I wanted fifty milliliters. You bought thirty milliliters. You must not have wanted to buy it for me." Then she threw the face cream at Ling's chest, saying how great Mrs. Cheng's daughter was, telling Ling, "I don't know why you were born. You're not even as good as shit."

Ling couldn't open her mouth as her mom chewed her out. She'd rather go shopping than go home to accompany her mom. She knew she wasn't good enough, but she felt she was trying the best she could for her mom. As a child, she worked hard to earn good grades, learned English to communicate with foreign customers for her mom, cooked meals for her mom after helping manage the stall, helped out with the shopping . . . Since she started working, she had voluntarily given her half of her salary every month, helped her manage her rental properties, and even taken her on trips during school holidays. Ling looked up at the seventy-inch ultra-HD TV on the wall. It had been purchased at her mom's request. She'd also given her the professional treadmill in the corner of the living room, as well as the massage chair, Italian glass dining table, and air purifier . . .

Her mom didn't use to speak so harshly. When Ling gave her a gift, no matter whether it was cheap or expensive, her mom would side-eye her and call her a worthless girl, but still say thank you. Why had she become like this? Was it all because Ling wasn't helping her or spending enough time with her this semester?

Now, Ling knelt in front of her mom. Observing her

mom's body curled up to fit the size of the sofa, she removed a bottle of perfume from a shopping bag and placed it beside her. Then she stood up and walked over to the window. The lights of Victoria Harbour scurried like ants before her eyes, converging toward the most primordial point. Ling silently murmured, *Which point was it? Which point was it?*

What was it that made her mom increasingly dissatisfied with her?

What was it that made her mom increasingly demanding?

Was it last year, when she had excitedly told her mom that she had a new colleague who was stupid and waited on her like a servant, so her mom assumed she'd been promoted to the middle of the hierarchy?

Was it the year before that, when Ling was praised by the principal, and she was so happy that she volunteered to increase her contribution to their household by 5,000 HKD, so her mom assumed she had a high salary and could satisfy her indefinitely?

Was it on her mom's birthday one year, when she gave her mom her entire month's salary, so her mom assumed she was rolling in the dough?

Or was it that her mom had always been this way, but she used to be able to handle it before, and now she couldn't?

Ling was sleepy, her legs sore after standing all day. She stretched, rubbing the dry corners of her eyes, the light in front of her blurring, leaving only her reflection in the window.

THESE DAYS, the principal seldom ate with the Chinese department. Ling would post tantalizing food pictures in the WhatsApp group and wait all day, but the principal never replied. The other teachers followed suit and all left her on read. In the chat column, Ling was only talking to herself. When she checked the chat transcript, she discovered the principal hadn't even clicked on the thread to see her messages.

With the change in the principal's attitude, everyone began dining separately, so one day Ling invited Ivy to have a meal with her. As soon as the lunch bell rang, Ling looped her handbag over her shoulder and met Ivy at the school office.

The Japanese restaurant used to be a cha chaan teng, but after being renovated by Link Real Estate Investment Trust, it had undergone a superficial upgrade. The principal preferred eating Western food, so Ling seldom came here, but she'd done enough homework beforehand to know which dishes were the highest rated, and what the latest specials were. As soon as Ivy sat down, Ling poured her tea and then ordered.

Recently, Ivy had gotten tattooed Korean-style crescent-moon eyebrows and begun applying a slight halo of orange-red eyeshadow on each of her double eyelids, dolling herself up like a Korean girl. After taking a seat, Ivy cupped her own face and began spouting off her beauty troubles. Ling thought, *It's good to be young—all troubles are simply trivial. If you complain, someone will comfort you; if you make a mistake, you'll always be given another chance.*

"Don't you think my skin's gotten worse lately? So many fine lines—my skincare products aren't sinking in . . ."

Leaning forward, Ling studied Ivy's face. She had a few pimples, but her skin was still delicate and translucent. At twenty-eight years old, Ivy was seven years younger than Ling. This was the prime of a woman's life. What wrinkles? But after Ivy's comment, Ling pulled out a few facial masks from her handbag. "The saleswoman gave them to me when I was buying makeup. If your skin is dry, this is the best mask for moisturizing."

Ivy picked up the masks and glanced at them before tucking them in her handbag, and continued to cup her face. "Alas, masks are useless. I'm starting to lose collagen—my face is sagging."

"If yours is considered sagging, what's mine?" Ling fished out her compact, peering left and right to check whether her makeup had smudged. When she'd set off this morning, she thought her makeup looked pretty good, but now, as she scrutinized herself in the compact mirror, she found that, no matter how hard she tried to conceal her flaws, two dark blobs of fat were clearly visible, and the fine lines that crinkled in the corners of her eyes were even more prominent beneath her makeup.

At the sight of Ling silently staring in the mirror, Ivy said, "As a woman ages, her looks start to go . . . sigh. Let's get plastic surgery together—whether facial bone contouring or Botox. Dr. Reboot is offering a twenty percent discount."

Ling chuckled, thinking, *Haven't you already had plastic surgery?* With big eyes and a high-bridged nose, she had thought many times that Ivy was a dead ringer for Lin Chi-ling. Out loud, Ling said, "Plastic surgery is so expensive. Twenty percent off is still at least two hundred or three hundred thousand dollars. How can I afford it?"

"Money's no problem. If you don't have enough, you can pay in installments."

"Makeup's sufficient . . ."

"Makeup's just an aid. Cosmetic surgery extends from the inside to the outside, making the entire person beautiful."

"I'm afraid that the more plastic surgery I have, the worse I'll look, and the principal won't recognize me." Ling had never seriously considered plastic surgery, but now, as she faced the mirror, she realized that no amount of makeup could conceal the traces of aging. After listening to Ivy, she was somewhat tempted. Although Ivy was the spitting image of a celebrity, she looked quite natural. There were no scars or abnormalities—it was as though she'd been born this way.

You . . . why do you ha-hat-hurt *yourself?*

Ling raised her teacup and drained the contents.

Seeing that Ling was deep in thought, Ivy took her phone from her handbag and found a close-up photo of her head. It looked different from the current Ivy, with single eyelids, a small nose, and a wide jaw, but it was clearly the same person. Criss-crossed black lines were drawn across the photo, resembling a cracked dish. "I'll let you in on a secret—actually, I've had plastic surgery. A few years ago, I asked a face reader to have a look at my face. He took one glance at me, and even though I didn't say anything, he knew I'd never been in a relationship before. He said my face was a jinx to any future husband, and I was doomed to live a loveless life. His words were spot on. I'd never had any relationship with the opposite sex, and no boys pursued me in school. I asked him if I could change my luck with plastic surgery. He said that as long as I changed my single eyelids to double eyelids to make my eyes more seductive, and softened my jaw, I'd be more attractive, so I decided to have plastic surgery."

Is Ivy showing me her before photo to persuade me to undergo plastic surgery? For women, plastic surgery was a huge secret. Ling blurted out, "If the plastic surgery's successful, of course people would chase after you."

"I'm not joking. Master Chan is really good. I read on an online forum that someone who used to be infertile had a baby after following his recommendation to have plastic surgery. Someone with cancer was cured after having plastic surgery. Maybe if you have plastic surgery, not only will those bags under your eyes disappear, but you'll also get a promotion and a raise."

"A promotion?" This was a good opportunity to change

the subject. Ling sighed. "Earlier, the principal said she might not renew my contract. After the school switches to Mandarin as a medium of Chinese-language instruction, surely she'll fire me and invite a mainlander to take my place."

"Hmm . . . I don't think so . . . but I have noticed that sometimes the principal likes chatting with newly immigrated students from China." Ivy snickered.

Ling covered her mouth with both hands. "Shit. I'm going to be fired."

"I've heard the principal say she thinks mainlanders are better than Hong Kongers—they work hard and are obedient. I often overhear her speaking on the phone in Mandarin when I go into her office. It seems like one day last week, she went to the mainland on business."

Ling was shocked. Recently, the principal had expressed her fondness for the mainland during her speech at school, but it hadn't occurred to her that she had official business there. "Does the principal really want to hire mainlanders as teachers?"

Ivy snacked on an appetizer. "No one's been in lately for an interview."

"Who was she on the phone with?"

Ivy shook her head.

"Besides me, is there anyone in the Chinese department who hasn't taken the LPAT?"

"So you haven't taken it?"

"Can you help me ask around?"

"I can try, but I can't promise I'll get an answer."

Overcome with anxiety, Ling picked up the teapot and poured Ivy more tea. "Just casually ask around. Hey, what do you think would happen if we took a picture of the principal to the plastic surgeon?"

Ivy laughed. "We'd become principals and could fire anyone we wanted."

"I'm interested in plastic surgery. I want to change my luck. Take me to see Master Chan some day." Ling and Ivy exchanged smiles. Just then, their server brought over a plate of salmon sushi. Ling plucked a piece for Ivy and topped it with wasabi and soy sauce. "You can't tell anyone I haven't taken the test yet."

"C'mon, relax." The words oozed out of Ivy's mouth as she chewed.

COULD PLASTIC SURGERY really change a person's luck? What a joke. If she were a celebrity, sure, but Ling was a teacher.

Plastic surgery was futile regarding her current predicament. Right now, doing a good job was of the utmost importance.

November was testing month. Ling had to juggle her junior secondary and senior secondary-school classes alongside preparing for the Joint School Oral Exam. Numerous tasks awaited her. She was working seven days a week, with little time for shopping, and she also missed her Mandarin classes. Her teacher from Beijing sent her text messages reminding her of her lessons, but she left them all on read.

As if she wasn't already busy enough with work, Tsui Siu-Hin in class 2D had to go and stir up trouble. Ling asked one of his previous teachers about him. It seemed that Tsui Siu-Hin was particularly fond of causing a scene in Chinese class—three months into the school year, and she still hadn't found a way to deal with him. In class, he loved asking boring questions, especially about who was right or wrong, and whether something was fair or unfair. Last month, Ling had given a lecture on the text "Niang" by the mainland author Bai Ling. She'd reached the part where the protagonist Dongdong pointed out the teacher's mistake in front of everyone. The teacher, however, was willing to admit her mistake, indicative of her humility. Ling tried her best to avoid using words like "right" or "wrong" or "integrity," but still, she struck a nerve with Tsui Siu-Hin. He stood up and shouted, "Why do so many people have a problem admitting when they're wrong?"

A student who'd been sleeping started awake, gazing up at Tsui Siu-Hin and Ling. Knowing it was useless to confront Tsui Siu-Hin head-on when he was in attack mode, she simply said, "When we do something wrong, we apologize."

"How come the principal isn't responsible for hounding Miss Yu to death, but students are punished for their wrongdoings?"

Ah, it was about Wai again. Ling stole a glance at the classroom transom window.

"Are you worried the principal will overhear when she passes by?"

The whole class roared with laughter. Heat blazed from the soles of Ling's feet all the way up to her ears. *During my last classroom observation, Tsui Siu-Hin must've seen that the principal wasn't satisfied with my performance, so he's bringing up the past to humiliate me.* Ling threw the textbook down on the table with a thud. The class fell silent. She surveyed the room, then picked up the textbook and continued discussing the text, ignoring Tsui Siu-Hin.

But Ling had only uttered two sentences when Tsui Siu-Hin cried out again: "You didn't answer my question."

What am I supposed to say? That's just how society is—the powerful are correct, and the powerless must accept it. Even though I'm a teacher, I'm not much better than you. Ling didn't want to engage Tsui Siu-Hin any longer. "Introspection is a good thing. We read in order to learn how to become more introspective. Okay, let's return to the text . . ."

Before she'd finished speaking, Tsui Siu-Hin had vacated his seat and was running around the classroom in circles, knocking down the schoolbags in the aisle, scattering books and papers all over the floor. "You're just like Mouse Yu—neither of you answers any questions."

Ling called out to him, but he kept on running, only agreeing to sit back down after he'd worn himself out running around for most of the class. Although he didn't cause an accident, he carried on like this for twenty minutes, and they fell behind schedule once again.

Tsui Siu-Hin's vow to never give up until he got an answer was a headache for Ling. She couldn't stand this kind of student. He wasn't an academic overachiever who killed himself studying—such students were self-revolving planets who churned out brilliant report cards like clockwork, never bothering their instructors; nor was he one of Ling's preferred "teacher's pets" who understood the ways of the world and knew how to suck up to the teacher. He was someone who considered himself smart, fixating on unnecessary details, finding fault with his instructors, delighting in challenging their authority.

No wonder Wai often mentioned his name and was reduced to tears because of him.

Recently, Ling had decided to teach Xiao Si's "Hong Kong Story." She scrawled *Hong Kong, a city with very hazy origins* on the blackboard. Ling's blackboard handwriting wasn't attractive. "Hong Kong" was too big, and the words below it were too small. From a distance, the full line seemed to have been blown askew by the wind. After she finished writing, Ling said, "Xiao Si is a famous Hong Kong author. She used to be a teacher for many years, and then worked as a university researcher. The beginning of the essay states that Hong Kong's origins are hazy. Does everyone understand what this means?

"After 1842, Hong Kong became a British colony, and the British ruled Hong Kong for more than a century. We've learned a lot about Western culture from the British. For example, most Hong Kongers know English—we can read English-language books and watch foreign TV dramas. However, Hong Kong originally was part of China, and has inherited many traditional Chinese customs, so we're a blend of Western and Chinese cultures . . ."

Ling turned her head to write on the blackboard. Suddenly, her back tickled, and a wadded paper ball landed at her feet.

"What's a 'colony'?"

Tsui Siu-Hin again. Ling took a deep breath and spun around, and her face tingled with sharp pain. Two paper balls rolled to the floor. The entire class burst out laughing.

Ling willed herself not to lose her temper. Walking over to Tsui Siu-Hin, she said, "Okay, I'll explain what a 'colony' is. The British made money selling opium to China during the Qing Dynasty. Opium is a drug. The Chinese government banned the British from selling opium and appointed an official named Lin Zexu to burn it. Since they couldn't make any money, naturally the British were unhappy, so they went to war with China. At the time, the British navy was powerful, with advanced weaponry and superior technology. China had no guns or artillery, and its military power was weak. As a result, China lost. Afraid that Britain would keep fighting, China ceded Hong Kong to Britain as a condition for peace. Because it was so far away from Britain and wasn't within the country's borders, yet it was forced to accept British rule, Hong Kong was considered a British colony. The territory didn't return to China until 1997. Does everyone understand?"

Tsui Siu-Hin glowered up at Ling like a crowing rooster. "The British bullied us—picking on the little guy paid off."

"Tsui Siu-Hin, what an interesting metaphor. However, this can't really be called 'picking on.' Becoming a British colony was good for Hong Kong. The British did a lot to build up Hong Kong, and they came here to do business, making the city richer and richer. They also brought Western culture, making Hong Kong a mix of East and West ..."

"Meaning, we're neither British nor Chinese—we're not anyone."

He was a gifted student all right. He'd raised a question that not only other second-year secondary school students hadn't thought of, but that even Ling herself had rarely considered. Ling coolly said, "We're Hong Kongers."

"So what?" Tsui Siu-Hin said in English.

"Don't underestimate Hong Kongers. The best thing about us is our strong adaptability. Due to having been a colony, we embrace Chinese culture without rejecting Western culture."

"Is having strong adaptability all that impressive? As long as there are benefits, and I can adapt, I don't care if I'm picked on. In the future, I'll treat everyone to lavish banquets, improving everyone's 'adaptability' at the same time."

After Tsui Siu-Hin finished speaking, the students whistled and asked him to treat them to a meal. Ling knew that Tsui Siu-Hin was trying to provoke her. Facing such an attention seeker, the best thing she could do was to ignore him. "Enough with this topic. Let's move on ..."

"Mouse Yu must've been colonized and couldn't adapt, so she ended up killing herself."

Ling pretended not to hear and kept on talking, but Tsui Siu-Hin's shouts drowned out her voice. "You didn't explain it clearly."

"I'll explain it to you after class," Ling said, turning her back to the students and starting to copy the first paragraph of the essay onto the blackboard. Halfway through, something whacked her in the butt. The pain startled her; then she felt something wet. Glancing down, she saw red liquid running down her dress to her feet. On the floor was a pencil case covered in red ink, resembling a pool of crushed entrails. Ling's heart suddenly stopped, the blood in her entire body coagulating in her ice-cold butt. In her ten years of teaching, she'd never seen anything like this! The other students held their breath as they watched the red ink streaming down her legs. Ling was so livid she could barely breathe. She wanted to slap him in the face.

"Tsui Siu-Hin, after school you will report to the discipline teacher!"

"I'm being colonized by the teacher. The teacher's lecture wasn't clear, and she even punished me—I can't adapt." Tsui Siu-Hin pulled a long face, trying to make his classmates laugh, but no one dared to crack a smile.

After class, Ling rushed to the bathroom to clean up. Her dress was made of cotton—no matter how much she scrubbed it, a faint red mark stubbornly remained, reminiscent of a menstrual bloodstain. Ling scurried back to the teachers' office and tied a large pink scarf around her waist. Accessorizing the yellow dress with a clashing pink scarf made it obvious that she was covering up something and undermined the two hours she'd meticulously spent getting ready that morning. Her colleagues said nothing but eyed her strangely. When she walked into her next classroom, the students cried "Wow!" and loudly asked her, "Miss, what happened?" Ling glared at them and carried on with class. She longed to run home and hide. She couldn't bear being so poorly dressed—how was this any different from being naked? But she couldn't just take the rest of the day off. A dirty dress was no excuse. When she'd previously left early on the pretense that her mother was in the emergency room, she had exhausted the goodwill of the head of the department. If she had any more accidental mishaps, the department head would complain to the principal.

What could she do about being picked on? *You'll just have to find a way through.*

DURING LUNCH IVY glanced at Ling's pink scarf and, without saying anything, dragged her to the staircase behind the teachers' office, walking to the bottom floor.

"I found something out." Out of breath, Ivy handed her crystal-adorned iPhone to Ling. "I accidentally discovered it today when I was helping the principal sort through staff files."

The back staircase was dark, and Ivy's phone screen was blindingly bright. It showed copies of the résumés and academic qualifications of all the faculty in the Chinese department. Ling wasn't interested in which universities her colleagues had graduated from. She quickly scanned the languages qualifications section, moving her fingers to enlarge the font to read the text. The head of the department had passed both the PSC and the LPAT, with an impressive grade of Level 1-B on the PSC and an equally impressive grade of Level 2 on all papers of the LPAT. Another Mandarin teacher, Miss Ko, had scored the slightly above-average grade of Level 2-B on the PSC, and just scraped by with an average grade of Level 3 on all papers of the LPAT. However, Miss Wu, Miss Ip, and the other teachers had only taken the PSC and not the LPAT. The last one was Miss Au's résumé. It only said that she had graduated from the Chinese department, but didn't indicate whether she'd passed the LPAT or PSC.

It turned out there were others like Ling who hadn't taken any of the Mandarin proficiency tests. She was over the moon. "Thank you so much!"

"Don't tell anyone." Ivy grabbed her phone back and immediately deleted the photographic evidence.

"Don't worry, I'm blind—I didn't see anything," Ling said.

Ivy shut off the phone screen, and the back staircase immediately fell into darkness. Ling found the darkness soft and comfortable, and wanted to lie in it for a lifetime. Just then, the bell rang, announcing the end of the lunch period. Ivy turned around and climbed up the stairs. Ling called after her. "Hey, do I need to make an appointment to have Master Chan read my face?"

"Are you really going to get plastic surgery?" Ivy turned her head.

"It won't hurt to see the master about my luck." Ling tried her best to appear interested.

AFTER SAYING GOODBYE to Ivy, Ling went back to the teachers' office. Miss Wu was sleeping with her upper body on her desk, snoring loudly. The head of the department held up an English textbook, muttering something. There was quite a distance between Ling's cubicle and the head of the department's, but she still heard the department head's voice. Sitting behind her, Miss Au wore headphones and silently corrected homework.

Ling grabbed a Form 2 textbook and walked over to Miss Au. Miss Au had on a Giordano black dress paired with Chanel ballerina knit flats. Her look was disproportionate. The Tiffany & Co. ring embedded with small diamonds was so dull and lackluster it was barely visible. While Ling's Céline dress with a scarf wrapped around it was awkward, she happened to be wearing a one-carat ruby ring . . . At second glance, the ruby ring and pink scarf weren't actually a bad match, but Ling took off the ring and tucked it into her pocket. "Sorry, I want to ask you something . . ."

Miss Au removed her headphones. Seeing it was Ling, she inched closer to her desk. She glanced at the scarf and said nothing.

"Thanks for lending me the worksheet on 'Hong Kong Story.' Do you have an answer key? I lost it."

Miss Au picked up a folder from her desktop, quickly found the answer key, and handed it to Ling.

Ling repeatedly thanked her, smiling. "Sorry . . . I don't know how to teach 'Hong Kong Story.' How do you teach it?"

Miss Au gazed at the homework on her desk. "I hand out the worksheets, then explain. I also have my lecture notes— do you want them?"

"Thanks, but there's no need. The materials you gave me aren't suitable for the 2C and 2D classes. The level is too advanced. By the way . . . did you teach 'Hong Kong Story' last year? The lesson is very difficult and isn't that suitable for Form 2 students."

"This is the second year it's being taught."

"This lesson seems like it might be better as part of the senior secondary curriculum."

"Last year, the head of the department said she wanted to raise the students' level, so I wanted to teach a bit more advanced." Miss Au raised her hand and glanced at her watch.

Ling continued, "Have you taught this lesson yet?"

"No. I'm still teaching 'The Foolish Old Man Moves Mountains.'"

"I'm worried we won't have enough time. By the way, how are your supplementary readings in Chinese going? I'm worried we won't be able to finish by the end of the semester."

"We've been doing listening exercises lately. We haven't had any time for supplementary readings. I'll have the students take it home to do if they can't finish."

"Have you all . . . finished your book reports?"

Miss Au glanced at her warily and then, without paying any further attention to her, resumed correcting homework.

Ling thanked her and tactfully walked away. Miss Wu's

snoring overlapped with the head of the department's recitation. Miss Au put her headphones back on.

UPON LEARNING THE news that Miss Au hadn't taken the LPAT, Ling was in a good mood all day. On a whim, she decided to go home early. She hadn't eaten with her mom in ages. She especially decided not to detain students after school to do their homework, and instead left work at six o'clock. First, she swung by IFC Mall. She picked out a dress from a rack at Céline and went into the fitting room. She undressed in front of the mirror. The red ink had not only stained her dress but also her white underwear, and there were streaks of what looked like menstrual blood between her legs. Ling dabbed at them with a tissue, but the red stains stuck stubbornly. Forget it—she'd go home and clean up in the shower. She lifted up the new dress, which was knee length and adorned with purple-red sequins, and spun around, seeing glints of purple in the mirror. She looked like a new person, and her confidence was restored. Instead of changing back into her original clothes, Ling walked out of the fitting room and asked the salesperson to cut off the price tag, then paid with a credit card and left wearing the new dress.

Before leaving IFC, she went to the high-end supermarket on the second floor to buy her mom's favorite Spanish cherries. It suddenly occurred to her that she might as well take a look at her mom's units. Since her mom had kicked out the Nepali man, Ling had rarely handled the rent for her. She'd been awful to her mom during this period.

Ling took the subway to Mong Kok and arrived at her mom's units. She opened the rusted iron gate and the narrow passageway appeared before her. There were five doors in the passageway. Her mom had divided the original 400-foot-plus flat into five smaller flats for rent. The passageway had no windows, and the scent of spices lingered. After the Nepali man moved out, an Indian man had moved in. Whenever he opened the door, a strong smell drifted out.

The other two rooms were occupied by South Asian refugees, who worked as unregistered laborers nearby, leaving early and returning late. Ling rarely saw them. The innermost apartment housed the much-complained-about newly immigrated mother and daughter, who were hated by just about everyone except her mom. They'd only lived there a month. Last time, Ling had called them to tell them the amount, and she'd received the money the next day. Other than the Nepali man, very few paid the rent on time.

But just because they paid the rent on time didn't mean that Ling liked them. Ling had the impression that tenants who were new immigrants were trouble. There was a mainland tenant who had stolen all the electrical appliances before moving out, as well as tenants from the north who threatened Ling every time she collected rent, claiming to be mainland gang leaders who'd kill her entire family if she chased down the rent again. She advised her mom not to rent to new immigrants, but her mom said, "There are bad people in all races." She didn't know if it was prejudice or not, but anyway, among all the various tenants she disliked the newly immigrated mother and daughter the most. She still remembered in August when she and her mom had shown the unit to the woman. The woman had dyed red hair, and thick eyeliner that had smudged onto her lower eyelids, resembling two hanging bike tires; as for her clothes, she wore a tight-fitting red shirt with blue pants; the bra underneath was too big and clearly just for show. Only an improper woman would deliberately exaggerate the curves of her body. But her mom disagreed, saying Ling was being too sensitive, and besides, the woman couldn't do anything with a child in tow. The child was about six or seven, with frighteningly large eyes, wearing a gray knock-off wedding dress and hiding behind the woman all the time.

Whenever the woman asked something, her mom kept speaking in Mandarin like a yes-woman. "Sure, sure, you need a bed, a refrigerator, no problem, we can do that." The woman constantly thanked her before and after, smiling shyly from time to time, as though she regarded Ling's mom as a benefactor. No matter what Ling said, her mom didn't listen. Her mom even whispered in Ling's ear, "You see what a good upbringing they have, more polite than you." However, the little girl's eyes seemed like they wanted to devour people, fixed tightly on her and her mom without blinking. Ling retaliated by staring at her with a stern teacher's gaze.

Standing in the corridor near the door now, Ling checked the electricity and water meters of each household, copying down the numbers for her mother. Just then, a man emerged from the mainland woman's flat. He was middle-aged, with a white shirt that barely covered his sagging belly. He passed by Ling, hurrying away without making eye contact. The woman stood in the doorway, watching the man leave. When she saw Ling, she softly said "Sorry" in accented Cantonese, then quickly moved to close the door. Ling noticed a red ribbon hanging in front of her door. In the dark passageway, the thick red color deeply pierced her eyes.

Every time, she only heard complaints from the tenants, but her mom always made excuses, accusing her of taking things out of context and specifically targeting the mainland woman. Now that Ling had seen it with her own eyes, could her mom still deny it?

A few years ago, she and her mom had encountered tenants involved in prostitution. A Hong Kong man and woman had been renting two adjacent subdivided rooms. The woman was somewhat attractive. Her mom said she was in it just to make a quick buck. The man was also good-looking and in good shape, and appeared to be her friend or boyfriend. A red light bulb hung outside the door of the woman's room. Clients lined up from outside the door to the stairwell. Every ten minutes, there'd be a new one, with moans of "oh oh ah ah" crying out from morning to night. Under the cover of the woman, the man also started doing business. At first, Ling thought he was a reputable man, but then on several occasions when she went to collect rent, she saw various men coming in and out of his room. The people to the left and right often complained. Ling wanted to throw them out, but her mom paid no attention, and only told Ling to raise their rent. Initially, each unit increased by three thousand, then by four thousand. Though they grumbled a bit, they still continued their leases. Her mom said they were raking in so much dough they had bought two units of their own within six months, and in fact could've gotten out of the game, but they couldn't stop now that they were turning a profit.

Until one day, a man pretending to be a customer lined up at the woman prostitute's door. When it was his turn, he went in, enjoyed himself, then suddenly handed over his police ID, handcuffed the woman, and broke down the door to arrest the man as well. Ling and her mom thought that since they had been caught by the police, it would have nothing to do with them, but the police called her mom and Ling to the station to give statements, suspecting they were running a prostitution ring. At the station, the female prostitute complained that the police officer hadn't paid for her services, while the male prostitute loudly claimed he was innocent and asked Ling and her mom to speak up on their behalf.

Her mom fervently asserted that it had nothing to do with them, stating that when she had rented them the units she hadn't realized they'd be used for prostitution (later, her mom said they'd told her at the beginning they were renting the units to "make money" and she had turned a blind eye, as long as they were willing to pay double the rent; after that, her mom kept raising it, earning at least 30,000 HKD from them every month, the equivalent of renting out eight subdivided flats). Ling and her mom went to the police station several times, but the matter still wasn't settled. In the end, they had to go to court, and her mom had to serve as a witness to prove that the tenants were engaged in prostitution; she also had to prove her own "innocence" and that she had no involvement with them.

However, even after the man and woman went to prison, the trouble still wasn't over. The police came again the following day to check whether there were any illicit activities going on. Several new tenants caught wind that there had been prostitution going on there and were hesitant to stay. Ling had to provide counseling sessions for the tenants, constantly convincing them to stay. It took two years to finally clear their tarnished reputation and for the cops to stop coming around. Ling warned her mom not to rent to suspicious people, hoping she had learned her lesson. Who would've guessed that now there would be another prostitute?

The woman was about to close the door, but Ling stepped forward and intercepted. "Illegal activities aren't allowed here."

The woman touched the back of her head. "Uh . . . we're *naught-naught-not* doing anything *eel-illegal*. I'm *suh-sorry*," she said in broken Cantonese.

Ling glimpsed a bunk bed on one side of the room, a red curtain hanging over the lower bunk. The little girl was on the top bunk. The girl stared intently at her, her big eyes like two sores oozing with black pus. On the other side, clutter was piled up like a cliff in the corner. A monogrammed handbag with LV printed all over it lay in the middle of the cliff, the LV diamond pendant hanging on the side of it extremely eye-catching. Although there was a fair distance between Ling and the handbag, because of her familiarity with name brands she knew it was genuine as soon as she laid eyes on it.

"How come there are men coming and going? How come you've tied a red ribbon?" Ling asked.

"It's a *duck-decoration* . . . The men are my—my *fronds-friends* . . . I'm *suh-sorry* . . ."

Eyeing the LV bag, Ling felt this woman was worse than the previous prostitute. She came from the mainland to Hong Kong, obtained Hong Kong resident status, did work that wasn't above board, and openly did her work in front of her child. Disgusting!

Ling wanted to kick her out right then and there, but her mom had the final say, so all she could do was warn her sharply: "Next time I catch you doing illegal activities, either I'm calling the cops or you're moving out."

"*Re-lease-lax*—relax, I'm *suh-sorry* . . ." The woman nodded vigorously, then turned to the little girl and said, "*See-say* bye-bye to Auntie." The little girl poked her head out of the bed and stared blankly at her.

Every syllable the woman uttered was like slipping on a greasy floor, swallowing up all the Cantonese intonation. *If you're going to speak it so unpleasantly, then don't speak it*, Ling thought. Moreover, she kept saying "I'm sorry" here and "I'm sorry" there—there was no need to put on airs. If she really had a good upbringing, she wouldn't come and pollute Hong Kong. Ling suddenly thought of Wai. Wai and her mom had lived upstairs from some ladies of the night, and it was possible that both mother and daughter had been turning tricks. Wai had wanted to turn herself into a mainlander, and this woman was born a mainlander, both from the same roots, really *cheap*.

Leaving Dundas Street, Ling walked home via the Ferry Street footbridge. Dundas Street was teeming with neon signs for nightclubs and saunas, the street a mixed bag of characters: shirtless laborers, men smoking on the roadside, and middle-aged women who always wore low-cut clothes . . . But once she turned onto Ferry Street, the scenery was completely different—clean and bright, with luxury residences and modern estates extending all the way out to the sea. The people in the street were much more respectable, and the sky above was extraordinarily vast. It was as if there were two worlds, new and old, an immense chasm between them. When she stepped onto the Ferry Street footbridge, her disgust from just then turned into a sense of inexplicable superiority, and her steps became lighter and quicker.

WHEN LING GOT home, her mom was sprawled out on the sofa watching TV, newspaper pages strewn all over the floor. Ling set the data for the electricity and water meters on the coffee table and took the cherries to the kitchen to wash them, then piled them on a Swarovski crystal plate bought from a previous trip to Switzerland, along with a smaller plate for spitting out the pits, and placed them on the coffee table in front of her mom. Her mom's eyes floated with the light and shadow of the TV. Taking a deep breath, Ling said, "I just saw a man come out of the mainland woman's flat. She really is turning tricks. Kick them out."

Ling assumed her mom would refute her immediately, or seize the opportunity to scold her for not coming home for dinner, or not buying anything for her. She didn't expect that her mom would keep staring at the TV, casually picking up a cherry, tilting her head back, and popping it in her mouth. "Turning tricks means more money. Add on three thousand to her rent. With her daughter, it can be kept under wraps."

"But if the police find out, there'll be trouble. Before—"

"Are you the one paying me rent? If she's willing to agree to the increase, I can get eight thousand a month."

Would her mom keep the mother and daughter, and evict the Nepali man, simply because they paid more money? Forget it—all the subdivided flats belonged to her mom. What right did she have to say anything?

Her mom picked up the small plate, making a *ding* sound as she spat out the pit, then popped another cherry in her mouth. Ling stared at the naked pit, a bit restless, feeling like she should find something to say. Although Ling was a skilled conversationalist and could talk to her colleagues no matter how different they were, when facing her mom she became tongue-tied. Lately, she'd been spending too little time with her mom—was her mom still angry with her?

A National Geographic program played on TV, the screen an endless grassland. It had just started to rain, the drops making a pitter-patter sound on the seventy-inch TV, making their home seem lush and green. Her mom had always been fond of watching nature documentaries, finding soap operas too boring. She said watching documentaries helped her to better understand the world. When she was a child, her mom used to watch the nature documentaries on Pearl TV with her, teaching her the truths of life, often saying that the world was cruel and one must learn to adapt to the environment and so on.

At this point, the camera showed a male African lion whose fluffy mane had been flattened by the rain, eyes drooping, braving the rain to forage on the grassland. A small fox was looking for a place to take shelter from the rain. Suddenly, its long ears perked up, sensing a lion nearby, and it took off running, the two animals running in the rain as if flying mid-air.

"Surely the fox is going to die." Ling tried to strike up a conversation.

In the camera lens, the fox darted away at full speed. At first, the fox was far away from the lion, but the lion ran so fast that soon it was only a horse's step away from the fox. The lion stretched out its claws and was about to catch the fox, but the fox suddenly accelerated and dodged it, the lion's claws slipping off the fox's body, coming up empty-handed. The lion stretched out its claws again, but the fox surged ahead, diving into the nearby woods with a whoosh. The lion didn't chase after it, and stayed wandering around the grassland, hanging its head in the rain. The camera followed the fox into the woods. The fox rested a while, and soon spied several mice hiding under a tree. It hid behind a bush. The mice, unaware of the predator close by, kept kicking their back legs while holding something to eat in their front paws. In no time, the fox sprang out, and only then did the mice realize they needed to escape. One of the slower runners was caught, and struggled beneath the fox's claws.

"The fox is smarter. The lion goes hungry, but the fox eats its fill," her mom said, pointing at the TV.

As soon as her mom opened her mouth, Ling sighed in relief. She deliberately asked her questions to keep the conversation going. "But the lion is the more powerful fighter."

"You've been with your ma so many years and still don't get it. It's not about size or strength, it's about being clever. The lion keeps chasing, alerting its prey, while the fox uses its brain. It's the same for people. Remember that."

Her mom's face was full of emotions, and she kept waving her hands. Ling couldn't refrain from laughing. "Yes, you're the smartest."

"Am I wrong? You don't necessarily have to be the strongest person—does everyone have to be Li Ka-shing? The most important thing is to be clever. Your ma may not be as success-ful as Li Ka-shing, but I know how to read a situation and deal with people. You know from when we worked my hawker stall. I wasn't part of the hawker management team, and I had no authority or power, but I never received any fines . . ."

Her mom really did know how to read a situation. She'd been a hawker for more than twenty years, and Ling had the impression that her cart had nearly been confiscated only once. Ling was just five at the time, and the hawker manage-ment team wasn't as strict as they were now. One evening, a few people in uniform had swaggered up to the stalls in the Ladies' Market holding small notebooks. Her mom knew that running off with the cart would raise suspicion, so she just left the cart on the street and dragged Ling to hide at the back of the street. When the hawker management team surrounded her cart and tried to push it away, her mom ran forward with Ling in her arms, then threw herself on the ground sobbing, saying how lonely and helpless she felt in Hong Kong, how hard it was to be a single mother . . . This was the first time Ling had seen her mom cry, tears and snot streaming down her face and into her mouth, salty. She didn't know why, but Ling also started crying with her. The manager of the hawker management team was an auntie who was pushing her cart and kept on yelling, "No, we have to follow the rules." But her mom clung to her feet and refused to stand up. The auntie tried to shake her off several times, but she was still caught in her mom's death grip. The auntie and her colleagues looked at each other, unsure what to do. After a long standoff, she finally said, "I never saw you." Her mom quickly sucked back the snot that was about to flow down, then choked up with sobs, said thank you, and dragged away Ling and the cart.

After that, when her mom was working her stall and saw the auntie from a distance, she sent Ling over to deliver snacks to the auntie and also had Ling ask the woman for her phone number. From then on, whenever her mom was free, she'd invite the auntie for dim sum, pay her greetings at Lunar New Year, and give her birthday presents. Each time before there was a crackdown on unlicensed street vendors, the auntie would give her mom the heads-up, and her mom would push her cart away in advance.

Then the auntie retired and was replaced with a male manager. Before the male manager came onto the scene, her mom had already figured out his habits from the auntie. He loved eating seafood, so her mom asked the auntie to give him a gift certificate for Lau Fau Shan seafood, and also asked the auntie to put in a good word for her. And so, not long after the male manager assumed office, her mom had already become familiar with him, and even privately invited him for dim sum.

The male manager was extremely tall. When walking side by side, both she and her mom would have to crane their heads up, making their necks sore. As soon as they sat down, before the waiter had even served their tea, the male manager blathered on and on about his successful investment experiences, boasting about how much he'd earned from stock trading and property investments. Her mom couldn't do anything but nod and serve him food, occasionally asking him to "teach her." The male manager was so pleased that not only did he pay the bill, he also placed two orders of har gow for them to take home. Sitting beside them, Ling felt it strange to see someone dominant as her mom turn into such a submissive woman in the presence of the male manager, but as soon as they left the restaurant her mom ranted, "He's so smug. His stock tips are bullshit." Fortunately, the male manager was long gone and didn't hear. From then on, the male manager would confide in her mom, always messaging her before inspections. When they met on the street, he pretended not to see her and just walked by.

ON THE TV screen, the fox tore apart the mouse's flesh piece by piece. The mouse became a mangled, bloody mess, with only its eyes still open, staring blankly at the sky. "So, the most important thing as a person is to be clever. Nature tells you that if you can't be a lion, being a fox isn't half bad—but most importantly, don't be a mouse."

Her mom spoke so seriously, as though she were a biologist. Ling wanted to laugh. "How miserable to be born a mouse."

"Nature is cruel. If you're on the lowest level, unless you evolve and become a stronger species, you'll go extinct."

"What about people?"

"People are a kind of animal. If they don't work hard, they'll be eliminated, just like animals."

Ling was both amused and angry. "If people are all animals, why don't you like cats and dogs?"

Her mom glared at her. "You can't let go of that Nepali man."

Her mom assumed Ling was making oblique accusations; in fact, Ling wasn't thinking of the Nepali man, but the "game" her mom used to play with stray cats and dogs. After finishing their work at the stall, she and her mom would push the cart from Nathan Road onto the side streets. At night, Shanghai Street and Canton Road were especially crowded with cats and dogs. They were light on their feet and quickly dashed out of the range of streetlights, but her mom always spotted them. She would stealthily push the cart over to where the stray cats and dogs were, and when the animals sensed danger and wanted to escape, she would thrust the cart forward at full speed. The cats were smart and would avoid the cart and escape, but if they encountered a dog, the dog would bark wildly at them. When Ling was little, she was scared of dogs and would hide behind her mom, but her mom would ignore her, saying, "You're so useless, you're even afraid of dogs—dogs are harmless," then charge at the dog. Her mom couldn't run very fast when she was pushing the cart, and it wasn't hard for the cats and dogs to dodge out of the way. However, on a few occasions her mom cornered the smaller cats and dogs, who had no way to escape. She would say, "Let's see how you escape now," then shove the cart at the dog or cat, hitting it over and over, the cracking of bones scaring Ling so much that she covered her ears. Soon, a pool of blood would flow out from under the cart. Looking as though she felt a sense of accomplishment, her mom would push the cart away. Ling didn't dare look back at the animal corpses, but just the two lines of dark-red rolling marks that stretched out along their way home were so shocking that Ling suffered from nightmares. Countless times, she dreamed that her mom pushed the cart against her over and over, her blood splashing all over the ground . . .

Ling didn't ask her mom why she liked playing "games" with cats and dogs, but as she grew older, she no longer was afraid or had nightmares. She only knew that her mom was still a child. Now that her mom wasn't a hawker, she didn't know if she still had a habit of playing games with cats and dogs, but watching the mouse about to be eaten on TV for some reason reminded her of those small, dead animals.

Her mom's voice cut through her thoughts. "How come you always think about that Nepali man who doesn't even speak Cantonese and only earns a few thousand bucks a month? Look at the people who earn money. I keep urging you to learn from Mrs. Cheng's daughter. She's making a killing from doing business, and has already bought her mom several properties. You? You still live at my place."

Clearly her mom had been happily chatting, but now she was angry again. Ling wanted to explain that she didn't blame her mom for driving away the Nepali man and was just joking with her, but her mom wouldn't listen. She raised the newspaper that was on the table. "When are you gonna buy me a flat?"

It was a front-page ad for luxury housing. A man and woman waltzed in a hotel-style lobby overlooking the night view of Victoria Harbour. The man was dressed in a suit, the woman in a red evening dress. Beside them in fine print were the words: $20,000/FOOT. This was at least ten million per unit.

Not wanting to upset her mother, Ling casually said, "Of course I'll buy one when I have the money."

"When will that be?"

"Some day."

"Really?"

"Some day . . . I think."

Her mom's anger turned to laughter, and she waved her hand in the air. "I'm waiting for you, I'm waiting for you!"

Her mom wasn't angry anymore. Ling felt relieved. *When will I save enough money to buy a ten-million-dollar unit? Forget it, just tell her what she wants to hear, do whatever she wants.* Ling turned to look at the window. That sliver of Victoria Harbour was sandwiched between buildings, like a malformed bone-shaped diamond. Ling's silhouette was superimposed on the diamond, the purple-red Céline sequined dress full of light, more dazzling than the lights of Victoria Harbour. The more Ling looked, the better she felt about her appearance, and her mood improved.

AT FIVE IN the morning, Ling woke up in a cluttered room. Last night was the best sleep she'd had since the beginning of school, without tossing and turning, without nightmares; a full six hours of sleep. When she got out of bed, instead of putting together pieces from here and there as she usually did, she fished out the most expensive Céline retro floral maxidress from the numerous shopping bags and spent more than half an hour curling her hair. Standing in front of the mirror, she spun around. She looked like a Greek goddess. After she was all made up, she tiptoed into her mom's room and stole the Rokkatei chocolates from the cabinet, which she'd bought for her during a summer trip to Hokkaido. Her mom was snoring loudly and didn't notice, luckily.

When she got to school, the teachers' office was empty, and the lights were still off. Ling walked over to her cubicle, removed the chocolates from her handbag, grabbed a random folder, hid the chocolates in her arms, and headed for the principal's office.

It was November and the weather hadn't cooled down much yet, but Ling felt chilly as she walked along the deserted corridor. When she came to the door of the principal's office, a gleam of white light shone through the crack of the door. The principal had already started work, but Ivy and her other administrative colleagues hadn't shown up yet. Ling raised her hand to knock, but after thinking it over she lowered it and paced in front of the office, contemplating what she'd say to the principal, making sure she was prepared before entering.

After a while, Ling was again on the verge of knocking, but just as her hand touched the door, it opened and the head of the department came out. The head of the department shouldered a handbag, with a magazine in her left hand and a Starbucks coffee cup in her right. It seemed as though she hadn't had time to drop her things off in the teachers' office before coming to see the principal. The head of the department avoided Ling's gaze and walked past her, the espresso and the perfume she was wearing mixing into a strange smell. Ling glanced back at the head of the department, who walked very fast, her figure disappearing into the early morning sunlight.

Ling felt strange, but ignored it. Smiling, she pushed open the door, sat down and handed the principal the chocolates. "My mom bought these on a trip to Hokkaido."

The principal accepted the gift, placed it in the bookcase behind her, and smiled at Ling.

The principal's desk was cleaner than it had been the last time Ling had seen her. The water glasses and file organizer had been put away, leaving only the Valentino staring at her like a beckoning cat. Ling stole a glance at the bookcase behind the principal. The snack cabinet was full of snacks; aside from the Kopi Luwak and Japanese dried fruit, there was also German sausage, Dutch cheese, and Japanese dried scallops, none of which were from Ling. Ling's heart sank, but she couldn't lose her morale, so she perked herself up and said, "I started teaching junior secondary this year. I have some questions I don't understand and would like to ask for your advice. Should the teaching pace be fast or slow?"

The principal looked at Ling and smiled. "It depends on the students. If they're smart, teach a little faster; if they're average, teach a little slower."

Her answer was a non-answer, as though Ling had asked a stupid question, but Ling kept on going. "The 2C and 2D classes I'm teaching are the worst classes in all of Form 2. Now I've almost finished teaching all the material that will be on the exam, and I also gave the students a practice exam—the grades weren't too bad. I see that Miss Au's class still has two texts left to teach. I don't know if I'm teaching too fast." Ling handed her the test papers for 2C and 2D, deliberately placing the two with the highest scores at the top.

"The head of the department told me all about it."

A question mark popped up in Ling's mind, and she

remembered the scene when the head of the department had brushed past her just now. "Also, may I be so bold to ask, can the teachers please keep it down in the teachers' office?"

The principal looked puzzled.

"Because Miss Wu often falls asleep and snores in the office, and the head of the department only cares about stringing together English words . . . They disrupt my work mood. This year, I have a lot more work than last year. Every day I stay until eight or nine. I want to concentrate on my work and do better."

The principal threw back her head and roared with laughter, as though Ling were a child who'd said something funny.

Ling didn't know how to react. After a while, the principal stopped laughing. "Do you think the school has many problems?"

"Actually, our administration is better than other schools'. I just don't understand other teachers' schedules—"

"If there's something you're not satisfied with, you can tell me directly." The principal cut Ling off.

"No . . . I just want to communicate with you."

"If there's anything you're not satisfied with, tell me directly. The school affairs will be quickly resolved. If you talk to outsiders, then I have to deal with both outsiders and the school administration, and it'll be more difficult."

Ling frowned, not understanding. The principal gazed at her for a moment, then said, "Ling, you're clever. But being clever isn't enough."

"Mhm . . . Of course I should learn from you, principal. I still have many shortcomings. If you think there's something I need to improve on, you can tell me any time."

The principal's expression softened. "How's your Mandarin?"

"It's coming along. You can test me any time."

"You've got this."

When Ling left the principal's office, the principal didn't say goodbye.

THE SUN GREW brighter and brighter, and the air in the corridor began heating up. The students arrived at school one after another, gathering in the sports ground to chat and laugh. Ling pushed open the door of the teachers' office. Most of the teachers were there, lining up in front of the kitchenette to make coffee. Colleagues in the Chinese department gathered around the head of the department, chatting. When they saw Ling come in, they all stopped smiling and went back to their seats.

Ling looked around warily and her eyes fell on the head of the department. Without so much as glancing at Ling, the head of the department took a sip of espresso, flipping through the magazine on her desk.

The *Mango Weekly*.

Ling went over to her cubicle at once, switched on the computer, and clicked the *Mango Weekly* website. After a while, the bell rang, accompanied by the sound of heavy footsteps and chairs being pulled out; her Chinese department colleagues seemed to have coordinated ahead of time to hurry out of the teachers' office as soon as the bell rang. Ling stared at the screen, her anxiety ballooning. In the "Breaking News" section, she read a report with the headline FILIAL TEACHER UNABLE TO FULFILL MOTHER'S WISH—COLLEAGUE FROM SING DIN: SHE DIDN'T PASS THE LPAT.

Ling quickly pressed the mouse, the clicking sound echoing the rhythm of her heartbeat.

Previously, the suicide of a Chinese teacher at Sing Din Secondary School caused a sensation in the city, and even the foreign media scrambled to report it. Although the police ruled it a suicide, the principal of Sing Din Secondary School, Wong Gam Wai-Lo, recently imposed a media blockade prohibiting faculty and students from discussing this matter, adding to the confusion. It's well known that teachers have a heavy workload and long working hours; however, under the trend of transitioning to Mandarin as a medium of Chinese-language instruction, Chinese-language teachers are under the additional pressure of passing the Language Proficiency Assessment for Teachers in order to keep their faculty positions. According to the exclusive news obtained by this magazine, Miss Ng of Sing Din Secondary School revealed that Miss Yu failed the LPAT, and Principal Wong threatened to dismiss her. Miss Yu came to a dead end!

Rep: Reporter

Ng: Miss Ng

Rep: What was Miss Yu usually like?

Ng: She was hard-working. She graded homework and tests on time. She was enthusiastic about teaching and cared about her students.

Rep: Was Miss Yu under a lot of pressure?

Ng: Every teacher worked hard, but Miss Yu not only had to handle her daily work, but also study for the LPAT. Miss Yu was a contract teacher. The school requires all Chinese teachers to pass the LPAT before they can renew their contract. I once heard her say she didn't go to bed till 3 a.m. after studying Mandarin every night. I can only imagine how much pressure she felt.

Rep: Did the pressure come from the principal?

Ng: Of course! The principal likes to hire contract teachers, then undercut them based on their qualifications. Miss Yu said that because she hadn't taken the LPAT, the principal hired her at only seventy percent of the teacher's salary. Miss Yu had hoped to renew her contract the following year, so she had to work hard in studying Mandarin. However, she faced many obstacles in the process. For example, the head of the department frequently interrogated her about her progress in learning Mandarin, and the principal summoned her to her office from time to time to scold her, and ordered her to speak in Mandarin during weekly assemblies. When she was alive, she often said that work was hard. Now that she's dead, I'm also sad.

Rep: How many contract teachers are there in the school?

Ng: Many. The principal wants to save money. I'm also a contract teacher . . .

Ling couldn't stand to keep on reading. She was so livid that the mouse was about to melt under her palm. Obviously, Ling hadn't said any of that. Obviously, although that reporter had promised not to disclose her identity, now—even though her given name wasn't mentioned—her surname was listed. Everyone knew it was her.

Ling quickly scrolled to the bottom. There was another interview. The reporter had also interviewed Wai's mother.

Miss Yu's mother is a mildly mentally handicapped person. She lived with her daughter in a tong lau flat of just over 200 feet. They were interdependent on each other. Yu's mother had taken great pains to care for her daughter for many years. Her daughter studied hard and became a Chinese teacher. She should have been living in comfort in her old age, but Miss Yu is now deceased. Yu's mother broke down sobbing when discussing her daughter's suicide.

Mother: Yu's Mother
Rep: Reporter

Rep: Did Bat-Wai show any signs before taking her own life?

Mother: I sensed a change in Wai in the beginning of June. One day Wai came home from school. I was shocked—she'd cut her hair very short, like a man. I'd never seen Wai like this. She said: "No matter what I do, I can't change." Then she hid in her room and wouldn't come out. I thought the pressure from work was too much and didn't want to bother her. But for several days, Wai didn't go to school, didn't eat, she just hid in her room. I knocked on her door, and she ignored me. I tried opening the door to call her for dinner, but found the door locked. I glued my ear to the door and listened closely, hearing the faint sound of sawing. I was so worried I forced the door open with a key. When I opened it, I saw the room reflected in red light, the computer playing a bloody scene, like something out of a horror movie. Terrified, I asked Wai to turn off the computer, but she didn't respond. She just looked at the screen and said: "I want to change myself." I didn't understand what she was talking about. I thought she was out of sorts from working too hard, so I urged her to take a break from work. A day later, she went to work, and I thought she was back to normal. Unexpectedly, she came home from work with an electric drill. I asked her what it was for, but she said nothing, slammed the door, and didn't come out all night. The next morning, I was awakened by the roar of an electric drill. I kept knocking on Wai's door, but there was no answer. Soon, blood was flowing out . . .

Rep: Why do you think Wai took her own life?

Mother: It's my fault . . . I collect trash on the roadside. I don't make much money. I didn't want her to follow in my footsteps. Wai was well-behaved and had been obedient since childhood. I asked her to become a teacher. She studied very hard and was finally admitted to the Education University. I was so happy at the time. Who'd have guessed that only two years after becoming a teacher, she'd be dead. Wouldn't it have been better if I had never asked her to become a teacher?

Below the article, there was a photo of Wai and her mother. Their distinctive upside-down-V eyebrows formed two upward arrows when placed side by side. *I thought Wai's mother was a prostitute, but it turns out she's a trash collector. However, what she does is none of my business.*

Ling clicked to the next page. The first thing she saw was a red pop-up dialogue box that read: EXPOSÉ: SING DIN SECONDARY SCHOOL HAS A RECORD OF SUCKING UP TO THE CCP. Below was a brief introduction to the background of Sing Din Secondary School and its sponsoring body, the St. David's Society.

> According to insiders, in recent years, the St. David's Society has been growing closer and closer to a certain mainland political group. This political group has been assisting the St. David's Society in purchasing units and land in mainland China, and injecting a large amount of funds into its affiliated schools. The political group hopes that schools affiliated with the society can attract more cross-border students from the mainland to study in Hong Kong, eventually turning into private secondary schools responsible for their own profits and losses. As a result, the schools affiliated with the society have all turned to embrace Mandarin-language education. Recently, the political group has been sending inspectors to the schools to monitor their educational policies, which has made Principal Wong extremely nervous about school governance . . .

No wonder strangers had been frequenting the school to observe classes lately! Ling hastily glanced at the page. The next one listed the principal's credentials.

1980 Graduated from the English Department of the University of Hong Kong, worked as manager of a trading company after graduation

1985 Established Transmit Trade Co., LTD., specializing in China-related affairs

1999 During the Asian financial crisis, the company went bankrupt

1999–2004 Served as the head of the English Department at Zan Sin Mei Secondary School

2004–2010 Served as vice-principal at Sing Din Secondary School

2010–present Principal at Sing Din Secondary School

According to sources, St. David's Society specifically recruited Principal Wong because of her business background and educational experience, hoping to boost the school's ranking. Thus, she was appointed vice-principal immediately upon joining the school, and after the former British principal retired, she was promoted to principal immediately . . .

Ling had never imagined that the principal had a background in business. No wonder she knew so much about investment. In retrospect, the principal ran the school just like a company, prioritizing outcomes and ignoring any educational philosophy. Moreover, the principal graduated in 1980, so she should be around fifty-seven or fifty-eight now and would retire in a couple of years . . . no wonder the head of the department had recently become the principal's yes-woman— was it to pave the way for her promotion?

But at this moment, Ling wasn't concerned about these

things. She kept scrolling through the page, just searching for three characters. At the bottom of the page, she finally found the reporter's name—Tsui Tsz-Yee. Tsui Tsz-Yee? Ling pushed aside the neatly stacked exercise books and, after searching for a while, finally found the note with the reporter's name written on it between the Form 4 compositions and Form 2 worksheets. At the time, Ling had written: *Wong Wai-Yee*.

She was played. What now? Find the principal and explain? Call that reporter and give her a piece of her mind? Sue the *Mango Weekly* for libel? Five minutes had passed since the bell rang. Ling tidied up the exercise books as quickly as possible and ran to class.

FLINGING OPEN THE door with a bang, Ling walked into the classroom, set down the textbook, and looked at the Form 5 students expressionlessly. The students looked up at Ling briefly, then continued what they were doing. Some were doing their English homework, electronic dictionaries and small notebooks filled with new vocabulary words spread out on their desks. Some had hidden their textbooks in their drawers, secretly studying for the upcoming geography test. Ling was generally very fond of this class of students. They were lively and fun. Before each lesson, she'd tell a couple of jokes to capture the students' attention, and they'd automatically stop what they were doing and focus on the class. But at this moment, Ling couldn't see anything. She picked up the composition papers with one hand and distributed them to the students. "For today's essay, put away all non-Chinese books." They passed the papers back with puzzled expressions. They'd never seen Ling so serious.

Ling opened the teacher's textbook and flipped to the section on teaching composition, randomly selecting the essay prompt "self-respect and respecting people." She began writing it on the blackboard with a clattering sound. As she wrote the first stroke of the character for "people," the chalk broke due to excessive force.

"Now we're in Chinese class. I hope everyone can learn respect. I'd like to ask everyone, what is respect?"

The whole class looked at her in complete silence.

When the students didn't respond, Ling became even more impatient. "I'm asking you, what is respect?"

Still, no students spoke.

A student sitting at the front timidly raised a finger. "Self-respect and respecting...?"

Ling turned her head and discovered that she hadn't finished writing the character for "people." She immediately added the final stroke. However, she wrote too forcefully, and the stroke was crooked, like breath that was exhaled but couldn't be drawn back in.

The students bowed their heads and copied the topic onto their composition paper. As they scribbled away, Ling turned around and looked out the window beside the teacher's desk. Outside the window were the outer walls of two buildings, a corner of the road reflected in the gap. There was a traffic jam: a bus stopped at the crosswalk, unable to move forward, pedestrians weaving in and out of cars. Ling blinked, her reflection overlapping with the traffic on the road, and sighed.

A student softly asked, "Self-respect and respect for others is...?"

Glaring, Ling walked over to the blackboard. "We discussed this already in the previous class. Did you listen? Self-respect means respecting yourself, neither excessively demeaning nor elevating yourself. Respecting people means respecting other people, without belittling them, and being considerate of their feelings."

The students lowered their heads, taking notes. Another

student asked, "So do we have to choose a position to write from? Agree with a certain aspect?"

"As I explained in the last class . . . for this type of open-ended question, explaining the relationship between the two, and presenting arguments for both sides, will achieve higher scores."

"But if you respect yourself, it's hard to respect others, and if you respect others, it's hard to respect yourself . . ."

The student looked confused, but Ling pretended not to notice. She sat down at the teacher's desk and started grading the homework that she'd give to class 2D later. Her mind, however, wasn't on grading. Cold air rattled down on her. She felt the air was heavy, and her shoulders were tired. She didn't know how to respect herself or others, and several times she wanted to call and chew out the reporter. If possible, she wanted to kill her. But now she was in class and couldn't use the phone. She slipped out her phone and quickly peeked at the WhatsApp message from her mom about overdue rent, then slipped it back into her pocket.

IT WAS HARD to wait for class to be over. Ling collected the students' essays, then had to teach another lesson for class 2D before taking a break. She hadn't even reached the door of 2D when she heard a burst of shrill laughter. She closed her eyes, took a deep breath, and opened the classroom door. The students seemed not to notice her; they were focused on chatting and laughing loudly with Tsui Siu-Hin. Ling walked to the middle of the classroom, slammed the book down on the table. After she banged it three times, the students finally quieted down. Ling didn't have the energy to scold the students anymore, so she picked up the textbook, whose cover had been wrinkled by the throwing, and said, "Turn to page sixty-four."

While Ling was lecturing, Tsui Siu-Hin kept making gestures and strange noises to attract his classmates' attention, but the students seemed to realize that Ling was different from usual and all stared at the blackboard obediently, afraid to utter a peep. Bored, Tsui Siu-Hin propped up his cheek and doodled on the cover of his textbook with a black marker. Drawing cartoon characters was better than him going crazy, as long as he didn't make a scene. Ling repeated the content from the previous class, saying that Hong Kong culture was a mix of East and West, making it difficult to distinguish its unique characteristics. She read aloud a section from "Hong Kong Story" that the teacher's manual marked as important: "Westerners come to Hong Kong in search of Eastern qualities, while Chinese people complain that Hong Kong is too Westernized. As for us? For a moment, we can't explain it clearly and can only go with the flow, raising our heads to accept the title of Chinese–Western Cultural Exchange Center.'"

As soon as she finished reading, Tsui Siu-Hin stood up and threw a book at her. "Why do we have to study this? I don't want to."

The book flew over the students' heads, landing at Ling's feet. Tsui Siu-Hin had drawn a pig nose over the lotus pond on the cover and erased the word "Chinese" in "Chinese Language," leaving only the word "Language." *Here we go again.* Ling sighed, bent down to pick up the book and screamed, "Sit down!"

Tsui Siu-Hin stood with his hands on his hips, his childlike eyes still fixed on Ling. Ling thought, *Let him stand there all he wants.* She looked up at the clock. There were still twenty minutes left. It would be over soon, it would be over soon. She kept on teaching, writing "Pearl of the Orient" on the blackboard, explaining the meaning of this nickname to the students. Realizing that Ling was ignoring him, Tsui Siu-Hin raised his voice and shouted, "Why won't you answer my question?"

Ling really wanted to answer that the head of the department required her to teach it. Many questions in the world don't have answers, and even if you get an answer, what can be changed? Ling glared at Tsui Siu-Hin and said in a neutral tone, "We're reading this to help everyone understand Hong Kong culture and identity."

"In summary, Hong Kong's origins are hazy, neither Chinese nor Western, but now it's becoming clearer. Schools are all switching to teaching in Mandarin. This lesson is useless. I don't want to study it."

The news reported earlier that morning had already spread among the students. Tsui Siu-Hin's words stabbed at Ling's heart, but the class still had to go on. "Just because you don't want to study it doesn't mean others don't want to. This is a school, not a home. You don't have a choice."

"Why are you forcing me?" With a loud roar, Tsui Siu-Hin charged out of his seat, walked up to Ling, and tore up the notes she'd prepared for the students into pieces, one by one.

The shredded paper swirled in the air, a few pieces floating onto Ling's feet. The itchy feeling ignited fury in her entire body. Those worksheets had taken her a whole night to finish, just to meet the principal's requirements and ensure that students wouldn't merely memorize the answers ... It was as though she saw the principal standing in front of her, slapping her face over and over. Ling couldn't control it anymore. She raised her hand and pointed at Tsui Siu-Hin, then shouted hoarsely: "You—go—back—to—your—seat—!"

Tsui Siu-Hin was taken aback, but he still stood his ground, confronting Ling.

"Are you deaf? Or crippled? Or born with brain damage?" Ling shouted hoarsely.

Tsui Siu-Hin was stunned. The corners of his mouth twitched involuntarily, but then he burst into a high-pitched laugh. "If you teachers and psychologists say there's something wrong with my brain, then there must be. Who I am is defined by all of you anyway!" Suddenly, he took out a lighter from his pocket. Before Ling could react, he flicked the wheel, and a tongue of fire quickly engulfed the remaining worksheets on the desk. Stretching out his hand, Tsui Siu-Hin tossed them aside, a ball of sparks swirling up from the floor.

Screaming loudly, the students rushed to stand up and stepped back. Two students sitting in the front row handed Ling water bottles, which she snatched, vigorously dousing the flames. Amid the chaos, Tsui Siu-Hin glanced at the burning embers on the ground, threw down the lighter, and fled out the door.

WITH TSUI SIU-HIN'S antics, it was impossible for Ling to dismiss class on time. She had to find the custodian to come and clean up the mess. When the recess bell rang, she had to mobilize students to hunt for Tsui Siu-Hin. Eventually, they found him in the boys' bathroom on the fifth floor. Ling didn't even have the energy to scold him when she saw him. She directly handed him over to the discipline team, then reported the incident to his class teacher. This was how she spent her break. When the bell sounded, she finally had time to return to her cubicle and take a sip of water.

Fortunately, she was free the next class period. She fished her phone out of her handbag, picked up the note with the reporter's phone number written on it from her desk, and rushed out of the teachers' office.

The back stairwell was quiet. Although recess was over, the noise from the sports field could still be heard. Ling dialed the phone number on the note, and a robotic voice sounded immediately. "The number you have dialed is not registered with any user."

Ling was so angry her hands trembled. She immediately searched for the number of the *Mango Weekly* online and called them. "I want to speak to Tsui Tsz-Yee."

"Is Tsui Tsz-Yee a reporter?" a young female voice asked.

"Yes."

"This is the tip line. Have you tried the human resources department?"

"What's the number?"

"2364756."

Ling called the number and asked if Tsui Tsz-Yee was there. A male voice on the other end said, "There's no one here by that name."

"But your latest interview about education was written by Tsui Tsz-Yee."

"Ah, Tsui Tsz-Yee is her pseudonym."

"How can I find her?"

"Who are you?"

"I need to ask her something."

"She recently transferred to the newspaper department. Why don't you try calling the newspaper department and ask?"

"What's her name?"

"Mavis Lai."

"What's the phone number for the newspaper?"

"3726472."

Ling wrote down the number, hung up, and silently exclaimed, "Fuck!" She called the number again. This time, a mature female voice answered. "Mavis Lai? There's no one here with that name."

"Is there a reporter named Tsui Tsz-Yee?"

"Let me check the name list . . . no."

"Wong Wai-Yee?"

"Wong Wai-Yee . . . has resigned."

"You published an interview about education in the current issue of *Mango Weekly*. I'm looking for the reporter who wrote that piece. The magazine lists the reporter's name as Tsui Tsz-Yee, but when I called, the magazine said she'd been transferred to work as a newspaper reporter. Now you're saying she's resigned? I want her number!"

"I'm sorry. The number's private . . . I really can't help you. If you want to complain, you can call the complaints hotline. We're the reception department."

"Are you playing games? Obviously I didn't say anything, but she made up fake news. I clearly told her not to publish my name, but she wrote my name. Now you're hiding a reporter. I want to speak to your manager!"

"I'm sorry, but the manager is busy now . . ."

The voice sounded familiar. Could it be that Wong Wai-Yee had answered the phone? "What's your name?"

"Mary."

"Don't play games. Also known as Wong Wai-Yee, also known as Tsui Tsz-Yee, also known as Mavis, and now Mary."

"Miss, I'm only a receptionist. My name is really Mary. My colleagues in the complaints department would be happy to help you . . . Sorry, there's a phone call coming in." The mature female voice suddenly switched to electronic music. Ling hung up and flung her iPhone on the floor, the screen cracking immediately.

Ling slumped down on the stairs, panting heavily. It wasn't until the recess bell rang that she picked up her phone and headed back to the teachers' office.

I CAN'T FIND the reporter, and the principal thinks I'm a mole, which isn't the case at all.

There's not a single sentence in the entire report that I said, and there's also the situation with the society and the principal's credentials—how would I know any of that? Anyone with common sense would know I'm not the whistleblower . . .

But will anyone believe me now? There's only one Miss Ng in the school.

During her free time, Ling called the number several times. The reply from the *Mango Weekly* was the same, refusing to tell her the contact information for Wong Wai-Yee/Tsui Tsz-Yee/Mavis Lai.

She searched the internet for information about libel. *400,000 to 500,000 dollars for a lawsuit—where would I get that kind of money? Plus, I don't have a recording of the phone call—how can I prove it?*

What can I do? Am I really going to leave Sing Din next year?

Ling felt backed into a corner for the first time in her thirty-four years of life. Now it was as though someone was strangling her, rendering her speechless.

During her free period, she paced outside the principal's office, struggling whether to report the incident to her; but now that there was "solid evidence," what else could she say?

Ivy was in her seat peeking at a fashion magazine when she noticed Ling's gloomy-looking face, so she called out to her, "The principal isn't in school this afternoon."

After she finished speaking, she looked around to make sure no one was nearby, then mouthed the word "mainland" and pointed upward.

Ling rubbed her hands and began pacing again.

"What happened?"

Ling bit her lip, wanting to ask what the principal was doing on the mainland. Was she really planning on firing her? But she forced a smile and said, "Nothing."

Ivy fixed her gaze on Ling, who immediately changed the subject. "Is Master Chan free today? How about we go get our faces read after school today?"

Ivy raised her eyebrows. "Sure! You seem troubled. You could probably use some guidance."

BACK IN THE teachers' office, Ling sprawled out on the swivel chair and slowly breathed in and out.

Sunlight reflected from Wai's wall of mirrors. Ling squinted at the spotless desktop, a full to-do list on the left, a cold cup of coffee on the right, piles of exercise books stacked up on either side. It was like she was trapped in a castle of light, with arrows of light shooting at her from all directions, with no place to escape.

Closing her eyes, Ling pinched the center of her eyebrows. Getting her face read might be a good idea. She really needed some direction. Although she'd suggested it to Ivy earlier, it had merely been an excuse to talk.

It was five o'clock on the dot. The head of the department, Miss Wu, and Miss Ip had already left work, while other colleagues in the Chinese department were still hard at work. Ling put the exercise books that needed to be graded into her handbag and went to the school office to meet Ivy. Ivy led her to board a bus to Kwun Tong, and soon they arrived at Mut Wah Street. Mut Wah Street was full of various shops, including snack shops, mobile phone shops, and pawn shops, densely packed like gapless teeth. Ivy led Ling into a commercial building, and they rode the elevator to the fourth floor. The corridor was dimly lit, and Master Chan's shop was located at the very end. It was a unit over a hundred square feet, with several umbrellas hanging on the wall. There was a gray iron desk near the window, with documents and books piled on top, a few chairs placed randomly beside it, all of them stacked with miscellaneous items. A woman in her fifties sat at the desk. She had upturned phoenix-like eyes, thin, curved eyebrows, and cascading black hair that seemed to have been treated with negative ions. She was reading a book with the title *The Sickness Unto Death* on the cover. Upon seeing them, the woman gestured with her hand. "Come in. Please have a seat." Surprisingly, it was a deep male voice. After speaking, the person moved the miscellaneous items and cleared two seats for Ling and Ivy.

As soon as they sat down, the master continued reading, paying them no attention. Ling observed that, while he had a feminine face, his arms were muscular like a man's and covered in body hair. After a few minutes, Master Chan said, "May I ask your age?"

"Thirty-four."

"What aspect are you inquiring about?"

"Career."

Master Chan nodded, playing with his long hair, flipping through a few pages of his book. He didn't seem interested in doing business. Instead, it was as though they'd disturbed his leisurely reading. Ling slightly regretted coming here with Ivy. Ivy nudged her shoulder and whispered in her ear, "He's effeminate, and a bit arrogant, but really accurate."

After a while, Master Chan's eyes left the book. He stood up slowly, sizing up Ling with his phoenix-like eyes. "Lift the hair in front of your forehead."

Ling pushed her hair aside. Master Chan craned his neck to study her side profile. "Hmm, your fate is very strong."

"Huh, is that unlucky?" Ivy asked.

"There will be many challenges in your life, but if you can endure them, you can achieve great things."

Master Chan spoke casually, his phoenix-like eyes firmly fixed on Ling's face. "Let's start with your forehead. You have a good, wide forehead, indicating that you were born into a middle- to upper-class family. Also, your forehead is high, which suggests you did well in your studies when you were younger and probably graduated from university. What is your profession?"

"A teacher."

"But ... you're really not suited to be a teacher. The middle of your forehead is slightly concave. People like you have a harder time finding work. Instead, you'd be better suited to developing an unconventional path."

"Unconventional path?" Ivy asked.

"It means working in a profession that fewer people pursue, and being self-employed, without relying on others." Master Chan pointed to the middle of Ling's forehead. "Touch here."

Ling gently touched her forehead, her finger wiping off a bit of white powder.

Master Chan smiled, and as he did, his face, which had a somewhat masculine profile, changed angle, now truly resembling that of a woman. "Even with makeup, that spot is still concave." It was as though he were mocking her heavy makeup. Ling hated this kind of smile.

"Or let me ask, why did you want to become a teacher?"

What did this have to do with face reading? What was he trying to find out? Ling thought to just give a perfunctory answer. "My mom wanted me to become one." Although it wasn't entirely true, it wasn't completely false, either. Her mom had always wanted her to do business and opposed her becoming a teacher, but since she was a child, her mom had also taught her to exchange the most significant return for the least amount of effort. She had studied Chinese because teaching was the easiest profession to break into and had long vacations and annual salary increases for permanent staff. Didn't this precisely meet her mom's demands?

Master Chan thought for a while. "You have a mole on

your temple, which indicates you have a strained relationship with your mom. Is she strict?"

Ling let out an "M-hm" sound.

"You're too filial, and you can't break away from your mom. Being too filial has an impact on your development. When I evaluate a person's career, I not only analyze aptitude, but also consider whether they pour their heart and soul into it. If you do whatever your mom asks you to do, then you're not suitable."

Ling chuckled. "Are you here to read my face or to counsel me?"

Master Chan wasn't angry. "I had a client who was a nurse. The pay and benefits were good, but she never liked going to work. She asked for my advice, and I said that, if she didn't like being a nurse, she wasn't suitable for it. I helped read her fortune and found she was suited for a career in a creative industry. She followed my advice and studied design in her spare time. The more she studied it, the more she enjoyed it. Then she quit her nursing job and became a designer. Although she makes less money than before, she's successful and is well known in the industry. Most importantly, she's happy with what she does."

Haven't I poured my heart and soul into being a teacher? How could I do it for ten years without pouring my heart and soul into it? I've even been learning Mandarin and will take the LPAT . . .

"What does it mean to pour one's heart and soul into it? Does it mean having a lot of enthusiasm for teaching?" Ling questioned.

Master Chan raised his arched eyebrows. The answer was in his eyes.

"How many such people are there in Hong Kong? Many people become teachers just for the money."

"This just reinforces you're not suitable for it. People who pour their heart and soul into something don't care about gains and losses. If you're only doing it because of environmental pressures, no matter how hard you work, you're not pouring your heart and soul into it. And, you'll never do it well because you're not doing it for yourself. Have you ever thought about what you truly enjoy doing? Besides making money."

For a moment, Ling was stunned. Clothes shopping? Makeup and beauty treatments? Were these just life's necessities, or did she truly enjoy them?

Smiling, Master Chan said, "If a person understands themselves clearly, then there's no need to come in for a face reading. Face reading is a process of understanding yourself. However, I can only provide general guidance. Your life is ultimately in your own hands."

"But I don't think that life can be controlled. There are many things not decided by me." *If my life were up to me, I wouldn't be in today's predicament.*

"Indeed, there are many things people can't control, but humans are different from animals . . . Animals are constrained by their environment. They only focus on finding food, and once they are full, they are satisfied. But humans are about more than just finding food, they also have thoughts and souls. Humans have choices and are not entirely constrained by their environment. The truth is, if you're unhappy as a teacher, why not try doing what you truly want to do? There are many choices in life besides making money."

"So, if you say I'm suited for a lesser-known profession and need to be self-employed, then what am I suited for?"

"Since it's lesser known, of course not everyone would think of it. You'll have to pave your own path."

Bullshit. I came here to have my face read in the hope of gaining some direction, to seek good luck and avoid misfortune, and you're telling me I have to figure it out myself?

Master Chan glanced at Ling and smiled. "Hong Kong people really lack imagination."

What kind of attitude is this? I paid you, and now I have to put up with your bad mood? Plus, you're a freak that's neither male nor female? Ling wanted to turn around and leave, but Ivy held her back. "If Ling continues to be a teacher, what will happen?"

Master Chan glanced at Ling's face, then flipped to another page in his book. "Your eyebrows are thick, which indicates you're good at socializing. However, if you continue in this job, sometimes trying too hard to please others may backfire. People may take advantage of you, and you may not know what you really want."

Ling's heart clenched, but she didn't show it. Ivy followed up, "You really ... want her to resign?"

"Your eyebrows are extremely close together, and there's not enough space between them. Because of this, you tend to be pessimistic and stubborn, which could negatively affect your career development. Additionally, your nose is relatively thin, and with a not-so-straight bridge, often referred to as a 'child's nose,' which suggests that you sometimes lack confidence."

"I don't think I lack confidence."

"Perhaps at times you don't trust yourself, especially in unsuitable environments, which makes you doubt yourself."

Ling eyed Master Chan coldly, not wanting him to think he'd hit the nail on the head.

"One thing you should really take note of is that your face is rather bony, with prominent cheekbones and sunken cheeks. Such an angular face shape, which calls to mind the Chinese character for 'king,' indicates a fate with relatively more twists and turns in life. However, if you can overcome them, you will become stronger."

"Does Ling's face shape put her at a disadvantage in the workplace?" Ivy questioned.

"Everyone's fate is different. Some people are suitable for being a teacher, while others are suitable for a lesser-known profession. You can't compare them."

Ling interrupted Master Chan. "Why can't we compare them? Some people earn more money than me, get promoted faster than me, and live better than me."

"Many people who come to see me just want to earn more money than others and get promoted faster . . . but why compare yourself to others? And why only compare these two things? If that's the case, then there are only two types of people in the world: those who make money and get promoted, and those who don't. In fact, there are many choices in life. Why do we have to pursue the so-called 'good'?"

That was just the way the world was. If you didn't work hard to survive, you'd be eliminated. If you didn't find food, you'd starve to death. Ling looped her handbag around her arm and started to get up, but Ivy stopped her with her hand, smiling apologetically at Master Chan. "Isn't plastic surgery an option?"

"I want to emphasize that I do not condone clients undergoing plastic surgery. Although one cannot control one's natural appearance, every face is unique. Why destroy it?"

"But the suggestion you gave me last time for plastic surgery really changed my luck, and many others have been successful as well," Ivy said.

"Plastic surgery can change your luck, but it's still disfigurement, you lose your original self, and surgery is risky. If something goes wrong, you can't turn back . . ."

Ivy had grown somewhat impatient. "What's wrong with disfigurement? Does it matter whether your appearance is original or not? Even if you don't have plastic surgery, no one sees your bare face when you have makeup on. And in the end, being beautiful is enough. No one knows what you originally looked like. As for the risks, if it's not right the first time, you can do it again. I've had plastic surgery twice."

"Why do people dislike themselves so much? The truth is, half of one's fate is determined by heaven, and the other is up to oneself. In fact, based on your facial features, if you're willing to quit your job and do what you enjoy, you can still achieve a lot . . ." Master Chan sighed.

YOUR FATE IS very strong.
  You don't know yourself.
  You're not suited to be a teacher.
  You're too good at pleasing others.

Although Master Chan was androgynous and arrogant, making Ling feel he wasn't entirely trustworthy, after leaving she began questioning herself. *I'm thirty-four years old—do I still not know myself? Is my fate really unlucky? Is my appearance really that bad?*

Saying goodbye to Ivy, Ling's heart was empty. Walking on the street, she didn't know where she was. Unconsciously, she arrived in front of the reflective pillars of a building, and stopped to examine herself in the mirror. She didn't know if it was the lighting, but the colors on her retro floral dress looked dull, her curled hair had already fallen flat, and her painstakingly painted face sank with gravity. *Is this me? Is this who I am?*

The street bustled with people. There were women dragging suitcases, and elderly people pushing carts full of cardboard. Ling stopped by the roadside. The street wasn't wide—many bumped into her as they passed by, tutting impatiently. She felt like dust, needing to be bumped into by people to avoid falling to the ground.

Suddenly, someone whipped by too fast, knocking her handbag into the air. The Valentino thudded to the ground. The zipper on her makeup bag inside wasn't properly closed, and a powder compact, tube of lipstick, and eyebrow pencil rolled out, scattering in front of passersby. Some didn't see the items and almost stepped on them. Ling quickly crouched down to gather her things. Glancing up, she saw that the person who'd bumped into her had disappeared. She inspected the contents of her makeup bag one by one. The mirror was intact, but the Armani powder was shattered, and the YSL lipstick had broken in half.

Ling threw the broken powder and lipstick into the trash can and continued walking forward. Soon she arrived at an intersection where people and cars zipped by her, forming invisible walls, and she didn't know where to go. Just then, her handbag vibrated. She pressed her handbag and waited for the vibration to stop, but it continued. She had no choice but to pick up the phone.

It was her mom's voice. "I have something to do tonight. Help me tell the mainland woman that if she's going to make money, she needs to tone it down and not disturb others. Also, add three thousand dollars to her rent."

Her mom hung up without waiting for an answer. Ling laughed. It was as though her mother was always by her side. Anyway, she didn't know where to go, and the crowd of people behind her pushed her forward. She might as well do what her mom said.

She took the subway to Yau Ma Tei and arrived at her mom's unit. The hallway was still dim, and the slapping of bodies could be clearly heard. Hearing someone come in, the Indian man opened his door and, upon seeing her, quickly said in English, "Noisy. Too noisy."

When she reached that woman's door, the red ribbon hung there as bright as ever, not a speck of dust on it. Ling knocked twice on the door, and the sound of slapping bodies stopped immediately. Some other movement continued, but after a few more knocks even that stopped. Then came some sort of rumbling sound. After a long time, the door opened a crack, revealing two terrifyingly large eyes. It was the girl. "What is it?"

A filthy feeling gnawed at her throat. Ling asked, "Your mom?"

"My ma is resting."

"Tell her to come out."

"Just talk to me."

The kid leaned against the door, arms crossed, just like a little adult. She was only six years old—did she have any idea what her mother was doing? Wasn't she ashamed? Ling shouted over the kid through the crack in the door, "I told you last time, illegal activities aren't allowed here. You're too noisy. People are complaining."

There was a rattling sound, and the door opened wider. The woman popped her head out. She had disheveled hair and a red robe. When she saw it was Ling, she lowered her head and said, "*Suh-sorry . . .*" Someone moved behind the curtain, letting out a few dry coughs. A man's voice. The woman rushed to apologize again, but Ling didn't know if she was apologizing to the man in the bed or to her. In the room, plastic bags were strewn all over the floor, laundry hung drying from the ceiling, and a makeshift sink was set up on a small squat toilet, piled with cooking utensils. Ling couldn't help but wonder, would a man really be happy seeking pleasure in a room like this? "I don't care what you do, but illegal activities aren't allowed here. Mrs. Ng said she wants to increase the rent from four thousand to eight thousand. You're lucky I'm not kicking you out." Her mom had only told her to add three thousand, but Ling unilaterally tacked on another thousand.

The woman's face twitched. "Why the *sod-sud-sudden*

in-increase in our *ruh-rent*? We *duh-don't* have that much money. I just came from the *main-loaned-land-mainland*, and I have my *duh-daughter*. I *cuh-can't fuh-find* a place that *fuh-fast—cuh*—can you *buh-bend* the rules?"

Ling was already in a bad mood that day. Seeing the woman's pitiful look made her hate her to the bone. "If you don't have the money, then move."

At that moment, the girl rushed out from behind the woman and grabbed Ling, staring at her with a freezing gaze. Ling saw herself in the girl's large eyes, and quickly turned away. The woman said, "*Suh-sorry* . . . When my *duh-daughter* and I came to *Huh-Huh-Hong* Kong, my old man *tuh-took* off. I *tuh-tuh-tried* my best to find a *juh-job*, but my *Cuh-Cantonese* isn't good. I *fuh-failed* many *in-interviews*. Everyone laughed at me for being a *muh-mainlander*, and I couldn't *fuh-fit* into Hong Kong society. I was *duh-duh-desperate* . . . I'm *suh-sorry* . . . I'll *tuh-try* to be *qu-quiet*. Please *buh-bend* the rules . . ."

It was the same old story of a woman coming to Hong Kong and being dumped by a man. Bend the rules? *Do you get sympathy because you act pitiful? When I have setbacks at work, who pities me?*

The man heaved a few more dry coughs. The woman glanced back, becoming even more jittery, apologizing to Ling over and over. The man turned around behind the curtain. The LV bag was mixed in among a pile of clutter, its logo faintly visible. She spoke so pitifully, but it was merely for show; and moreover, she had no taste at all. Only mainlanders liked LV, especially this kind of monogrammed handbag, where they treated the logo as if it were a sticker to be pasted onto their bodies.

"You can pay the rent by selling that LV bag," Ling said.

The woman's face turned red, and in her flustered state she spoke Mandarin. "No . . . I'm afraid that people will look down on us, and I don't want to face discrimination. We're not those wealthy mainlanders who come buy houses . . . we're really very poor . . ."

The woman blinked, and tears streamed down her face. The girl clung to her even tighter. Discrimination. Discrimination. Ling inadvertently recalled her experiences over the past few months—meeting with the principal, being targeted by colleagues, taking Mandarin classes, taking over Wai's classes, the reporter . . . *You mainlanders say you face discrimination. I'm the one facing discrimination!* Ling pried the girl's hands off her. "Anyway, the rent will be increased to eight thousand next month. If you don't have the money, you should leave as soon as you can."

THE WOMAN'S WORDS "I couldn't fit into Hong Kong society" felt like two hands continually slapping Ling's face. She felt an ironic pain, as if a dying tiger had come to her and begged her to tear off a piece of flesh for it to eat, but she herself was already on the brink of death.

When she got home, the living room was pitch black. Her mom hadn't come back yet. She opened the door to her room. It was a mess, as though it were shopping bags that lived in the room and not her. She paused in front of the door. There really wasn't anywhere to stand! Ling sighed and struggled to step over the shopping bags to get to her bed, where she sat down and held her head, taking deep breaths.

The nearly overflowing pile of mail on the dressing table caught her eye. The large words on the envelopes reading BORROWING MONEY IS CONVENIENT, AND REPAYMENT IS SUPER EASY always seemed to be forcing themselves on her. She was two months behind on her credit card. It was probably over three hundred thousand dollars by now. She didn't want to open the letters; she just wanted to burn them.

That master also told her to resign and switch to a lesser-known profession—with three hundred thousand dollars of debt, how could she resign?

Ah, forget it. Ling pinched the space between her eyebrows, pushed aside the makeup on the table, and took out the MacBook underneath. She thought of Wong Wai-Yee/Tsui Tsz-Yee/Mavis Lai—she really wanted to know their real identities. She typed the three names separately into Google, followed by the terms "*Mango Daily*" and "*Mango Weekly*." Wong Wai-Yee wrote political news for the *Mango Daily*, but she stopped writing after 2016, and had nothing to do with the *Mango Weekly*. Searching for Tsui Tsz-Yee only brought up celebrity photos and a bunch of entertainment news. Mavis Lai was a young model, and *Mango Weekly* had published some revealing photos of her. There was also another Mavis Lai who was a netizen who once commented "stinky man" under a news article about sexual assault in the *Mango Daily*, garnering over thirty likes. Ling scrolled the mouse, wanting to see what else Mavis Lai had said, but the comment thread quickly ended. None of these were who she was looking for. She'd been completely played—what else could she do? Ling's heart sank. She aimlessly scrolled the page. Just then, a row of words at the bottom of the *Mango Daily* website caught her eye: USER LOGIN | PRIVACY STATEMENT | TERMS OF SERVICE | ADVERTISING | CONTACT US | RECRUITMENT. On impulse, Ling clicked on RECRUITMENT to have a look.

Reporter (AW-24)
University graduate
Proficient in Chinese and English, fluent Mandarin
A good sense for news
Two years of work experience
Interested parties please send your résumé and salary expectations to Miss Cheung at recruit@lastdigital.com.

Senior Editor (EW-34)
University graduate
Proficient in Chinese and English, fluent Mandarin
Two years of work experience
Relevant experience preferred
Interested parties please send your résumé and salary
expectations to Miss Cheung at recruit@lastdigital.com.

There were several other positions available, including
office assistant, marketing manager, and public relations, all
with similar hiring requirements.

Ling asked herself if she met most of the requirements,
other than Mandarin. What was "fluent Mandarin?" She
randomly entered a job search website and clicked on "education." Fluent Mandarin was required both for Chinese tutors
and teaching assistants in cram schools. Then she clicked on
"service industry": salespersons, administrative assistants, and
marketing directors . . . The content was similar, as though
only the company email and contact number had changed.

Ling kept searching and found that only security guards,
cleaners, porters, and cooks didn't have any language requirements.

Standing up resolutely, Ling faced the full-length mirror
on the wall, straightening her clothes and taking a deep breath.
Imagining the person in the mirror was an interviewer, she
introduced herself in Mandarin, pronouncing her name as
Wu Zhiling instead of Ng Tsz-Ling, and her school's name
as Shengdian instead of Sing Din. "Hello, I am Wu Zhiling.
Thank you for giving me this opportunity to have an interview. I have been a teacher at Shengdian Secondary School
for ten years. I want to be a reporter because of my excellent
oper-observation skills. As a reporter, an excellent observation
ability can help me *discolor-discover* new *top-axe-topics* . . ."

She couldn't go on. *Why am I so nervous, as if someone is judging me? Obviously it's only me in the mirror.* Ling remembered the Mandarin notes she always kept in her handbag. She picked up her handbag and looked at them, realizing she'd only reviewed one-third of them so far. A strong sense of powerlessness rushed over her, and she mused that the prostitute who said she couldn't find a job was better than her, because at least she knew Mandarin . . .

Suddenly, her mom's face appeared in the mirror. Ling's heart raced, like a kid caught looking at a pornographic website, and she quickly closed her computer. Her mom pushed open the door and stepped over Ling's shopping bags, *whack whack*, as though she were playing soccer. "What're you up to? You seem so nervous."

Ling shook her head nonchalantly.

"I saw you browsing a job search site just now. Are there problems at work?"

"Just looking out of curiosity."

"Every day you say you're busy and don't answer my calls. You work so hard and are still being kicked out?"

"I really was just looking out of curiosity." Ling thought to herself that being hardworking and whether one was fired were two entirely different things.

"That idiot head of something-something got fired because she was born a real dumb-dumb. Did you get fired too?"

"Even if I kicked the bucket, nothing would happen to the head of the department. She has a high position and power."

"Now I remember . . . the one who died is . . . Wai. I don't know why, but I often mix up Wai and the head of the department."

Ling's heart twitched. She didn't want to discuss it any further. "Where were you just now?"

"From the time you were young, your ma taught you not to

offend people. If the boss asks you to do something, you must do it. You have a bad temper. Even when your ma asks you to do something small, you don't want to. I ask you to come home for dinner and you don't. Out there at work, you're bound to offend people more than sweet-talk them."

Did I offend someone? Who did I offend? Ling couldn't help but smile wryly, though her mom didn't see. "I always say, a two-faced official talks from both sides of the mouth, and a boss gives you the third degree—three strikes and you're out. You should try changing that foul temper of yours."

"Okay, okay, my temper's foul, and yours is sweet. Go away, I'm busy . . ."

Her mom snorted. "All this talking back, completely different from your ma. Ma just wants to teach you the truths of life. When Lin Biao was in power, the People's Liberation Army entered your ma's village. The Red Guards held meetings with us every day, asking us to point out other people's mistakes. Those who refused to criticize others were eventually denounced themselves, and many of my neighbors were forced to commit suicide. Your ma is obedient—when the Red Guards wanted me to denounce someone, I denounced them. Even if that person hadn't made any mistakes, I'd come up with a few mistakes for them. That's why the Red Guards liked me . . ."

Whenever her mom was happy, she chattered on about history. Red Guards, the Cultural Revolution . . . Ling had heard it all many times. Recently, her mom had been giving her dirty looks and scolding her for no reason. Today, she seemed to be in a good mood—what had happened?

Once her mom started talking, she couldn't stop. "The former village head was very kind to us. He worked at the municipal government and often helped us buy oil, and he sold us rice at a fair price. When the Red Guards entered our village, they took the whole village to the village head's house at night. The village head had a good family background and was the first to be denounced. The Red Guards pushed all of the village head's books to the ground, looted all the rice and oil from his house, and then stuffed an ink-stained glove into his mouth. Two Red Guards each grabbed one of the village head's hands and forced him to kneel down. Isn't it shocking? Everyone was scared out of their wits, and we all exchanged glances. The Red Guards loudly ordered everyone to point out the village head's mistakes. A long while passed, and no one dared to speak up. I volunteered, saying the village head was a member of the petty bourgeoisie who'd hoarded a lot of money. The Red Guards took him out and beat him on the spot. At the moment, everyone looked at me, thinking I had no conscience. What could I do? If I didn't denounce him, the Red Guards would've denounced me. At that time, no one else would speak up. After a couple of months, the Red Guards pressured everyone day after day, and people all denounced each other. Even your ma was denounced.

"In the past, your ma really was so miserable. I had to proactively give Red Guards rice and oil from our home, and even went hungry so the Red Guards could eat their fill. I also had to help them collect intelligence, taking them to the homes of the petty bourgeoisie and ransacking them, exposing neighbors' wrongdoings. After the reform and opening up, many people chewed me out for being so cruel and contemptible, but what could I do? Was I supposed to fight the Red Guards? If I didn't kiss up to the Red Guards, your ma would've died long ago—how could people talk about having a conscience?

"So, I'm telling you, never ever engage in confrontation. China's had so many dynasties but, till now, has there been a true revolution? No, it's always been one emperor overthrowing another. Your ma knows more about Chinese history than you do and has personally experienced it. Chinese people are most afraid of chaos. In short, when power is in someone else's hands, be clever, don't offend people, and then you'll surely benefit."

Mom must've been watching too much news on TV recently and thinks I'm one of those angry youths protesting in the streets. She doesn't know me very well. Ling couldn't help but smile.

After a while, her mom stretched. Ling assumed she was finally tired, and stood up to ask her to leave. To her surprise, her mom sat still, staring at the Mandarin notes on Ling's desk. Ling wanted to put the notes back in her bag, but it was too late. Her mom snatched them. "You're studying Mandarin? Is your school teaching Chinese in Mandarin?"

Ling didn't want to talk. Her mom seemed to understand. "There's no choice. The mainland has money now, and we have to align ourselves with them no matter what. Look at Mrs. Cheng's daughter, she's so clever, going to the mainland to do business, buying several flats."

Ling sighed. In her mom's eyes, everything would be easy if she became Mrs. Cheng's daughter. But she wasn't anyone else and could only be herself.

Suddenly, her mom thought of something. Widening her eyes, she leaned closer to Ling's face, examining her. "Hmm . . . Repeat after me, 'Hello, the weather is nice today,' in Mandarin.'

Ling was confused, but her mom looked expectant, so she repeated, "Hello, the weather is nice today."

"Your pronunciation is so standard! You'll have no problem learning Mandarin."

Ling laughed in spite of herself. *I want to use Mandarin to teach. It's not just a matter of saying hello to someone.* Her mom leaned in closer, almost cheek to cheek with her. "You look so much like me. You should have a talent for languages.

I taught myself English and made money from it, and foreign customers praised my good English."

In the past, in order to do business with foreigners, after returning home each night her mom would sit by the bedside holding a small black book-like Instant-Dict translation device, continually pressing the sound key, following along with a strange and rigid male voice reciting English word by word. *Come to have a look. It's the latest series. Three hundreds. One thousands. Sorry, my English is bad. Thank you. It is from France. I can show you. Red green black handbag tote clutch...* Every night, Ling fell asleep to her mom's tongue-rolling Rs and hissing Ts, Ss, and Ks.

Her mom followed along with Instant-Dict for two months. One day, a foreign customer paid, then gave her mom a thumbs-up and said, "You got an American accent. Your English is good." Her mom didn't know what the English word "accent" meant, but she understood the second sentence and laughed uncontrollably, repeatedly saying "Thank you." After the customer left, her mom instructed Ling to ask her teacher at school what an "American accent" was. The following day after school, Ling explained to her mom that "American accent" referred to the way that Americans spoke English. Her mom was so happy that, as she pushed her hawker cart, she muttered to herself in an awkward mix of Cantonese and English, "Your ma *American accent*, haha." Seeing how over the moon her mom was, Ling added, "My teacher said few people in Hong Kong have an American accent. Usually only Americans have it." Her mom was even more pleased.

But upon hearing her mom speak in such a seemingly fluent manner, some foreigners thought she really knew English and asked all sorts of questions, such as whether the items were genuine, and why they were so much cheaper than the market price. Her mom couldn't speak, so she pushed Ling out to deal with them. At that time, Ling was still young and didn't know how to answer all the questions in English and just stood there. After the customers left, her mom twisted her ears and scolded her. "You've studied so many books, and you still can't speak. You haven't learned shit!"

Ling's ears were blazing hot, and her eyes welled up with tears. "I got a ninety on my English test."

"Don't talk back! If your English is poor, study harder, lazybones! I'm telling you to study English with Instant-Dict every day. Go practice spelling." Her mom was loudly telling her how to learn English in front of passersby. She glared at her, trying to hold back tears.

"Use the method your ma used to learn English before. Find a few common Mandarin sentences used in class and read them out loud every day from a Mandarin-language website. Speak like a mainlander, and you won't have any problem," her mom said.

Though her mom no longer twisted her ears, Ling still found her words piercing. "Do you think learning a language is only about knowing how to say a few phrases? Times have changed."

Her mom pursed her lips. "Is it humiliating to only speak a few words? I was able to earn a living."

Anyway, no matter how she explained it, her mom didn't get it. Ling just wanted to send her away. "My Mandarin is very good. This year, the principal trusts me so much she asked me to teach two additional junior secondary-school classes. Who knows, I might even be promoted next year."

"That's great." Perking up, her mom took out a newspaper folded into a small square from her pocket and handed it to Ling. Ling opened it and saw it was a real estate advertisement. The newspaper was crammed with small squares filled with unit area and price, along with a couple of advertising slogans such as "beautiful southeastern view" and "practical layout." Her mom had circled a few units with a red pen, and she pointed to those red circles. "Which one do you like?"

Ling was taken aback. "Why do I have to choose? Buying property has always been your thing."

"Help me choose."

Ling randomly chose a three-bedroom unit for 8.5 million HKD. Before she could say anything, her mom snatched the newspaper, smiled at her, and stepped over the shopping bags strewn on the floor as she left the room. Ling didn't know what was going on, but finally her mom was gone. She sighed in relief, looking up at the full-length mirror beside the table. The person in the mirror, with her single eyelids and prominent cheekbones, slightly resembled her mom. She suddenly found the person in the mirror ridiculous, but after laughing, she wanted to cry.

IN THE MORNING, Ling looked at herself in the mirror. Her eyes were bloodshot and sunken. She'd applied several layers of powder, but fine lines still hung like tree roots beneath her eyes, and her deliberately curled lashes had lost their curvature. Ling moved the mirror. On the other side of it, the head of the department slowly walked to her cubicle, carrying her old Valentino bag and a Starbucks cup.

Ling closed the compact mirror and shut her tired eyes.

The previous night, Ling had been plagued by nightmares. She dreamed she was in a square with a group of people behind her, and a man and woman standing far ahead. She recognized the woman but had never seen the man before. The couple stood there with their mouths open, but Ling couldn't hear what they were saying. The people behind her kept shouting, "Denounce them, denounce them." There seemed to be a large number of them. They kept crowding around her, pushing her ahead, her legs out of her control, unconsciously following the thrust forward. Glancing back, Ling was surprised to find there was an army behind her. All the soldiers had human bodies and wolf heads, were clothed in yellow robes, and brandished weapons, their faces ferocious. The one at the front was fully a wolf, draped in white feathers like an eagle. The wolf flew straight to her and pointed a gun at her, its claw on the trigger, yelling, "Denounce them!" Terrified, she wanted to scream for help, but her throat was mute and she couldn't make a sound, so she had to force herself to slowly approach the couple. As she got closer, she discovered it was Wai and the village head, their eyes brimming with fear. Wai raised her drooping upside-down-V eyebrows and said, "Why won't you *ha-help* me?"

I don't have a choice, I don't have a choice . . .

Ling awoke with a shudder. She was so exhausted that she couldn't help but doze off again, and dreamed the same nightmare from the previous night. She took a deep breath.

Just then, she saw a note on her desk signed by the head of the department: *Today at noon, the principal and the Chinese department will have lunch at Fook Choi restaurant.* The head of the department must've left it when she'd nodded off. How reckless to be caught sleeping by the department head! She quickly took a face mask from the drawer and placed it over her nose and mouth. If anyone asked, the mask would provide a good excuse, even though she wasn't sick.

Suddenly, she heard a peal of laughter behind her. A group of Chinese teachers whispered and laughed loudly. "Spending so much time doing sneaky things and talking behind people's backs—she should just focus on her own work." It was Miss Au's voice.

"She seems very fond of the department head and principal, all decked out in Céline and carrying a Valentino," Miss Wu said.

"But that's not how studying works. Maybe she thinks that wearing Céline will make her French and carrying Valentino will make her Italian, and thus more noble," Miss Au said, and everyone laughed along with her.

The head of the department sneered. "Everyone can buy brand-name items now, it's just a matter of swiping a credit card. Maybe she thinks that work is like wearing clothes— she wears different clothes depending on who she meets; but work requires practical strength."

In the past, Ling would definitely fight back when she was picked on, but at that very moment she was worn out. The clothes on her body and makeup on her face seemed to have disappeared without a trace, leaving only her face mask as powerless protection.

Daughter, the mainland woman is up to no good. Handle her for me.

Ling's mom kept frantically sending text messages and calling, so Ling hid her phone underneath the tablecloth. In the small private room of the restaurant, a group of teachers sat around a large round table. There was no head seat at the table, but the principal sat in the center. Next to her was a middle-aged woman with curled hair that looked like black cookies, and two sagging cheeks that formed four right angles. She was wearing bright red lipstick and a black suit trimmed in silver. The head of the department was busy pouring tea for the middle-aged woman, who was sitting directly opposite Ling. There was a tray of purple butterfly orchids on the lazy Susan in the center.

"I'm very glad that Principal Luo has come to eat with us today." It was the first time Ling had heard the principal speaking Mandarin. She spoke slowly, checking the pronunciation of nearly every word before saying it.

Ling had assumed it was just a regular meal gathering. She hadn't expected this woman, Mandarin-speaking Principal Luo, to also come. Ling glanced at her phone and then looked up, smiling even though she was wearing a mask and no one could see her expression.

"Help me decide what to order." The principal handed the menu to Miss Au, and said to everyone, "It is truly our honor to have Principal Luo assist us next semester at Sing Din Secondary School."

Assist? What kind of assistance? The head of the department led the applause, and everyone clapped along, smiles plastered on their faces.

The head of the department glanced at Ling. "Yes, I forgot to make introductions. This is Luo Guihong, principal of Nanjing No. 1 High School."

The principal reached out and shook hands with Principal Luo. "Welcome! The reform of our Chinese-language curriculum depends on you."

Reform?

"We've decided to convert the school to teaching Chinese in Mandarin next year, and we need to rewrite the curriculum. We really need your advice." The principal took a sip of tea, sweeping her eyes over the teachers. "Some of you may not know . . . Sing Din Secondary School is participating in the China–Hong Kong Teacher Collaboration Program, and Principal Luo will arrange for some teachers to come and assist us."

"Nowadays, education in mainland China is much better than in Hong Kong. I heard that Nanjing High School's Chinese language scores are even better than those in Singapore. Hong Kong is really declining," the head of the department said.

"You're all too modest. I appreciate your flexible teaching

methods and hope that in the future we can learn from each other and grow together," Principal Luo said.

"It's imperative for our students to learn Mandarin well. Many parents have requested that we switch to teaching in Mandarin, fearing that their children won't be able to connect with the mainland," the principal said.

"That's right; compared to Mandarin, Cantonese is just a dialect, and too vulgar." The head of the department laughed.

The principal nodded, and everyone followed suit. Principal Luo smiled without saying a word.

"Ninety percent of our Chinese teachers have passed the Language Proficiency Assessment for Teachers and are absolutely capable of promoting Mandarin education." The corners of the principal's mouth were turned upward forcefully, her cheeks folded like candied fruit. "Teachers, please introduce yourselves briefly in Mandarin, just a sentence or two."

So suddenly? Ling's heart raced faster. She quickly lowered her head, tapped her phone under the tablecloth, and typed "Mandarin pinyin website" into the search bar.

"I'll start. I'm Lu Xue, the head of the Chinese department at Shengdian Secondary School. If our Mandarin isn't up to par, or we're not teaching well, we'd like to trouble you to please give us feedback," the head of the department said, pronouncing both her and the school's names the Mandarin way instead of introducing herself as Lo Syut and the school as Sing Din.

"Don't say that . . ." Principal Luo didn't have a pure Beijing accent, but Ling couldn't place it.

"I'm Hu Huihua. I specialize in teaching senior secondary school. I look forward to learning from you in the future," Miss Wu said, referring to herself by her Mandarin name rather than Wu Wai-Wah.

"I'm Ye Meimei. I welcome your suggestions," Miss Ip said,

using the Mandarin pronunciation of her name instead of Ip Mei-Mei.

Other than the head of the department, everyone stopped at one or two sentences. Even Miss Ko, who taught Mandarin, didn't say much. Wasn't now the time to show off? In October, everyone had been scrambling to write their names on the sign-up sheet for the weekly assembly—why be quiet now?

Ling's phone vibrated again. Her mom sent a few more urgent text messages, asking her to contact the mainland woman. Ling typed In a meeting, then switched to the Mandarin pinyin site, silently reciting the pinyin on the page.

Before long, it was Miss Au's turn. Like the others, she introduced herself by her Mandarin name instead of Au Cheuk-Wing. "My name is Ou Zhuoyong, and I mainly teach junior secondary school. I love teaching and hope to have the opportunity to learn from Principal Luo in the future."

Amid the chaos, Ling glanced up. Miss Au spoke very standard Mandarin. Hadn't Ivy said that she hadn't taken the LPAT yet?

"Are you from the northeast?" Principal Luo asked.

"My grandma is from Shenyang. She took care of me when I was young, so I had a lot of opportunities to speak Mandarin."

"No wonder. What's your PSC score?" Principal Luo asked.

"I haven't taken it yet. In the past few years I've been busy with my advanced studies, so I didn't have time to prepare. I'm not very confident. I plan to take both the PSC and LPAT this year. I might be the only teacher in the Chinese department who hasn't passed yet." Miss Au laughed.

"You speak well—you shouldn't have a problem," Principal Luo said with a smile, and the principal also nodded happily.

Miss Au sat down. It was Ling's turn. Everyone praising

Miss Au had given Ling even more pressure. Her phone kept vibrating. She gripped it tightly to prevent it from making any noise. "Hello, I'm Wu Zhiling. I specialize in teaching senior secondary. This year, I'm trying to teach junior secondary. I also think it's imperative that our school switch to teaching in Mandarin. The entire country of China communicates in Mandarin, and if we don't, we'll be marginalized. I hope that Principal Luo can give me guidance in the future."

Ling felt she spoke quite standard Mandarin. She had even silently recited it to herself just now. However, Principal Luo only nodded and didn't say anything.

"Ling, your Mandarin has improved rapidly." The principal turned to Principal Luo and went on, "This teacher is now working diligently to learn Mandarin. She'll take the LPAT in March of next year."

All eyes focused on Ling. Ling smiled awkwardly. "I might have an accent. Please give me advice—"

The head of the department cut her off. "Is someone calling you?"

The screen flickered between her fingers. Ling stammered in reply, "Ah . . . yes . . . it's not important."

Principal Luo smiled and said, "No worries. Take the call first."

Ling's face was blazing hot, and her mouth trembled behind the mask. "Then . . . I'll excuse myself for a moment."

Ling left the private room and frantically tapped on the phone screen, hanging up on her mom. She never called at the right time, and she chose to call at this particular moment! In the restaurant hall in front of her, government officials were busy pouring tea and keeping accounts, and uniformed waitresses were pushing dim sum carts, every table lively with chatter, while Ling was like a soldier expelled from the battlefield, abandoned by the world.

The phone rang again.

She answered. "Have you called enough?"

"Can you lower the rent?" The voice spoke Mandarin.

As soon as Ling heard it, she knew it was the daughter of that mainland woman. She was about to explode. "Your mom's turning tricks—why are you helping her? Have you no shame?"

"Damn it! Do you think you're something special? Who do you think you are?" The girl hung up the phone. The waitress approached carrying a tray, her legs shining white beneath her high-slit skirt, with measles-like goosebumps all over. Just then, Ling's phone rang again. She was so angry that her hands trembled, and it took her a few tries to press the answer button.

"Why aren't you answering the phone?" Her mom.

"I'm helping you get rid of that hooker."

The phone was quiet for a second, and then her mom suddenly started yelling. "What's the matter with you? Talking to your ma this way."

Ling immediately hung up, then turned off the phone. Annoying, annoying, annoying. She closed her eyes, placed her hand on her chest, and tried to calm her breathing. After a while, she pushed open the door to the private room and walked in. Everyone inside was all smiles, the table overflowing with dishes: broccoli stir-fried with sliced cuttlefish, steamed grouper, baked lobster with cheese, deep-fried crab claws, and a plate of white cut chicken in the middle. The principal was in the process of picking up a chicken leg to serve Principal Luo, the leg white and flawless beneath the light. Ling suddenly wanted to vomit, but instead burped out a sour gas.

As she was wearing a mask, no one noticed her strange expression. She returned to her seat. Everyone was too busy eating to look up at her. "This restaurant is delicious. We often eat here," the principal said, smiling.

"I thought Hong Kongers preferred Western food." Principal Luo took a bite of the chicken leg.

"Chinese food is delicious, and Chinese culture is extensive and profound. Sometimes, when we tire of eating Chinese food, we'll switch to eating Western food." The principal poured tea for Principal Luo. "We really like the white cut chicken here, it's very famous," the head of the department said.

At this point, Ling could no longer control the acid in her mouth, which was about to gush out. With no time to apologize, she rushed to the bathroom.

THE DOCTOR GAVE her two days of sick leave. Acute gastroenteritis.

Ling tossed and turned all night and didn't fully wake up till two thirty the following afternoon. The shopping bags strewn on the floor looked like enlarged monsters in the sun, while the Mandarin notes, credit card letters, and student exercise books lay quietly in a corner where the beams of light didn't reach. As Ling took this in with half-closed eyes, her scalp tightened, and she wanted to keep on sleeping, but she'd already taken a sick day and if she didn't get back to work, she'd fall behind. Ling rubbed her burning forehead, struggling to get out of bed.

She opened the bedroom door. The TV in the living room was making a fuzzy noise, the afternoon sun streaming through the gaps between the buildings, making the living room bright and airy. Her mom sat at the dining table, eating French toast while reading real estate advertisements, a bowl of takeout congee beside her. Ling approached the dining table, sat down, and lifted the lid of the takeout bowl. The steam from the congee blurred her vision. Staring at the TV, her mom said, "I took care of the issue with the mainland woman. Her daughter called me and said her mom wanted to kill herself. I was having dim sum with Mrs. Cheng at the time and wanted you to handle it, but you said you were in a meeting and weren't paying attention to me. I had no choice but to leave halfway through and take care of it myself."

Her mom's words stung, pricking Ling's tired and aching body with shards of tingling pain.

Without waiting for Ling to reply, her mom continued, "I went over there. The woman was standing on a chair, a rope dangling from the ceiling. The woman grabbed the rope and wanted to hang herself. The little girl kept crying, 'Mom, don't die.' The woman said, 'Mommy is sorry.' As soon as the little girl saw me, she immediately ran over to me and begged me to persuade her mom not to kill herself. The woman had been at it for a few minutes but couldn't bring herself to do it, so I knew she was trying to trick me into lowering the rent. I pulled her down and said, 'You're turning tricks in my unit. I don't want to kick you out, it's just a hike in rent. If you want to die, please go somewhere far away and do it, don't pollute my place. If you die in my unit, will anyone else want to live here?' She sat on the floor and kept crying. The little girl pointed at me and scolded me, 'You look down on us.' I said, 'I do look down on you. You come to Hong Kong, and there are so many things you can do, and you go turn tricks. And you turn tricks just to buy luxury brands.' Am I wrong? If you have money to buy luxury brands but don't have money to pay rent, then buy one less designer bag and you won't have to resort to turning tricks."

So it was suicide. In the past, some tenants had used suicide as a threat to demand lower rent, but Ling had reported them to the police. *If you don't have the money, move out or work hard to earn it. We're not a charity.*

"The woman sat on the floor weeping and wailing. It was

so annoying. I tossed her two hundred bucks and told her to move out as soon as possible. The little girl was also pissed off and kept asking me to cancel the rent. I told them to get out as fast as they could or I'd take back the two hundred bucks."

Ling didn't know what to say. Feeling guilty, she covered the congee and quietly watched TV with her mom. The TV was replaying last night's National Geographic program, the blue and green Earth reflected in the camera. It suddenly focused on a primate in the forest with a big head and small body, arms longer than its legs, walking hunched over with its legs bent, supporting itself with its fists. A few seconds later, the primate's waist straightened somewhat, its arms became shorter, and it no longer walked with its fists; but its legs still weren't fully straight, and it was slightly hunched over. After taking a few more steps, the primate's head became rounder, its waist straightened even more, and its fur lessened, revealing rough muscles; but it still didn't stand upright when it walked. A few seconds later, the primate finally turned into a human, wearing a grass skirt, carrying a spear on its shoulder, chin up and chest out, shoulders squared, no longer like an animal. In just one minute, humanity had undergone billions of years of history; but Ling hadn't paid attention. Other than the suspenseful music coming from the TV, there was no other sound in their home. Ling was calculating what to say.

But her mom spoke first. "Yesterday I called to tell you that our unit has been sold. I signed a provisional contract for ten million."

She sold the flat?

"I bought it seventeen years ago for two million, and now it's worth eight million. But the broker helped me negotiate and raise the price to ten million. Why not sell it?"

Ling stared at her mother blankly, unsure what was going on.

"I've thought it over. After selling this unit, you can buy one and register it in both of our names."

"Huh?"

Her mom didn't answer, and kept eating her French toast. Ling felt like a large rock was pressing on her chest. It took a long time before she could squeeze out any words. "But . . . you didn't ask for my input."

"I called you yesterday. You hung up on me."

"Are you retaliating against me now?" Ling stared, feeling the air flowing in and out of her body, leaving her hollow. Suspenseful music continued to play on the TV as a primitive man in a grass skirt chased a deer with a spear. With a single throw, the spear pierced the deer's hindquarters, causing it to fall to the ground.

Seeing that Ling wasn't eating the congee, her mom took it and started eating it herself. "I asked you before which unit you preferred."

"At the time, you didn't ask me to buy a place."

"You promised me you would."

"I said when I have money." Also, she'd just been joking.

Her mom glared at her. "If you don't want to buy property, then go rent a place on your own."

"Aren't you going too far? How can I afford to buy property?"

"I used to be a hawker, and still managed to earn enough to buy a few flats. You've been a teacher for ten years, you don't have to endure the elements, and you're a professional. How can you not afford it?"

"Times have changed. A unit used to only cost a few hundred thousand, but now it's ten million. I can't even afford the down payment, and the school . . ." Ling couldn't go on.

"If this school doesn't work out, find another one. Mrs. Cheng's daughter has already bought several flats. If you bought fewer name-brand clothes and bags, you'd have enough money to buy a place."

"You have your fair share of the name-brand clothes and bags I bought."

Ignoring her, her mom crossed her legs, and continued to watch TV. Ling couldn't take it anymore. "I've been supporting the family, buying you gifts, helping you deal with rental matters, satisfying all your needs. What else do I owe you?"

Her mom turned her head and looked at Ling, her gaze lingering for a long time. "I gave birth to you. You owe me your whole life!"

The dust between Ling and her mom tumbled restlessly. This home they had lived in for more than ten years had begun to develop mold on the walls, the pale-yellow leather sofa was peeling, and the professional treadmill, massage chair, and air purifier were all covered in a thin layer of dust.

Ling suddenly felt the flat was hot and stuffy. Her entire body was burning hot. She couldn't stay there any longer. She went back to her room, threw on a random dress, dabbed on some concealer to cover up her wrinkles and freckles, then grabbed her handbag and rushed out the door.

LING WALKED FASTER than usual, rushing through red lights and ignoring the blare of car horns, wanting to get as far away from home as possible.

She didn't know where she was going, and unconsciously ended up on her regular route to work. Walking the same route day after day had become a habit that surpassed any thought.

However, the closer she got to school, the heavier her mood became. When she was almost at the school, she turned in to a fashion boutique and wandered around. The slipper-clad salesperson told her to take her time looking, then resumed playing video games at the counter. Ling flipped through hangers without focusing on any particular item of clothing. *I'm off sick today and don't have to go to school; but there's too much work, and the head of the department and the rest of them are all so nosy ... Well, forget it—since I'm already here, it seems inexcusable if I don't check in at school.*

At 4.30 p.m., just as the school bell rang, Ling bowed her head and shrank her body, climbing the stairs against the crowd, avoiding saying hi to her students. When she'd left home, she had barely put on any makeup, and she didn't want anyone to see her face.

When she saw Ling walking up to the second floor and passing by the principal's office, Ivy was so surprised that she covered her mouth with both hands.

"Sigh, I have so much work that I have to come in even on a sick day," Ling said.

Ivy eyed her sympathetically, handing her a mask. Ling understood Ivy's intention.

"I really need plastic surgery. Even with light makeup, I don't look presentable." Ling smiled bitterly, immediately putting on the mask.

Ivy stretched out her finger, signaling to Ling to look in the direction of the principal's office. Four young women, all in their twenties, sat outside the office. The woman sitting on the far left wore a white lace shirt with a gray skirt, her clothing free of any extra wrinkles. The two in the middle wore ordinary suits of no discernible brand, but they were well coordinated. The three women sat upright with their legs crossed, folders containing their academic qualifications balanced on their laps. Ling glanced at the woman sitting closest to the principal's office and did a double-take. The woman wore the same style of Céline dress as her, except where Ling's was yellow, this woman's was black. The woman was bent over her phone. Ling saw her typing a line of simplified characters on Weibo.

Ivy whispered in Ling's ear, "They're all mainland students who came to Hong Kong to study . . . The head of your department is inside . . ."

Ling's heart skipped a beat. "Is the principal hiring Wai's replacement?"

"Today, I overheard the principal on the phone. She plans on hiring a Chinese teacher, and as for the rest, it seems like she'll hire whoever is suitable as a TA . . ."

"Is she planning on firing anyone?"

"I haven't heard anything like that, so it should be okay . . ."

Ling tried to force a smile, but the mask hid her expression.

The young women heard them chatting in hushed tones and looked up. The woman wearing the same dress as Ling quickly put away her phone. In Ling's eyes, they all looked the same: no crow's feet, bright, fair skin, and light makeup.

Seeing the young women glance their way, Ivy loudly said in Mandarin, "This is Miss Ng, a very experienced Chinese teacher at our school."

The young women all put on their best smiles, and the one wearing the same dress as Ling awkwardly nodded. She had a slender figure, the black dress highlighting her smooth, white legs. In contrast, Ling's legs were naturally thick and covered in blue veins from standing for long periods.

Ivy leaned closer to Ling and whispered, "Everyone loves Céline . . ."

The truth was, she wanted to crawl into a hole. Ling no longer heard what Ivy was saying. She just wanted to escape from the scene, escape from herself.

WHY COME BACK? Anyway, no matter how hard I try, I can't change anything. What am I doing wasting this day off?

Plus, I'm wearing this embarrassing dress.

Ling rushed into the bathroom, not wanting to see anyone. Standing in front of the full-length mirror, the dress looked more and more off, stick-straight with no tailoring, love handles sticking out, the color monotonous and gaudy. Why hadn't she chosen black—was her eyesight that bad? Why'd she come back wearing a long dress when she knew her legs weren't long enough? She wanted to find something to hide it. A silk scarf tied around her neck or a brooch would be good, anything to avoid people thinking it was a Céline dress; but, rummaging through her handbag, she only found the pink scarf. She suddenly remembered: wasn't the dress she had on the one that Tsui Siu-Hin had dirtied? Ling turned around and looked at the back, where the red stain on her buttocks still lingered faintly even after being put through the washing machine.

Ling wanted to remove her high heels and smash the mirror.

Just then, someone approached her in the mirror. The discipline teacher, Miss Ho. Miss Ho was in her forties, taught mathematics, and held the same high-level rank as the head of the department. She was slim and liked to wear pencil skirts. Ling had previously had very little interaction with her. Miss Ho had just finished class. With her math textbook under her arm, she rinsed the chalk dust from her hands under the faucet. Glancing up at Ling in the mirror, she said, "I thought you were off sick today and wouldn't be in. By the way, I'm meeting with Tsui Siu-Hin's parents later today. Since his class teacher has a competition in the afternoon, and you're here, could you explain Tsui Siu-Hin's situation on her behalf?"

"I'm really busy . . ." The mask muffled Ling's voice. Not hearing what she had said, Miss Ho shook the water off her hands, took the book from under her arm, and swayed away in her slit skirt.

In fact, it had nothing to do with Ling. She wasn't Tsui Siu-Hin's class teacher, only his Chinese teacher. However, Miss Ho was high-ranking, and now that she was gone it was too late to refuse.

Ling tied the pink scarf around her waist and followed Miss Ho to the conference room on the third floor.

There was an oval conference table in the center of the room. Miss Ho sat on one side organizing paperwork, while Tsui Siu-Hin and a slightly chubby long-haired woman sat on the other side. The woman wasn't wearing makeup and had a head of fluffy curly hair. She was probably Tsui Siu-Hin's mother. Ling took a seat beside Miss Ho.

Miss Ho asked Ling to retell what had happened with Tsui Siu-Hin in the classroom, then said to Mrs. Tsui, "Siu-Hin has always had behavior problems, but this time it's really serious. Setting a fire in the school endangers the safety of others. We considered reporting it to the police, but in order to protect Siu-Hin's future, we decided not to. I hope you understand."

The subtext of what Miss Ho was saying seemed to be that they were persuading Tsui Siu-Hin to drop out of school. Mrs. Tsui appeared worried, while Tsui Siu-Hin looked up at the ceiling and whistled.

"Actually . . . Ah Hin may be rebellious, but he's kind-hearted on the inside . . . Ah Hin, apologize to the teacher . . ." Mrs. Tsui trembled as she spoke. Most parents would put up a fight, but this mother was really weak—no wonder Tsui Siu-Hin was so unruly.

"I don't think I'm wrong. Why do we have to study that outdated lesson on 'Hong Kong Story'?" Tsui Siu-Hin retorted.

"At school, students must obey their teachers. They can't just do whatever they want," Miss Ho said.

Tsui Siu-Hin stood up and slammed hard against the table, but the conference table was heavy, and his delicate hands only budged it a little. "You teachers have the final say in everything."

Mrs. Tsui repeatedly told him not to act this way and held him in a death grip, but he struggled and broke free from her.

Miss Ho tried to smooth things over. "Actually, Siu-Hin is very smart. If he applies his intelligence to his studies, he'll achieve great things in the future."

Tsui Siu-Hin pointed at Miss Ho and shouted, "I don't need you adults to define my future!"

Mrs. Tsui quickly tugged at him to sit back down, but he pushed her away. "What business is it of yours? Who are you to me?"

"Sit down. What kind of attitude is that toward your mom?" Miss Ho snapped.

Tsui Siu-Hin glanced at Miss Ho and smiled. It was a kind of contemptuous smile—whenever a teacher made a mistake, he assumed this scornful expression. Mrs. Tsui looked at Tsui Siu-Hin, then at the teachers, then lowered her head and took a deep breath. "We . . . adopted Ah Hin, but we've always treated him as our own son."

Both Ling and Miss Ho were shocked. They'd never imagined that Tsui Siu-Hin was an orphan.

"I don't need you to treat me as your own son. I don't want to be responsible to anyone. I've said before that I don't want to study in this school, but you force me to. I don't want to attend extra classes, but you force me to. I don't want to see a psychologist, but you force me to. You say I have ADHD, and that I also have antisocial personality disorder . . ." Tsui Siu-Hin swept his gaze over everyone present. "Why do you always force me to do things?"

They were stuck in a stalemate for a while. Miss Ho's expression didn't change, but her tone softened. "We sympathize with Siu-Hin's situation. If he shows remorse, writes a sincere apology letter, and genuinely changes, we can give him another chance."

Mrs. Tsui urged him to apologize, but he said, "I won't write it."

"If you won't repent, you'll have to leave the school. Would you rather dig in your heels and pay the price?" Miss Ho said.

"It doesn't matter. I just want to have a choice."

THE STREETS OF Mong Kok were bustling at night. At the intersection of Soy Street and Sai Yeung Choi Street, someone was crooning Faye Wong's "Because of Him" in Cantonese. It was a song about a man making her courageous and teaching her that every story only ends in parting. The singer was around the same age as Ling, wearing an oversized black dress, standing beneath a blue tarp, holding a microphone, her eyes closed, completely immersed in the moment. A group of middle-aged people surrounded the singer, some singing along, some lightly clapping along to the beat.

Not far from the singer, a group of middle-aged women were dancing. They were decked out in heavy makeup, wearing short off-the-shoulder dresses studded with sequins paired with fishnet stockings. A loudspeaker played an old Mandarin tune sung by someone with a perpetually pinched nasal voice. The women swayed their bodies out of sync with the beat. Most passersby just took a quick glance and walked on by. On the other side, a short Chinese man in a wide-brimmed hat strummed a guitar and belted out The Beatles' "Yesterday" in standard British English, while an assistant next to him adjusted the loudspeaker. Perhaps because he was singing in English, there weren't many spectators compared to the woman singing Faye Wong.

Ling rarely came to Sai Yeung Choi Street. After school,

she either went to Dundas Street or IFC. Now, standing and listening to the singer, she found it quite strange. The singer didn't sing particularly well, she couldn't quite hit the high notes in the chorus, and her pitch was off-key. Ling also didn't care much for Faye Wong. However, she didn't feel like going to IFC. She looked down at her yellow dress. She wasn't in the mood for shopping. She didn't want to set foot on Dundas Street, either. Ten minutes earlier, her mom had sent her another text message. Remember, you have to sign the purchase agreement for the flat tomorrow. Also, I'm going to play mahjong tonight. Remember to collect the rent for me. Her mom had already forgotten their argument from earlier in the afternoon. Ling slid her phone back into her handbag, leaving the message on read.

Ling's thoughts drifted to the meeting just now. She suddenly felt a little envious of Tsui Siu-Hin. Because he was an orphan, couldn't he ignore parental expectations and teachers' teachings, and just do whatever he wanted? His adoptive mother didn't seem like a mother at all, merely a guardian . . .

—I just want to have a choice.

Do I also have a choice? Can I just do whatever I want? Quit my job? Skip the LPAT? . . . What else can I do if I don't? Travel for a year? But where can I get the money? . . . Do volunteer teaching? A lesser-known profession? Work in a funeral home? Don't be ridiculous . . . What about my 300,000 dollars in credit card debt? What about my mom?

I'm not an orphan. I have a mom, a principal, a job, debts, and many, many other things I can't get rid of . . .

Enough, enough. Her head throbbed as though someone was drilling into it. Ling looked up—the sliver of night sky fragmented by towering buildings was surprisingly small, full of sharp angular edges that could stab someone at any moment. She felt suffocated.

She needed something to numb her chaotic mind. She didn't want to watch aunties dance, or listen to old English songs, so she stopped here and listened to "Because of Him." Some of the people nearby dispersed, and new ones joined, but the area was still swarming with people. She stood by the loudspeaker, her insides vibrating along to the thumping of drumbeats. The singer sang about grasping a man's hands, hoping to make him forever hers, never caring much for freedom. Alas, she came to realize that she'd have to wipe away her own tears, as eventually the man would fly away and be gone.

When the singer sang the two syllables "freedom," her brows furrowed, and she gripped the microphone tightly, lost in emotion. Ling had heard this song back in primary school. Her mom had liked singing along with the cassette tape because there was a long section of English lyrics in the second half of the song, so she could learn English in the process. Ling never really paid attention to the lyrics when she was young, just made fun of her mom for singing the English parts without understanding what they meant. Now, every word and every phrase resonated in her ears, and Ling found them quite uncomfortable. The lyrics said that the singer had finally obtained freedom, but she was complaining that the man flew high and far and then was gone. Why not simply admit that heartbreak was painful? Was claiming independence and self-reliance because a man didn't love you true freedom?

She recalled one time when she was practicing for oral exams with her senior secondary school students. She asked them to discuss the following statement: "Life is precious, and friendship is even more valuable; for the sake of freedom, both can be abandoned." All five students had agreed with the statement. After ten minutes of discussion, when it came to the five-minute mark, they all just stared at the timer in a daze.

Perhaps the students believed that it was politically incorrect to disagree with the value of freedom. Ling had smiled, stopped the timer, stood up, and analyzed with them how to argue the pros and cons.

"The pro viewpoint that everyone agreed on just now is that freedom is the foundation of human existence. If there's life without freedom, everything would be controlled by others, and there'd be nothing to live for. Some students also pointed out that freedom is precious because freedom isn't just about fighting for one's own freedom, but also for the freedom of others, and even the freedom of the nation. Some gave the example of Sun Yat-sen, stating that, if people only pursued their own interests and didn't fight for the Chinese people to escape from imperial rule, society wouldn't have changed . . ."

The students bowed their heads and took notes. Ling paused before continuing. "What about the con viewpoint? Think carefully and refute me."

The classroom was quiet for a while, then a student shouted out, "If there's no life, then even if there's freedom, there's no life to enjoy it." The other students laughed. Then Ling had said something, but she'd forgotten what it was . . .

If she were the one taking the oral exam now, how would she answer?

The loudspeaker blared in Cantonese, while the other singer sang in English, the two tracks overlapping. The people standing around sang along, amid the Mandarin dance music and the old English song playing nearby . . .

Enough, enough. So noisy.

The Faye Wong singer trilled about how losing her man made her realize she didn't need his embrace, that there was no need to cry or become angry. She was off-key again.

The lyrics from "Yesterday" sounded in her ears, musing about how sorrows that once seemed far off now lingered, mixing with the old Teresa Teng Mandarin tune "The Story of a Small Town," which cheerfully detailed the various tales of a small town, replete with joy and happiness.

So noisy, so noisy . . .

If you teachers and psychologists say there's something wrong with my brain, then there must be. Who I am is defined by all of you anyway.

Because of the man, the woman understood that every story only ended in parting . . . The small town replete with tales of joy and happiness . . . The woman now singing in English about being let down, being merely human . . .

Have you ever thought about what you truly enjoy doing? Besides making money.

The woman in the Beatles song leaving without explaining why, the man yearning for yesterday . . .

I just want to have a choice.

You don't understand yourself. You're too good at pleasing others . . . Stop thinking about it, so noisy, so noisy—

The man no longer the person he once was . . . Something that resembled a painting and a song . . . The large harvest of the small town . . . Every story only ending in parting . . . Believing in yesterday . . . *Can I return to the past? The past used to be so good . . .*

Humans are different from animals . . . Humans have choices and are not entirely constrained by their environment.

She was only human . . . only human . . .

So noisy, so noisy! Ling was dizzy, as though she'd been spinning in circles for over thirty years, no, a hundred years, or even thousands of years, and she still was unable to break free . . . She was so tired, so very tired.

Out of nowhere, she felt a cool sensation on her forehead. Looking up, she saw orange-yellow arrows shooting beneath the streetlights. Suddenly, the rain grew heavier, and the people on the street rushed to seek shelter beneath the eaves. The singer crooning Faye Wong stopped mid-song to quickly cover her audio equipment with a cloth, while the singer of the old English song hid beneath an awning and continued singing, determined to finish the song. The aunties swiftly moved their speakers beneath the eaves. The street quieted down in an instant and, when the singer of the old English song finished, only the drip-drop of rain on the streets remained, growing more and more intense, like the sound of a machine gun firing, pure and tranquil.

Ling didn't take cover from the rain. The rain was heavy, the red and green neon lights on the streets seemingly coated in a layer of white jelly, as though it were a bleached rain. In less than a moment, the rain soaked her ankles, her high heels sloshed with water, and the heels became stuck, every step painful. She was drenched from head to toe, the taste of makeup flowing into her mouth, her false eyelashes long disappeared. Her yellow dress had turned a dark yellow, and the pink scarf had lost its warmth. When the wind blew, it was as cold as a knife cutting through layers of her organs. But the chill unexpectedly lifted her out of her exhaustion. People who were taking refuge from the rain gave her strange looks, but she was in a state of extraordinary excitement, and her shivering body was still oozing a little heat. It was as if something was being cleansed, washing away the stain on her dress, washing away the dress on her body, washing away her makeup, washing away her skin, washing away her organs, washing away her brain, washing away her thoughts ...

Just then, a stray black dog passed by, its sopping wet fur stuck to its body, feebly turning around to shake off the water droplets. She thought of her mom, who hated stray cats and dogs, maybe all animals. The dog stared at Ling wearily, lowered its head, and shuffled off toward the trash can at the side of the road. It sniffed around and found a McDonald's paper bag next to the trash bin. It bowed its head to eat something, took a couple of bites, raised its head to bark twice, then resumed eating. Did it come to scavenge for food while there was no one gathered smoking around the trash can? The people under the canopies were either looking down at their phones, or looking curiously at Ling, or looking at the dog. Ling stood in the rain, observing the dog. It wasn't afraid of getting soaked in the rain or of eating garbage—it knew what it wanted. If it couldn't scavenge for food during the day, it would eat at night. If it couldn't find food at night, it'd eat on a rainy day . . .

Soon the rain subsided, and the water flowing toward the drain gradually was reduced to slight ripples. The dog left, and more people came out onto the street, many of them holding umbrellas and heading toward Sai Yeung Choi Street South. Ling glanced down at the water at her feet, seeing her reflection in the puddle. The makeup she'd applied that morning hadn't completely dissolved. Streaks of foundation ran down her face, and her eyeliner was smudged, black tears streaming down her face. However, in the next instant, someone stepped in the puddle in front of her, and the wronged ghost in the water shattered into indescribable colors.

Suddenly, she had an epiphany. *People say that change is constant. Perhaps it's just as my Mandarin teacher said—I'm too arrogant. I just need to change a little more, then everything will be all right, won't it?*

THE DAY BEFORE Christmas vacation, the school only had half a day of classes. As soon as the bell rang, students couldn't wait to leave the campus. Most teachers went home after having lunch. The teachers' office was deserted, with only Ling and a few colleagues who taught other subjects staying behind to finish up work. The winter sunlight lazily leaked through the crack in the door, folding and unfolding like a fan. Ling was working when from a distance she saw Ivy approaching. The principal had already left work, so she probably wasn't there to deliver a message from her. Ivy walked toward Ling's cubicle with a huge smile on her face, her cut double eyelids almost swallowing her eyes.

"Last week, the head of the department had an interview at an international school. That school called to ask about the department head's qualifications. When the principal found out, she promoted the head of the department to vice-principal. Also, Miss Au has been looking for a new job. I have a friend who works in an administrative position at another secondary school who saw a Chinese teacher surnamed Au from Sing Din Secondary School go for an interview . . . It's not just the Chinese department. Lately, a lot of teachers have secretly been going on job interviews. The environment at Sing Din Secondary School is getting worse and worse."

Ivy cheerfully relayed this news to Ling. Ling used to care a lot about these things, but now her mind was elsewhere. Glancing at Ivy, she said, "As for me, I've decided to get plastic surgery. Does Dr. Reboot have any discounts?"

Ivy opened her mouth wide, taking a moment to speak. "Yes, yes . . . It's twenty percent off, but I've had plastic surgery with Dr. Reboot before so, if you mention my name to the staff, you'll get an extra thirty percent off . . . Did you decide to get plastic surgery because you saw Master Chan? As I said, Master Chan is very accurate."

Ling smiled softly at Ivy.

A few days earlier, Ling had gone to Kwun Tong to visit Master Chan again. Master Chan's shop was still messy, with too many books piled up on the desk to have room for writing, and the floor strewn with clutter. There were even more umbrellas on the wall than the last time she was there. That day, Master Chan wore a pair of powder-blue workman's pants and workman's shoes, his long hair in two braids, and he still sat there reading. When Ling opened the door, Master Chan looked up from his book. He recognized her at once and smiled.

Ling didn't want to look directly at his strange face. Before entering, she said, "I'd like to have plastic surgery if it can change my luck."

Master Chan kept on reading. After a while, he said, "Why does everyone in this generation want plastic surgery?"

Ling wasn't angry. She'd searched online for information about the master. Every customer who'd visited described him as effeminate and condescending, but he was still highly sought after. Talented people were inherently arrogant, but since she was a customer, Ling wasn't willing to lower herself to beg him. "Even if I get plastic surgery, it might not necessarily be effective. Can't you help me change my fate?"

Master Chan smiled, and pointed with his hairy fingers to the umbrellas hanging on the wall, gesturing for Ling to remove them.

Ling took down the umbrellas one by one. Behind each umbrella, there was a small bulletin board filled with thank-you cards from clients and post-plastic surgery photos, stacked on top of each other thick like tree rings. In those photos, everyone, regardless of sex, had oval faces, full cheeks, big eyes, and high-bridged noses. The content of the thank-you cards varied, but they all said that, although Master Chan objected to their plastic surgeries, they were still grateful to him for helping them to successfully conceive, get promoted, or snag a rich husband . . .

Master Chan glanced at Ling. "Sooner or later, I'll throw away those photos and thank-you cards on the bulletin board.

I really don't understand why everyone wants plastic surgery. Aren't you afraid of ruining your appearance? As soon as you go under the knife, your original face will be gone. You're the only one in the world with your unique face—can you really bear to destroy it? Moreover, there is always the possibility of a botched surgery. I've heard of many cases of botched plastic surgeries in the past."

Ling had already considered these questions before coming to see Master Chan. She remembered Ivy saying that, if the plastic surgery was flawed, you could just do it again; as long as you had the money, there wasn't anything that couldn't be solved. After all, a person's face was constantly changing, looking different from childhood to adulthood. Ling had long forgotten what she looked like as a child. *Plus, as Ivy said, whether or not I have plastic surgery, I always wear makeup—I see my made-up face way more than my bare face, so what's the difference between original and not-original?*

Master Chan continued, "Aren't you afraid of having the same face as someone else? Look at the beauty pageants in Korea. All of the contestants have the same face."

Ling smiled noncommittally. After meeting Master Chan with Ivy that day, she had bought an introductory book to face reading and learned that a full forehead, phoenix-like eyes, a symmetrical face, and a thick, high-bridged nose were all signs of a good fortune. She reflected on the principal's face; it pretty much checked off all the boxes for a good fortune—no wonder her career had skyrocketed. Last week, she'd deliberately stayed at work until 11 p.m. With the teachers' office empty, she turned on the light for just the Chinese department and walked over to Miss Au's cubicle at the back. Miss Au's bookcase was full of exercise books, and her computer and keyboard lay quietly on the desk. There were several photos pinned to the partition, including ones of her with her boyfriend and her with the principal. Yes, Ling wanted to get a closer look at Miss Au's photo with the principal. The principal's arm was draped around Miss Au's shoulders, and Miss Au smiled brightly. The principal's face was long and square, and Miss Au's face was round. They shared a slight resemblance, and their smiles were similar.

Then Ling walked to the head of the department's cubicle. Her desk was lined with IELTS textbooks and Starbucks tumblers. There were two picture frames in the center, one a photo of her daughter, the other a photo of her with the principal. It was taken at the graduation ceremony. The principal and head of the department stood shoulder to shoulder, both holding Valentino handbags. They both had deep nasolabial folds, and when they smiled, both had double chins.

Ling walked past her Chinese department colleagues' cubicles one by one. Some teachers displayed family photos on their desks, while others had photos with their students, but everyone also had an extra photo with the principal. Squatting down, Ling scrutinized their photos with the principal. The more she looked, the more she felt that, although everyone's appearance was different, they all bore some sort of resemblance to the principal, whether it was their eyes, ears, mouth or nose . . .

Ling resolutely returned to her cubicle and picked up the photo of her and the principal on her desk to examine it closely. It was taken on the principal's birthday, and Ling had specifically brought an instant camera to take a selfie with the principal. The principal held the millefeuille cake Ling had bought for her, and Ling smiled, making a victory sign. Now Ling could no longer feel the same happy mood as back then. She didn't look one bit like the principal. Her face wasn't round enough, her lips weren't full enough, her earlobes weren't round enough . . .

Seeing Ling was silent, Master Chan shrugged and said, "Hong Kong people like taking shortcuts and only care about making money . . ."

"That's right. I'm that shallow. Don't waste your breath. Just tell me the direction of where to go for plastic surgery. I'm in a hurry."

ON THE FIRST day of Christmas break, Ling went to a private hospital to undergo plastic surgery. Before she went into the hospital, she was a little nervous. After all, it was her first time having any sort of surgery, and it was on her face no less. The day before, she had spent the whole night packing her bags, including ice packs for after the facial bone contouring, cooling gel patches, straws, sunglasses to protect her eyes after having double-eyelid surgery, a wide-brimmed hat to use as a disguise when she left the hospital, a mask . . . Of course, the most important things were her credit cards. She checked her wallet over and over to make sure she had three cards, each with a credit limit of 100,000 HKD, which when combined would be enough to pay for the surgery.

Ling had an appointment to meet the doctor at 10 a.m., and arrived at the hospital at nine thirty ready to proceed. As soon as she set foot in the hospital, she received a message from her mom reminding her to follow up on the renovations for their new flat when she came back. Last night, she had told her mom she was taking students to the mainland to attend a seminar on China national affairs and wouldn't return to Hong Kong until five days later, instructing her mom not to call her. She didn't tell her mom she was undergoing plastic surgery, but she wasn't worried that her mom would be angry with her. Ever since the mainland woman and daughter had moved out, her mom no longer asked her to handle rental matters, complaining that she was biased against mainlanders and refusing to let her intervene. The fact was, after she signed the contract for the new flat, her mom was finally satisfied. Now, most of her mom's tenants were prostitutes, both Hong Kongers and mainlanders. Her mom often praised the former mainland woman tenant, saying that although she "was in that line of work," she had a good upbringing and kept the room well maintained; after they moved out, there wasn't even any need to wipe any dust or grime, so it could be rented straight out again. Ling didn't care about that woman now, and just focused on paying the mortgage.

But where would the money for the mortgage come from? The monthly payment was 25,000 HKD, but Ling's salary was only a little over 30,000 HKD, and her contract might not be renewed next year . . . If her mom asked her to buy another unit . . .

No. Nothing will happen. I'm at the hospital.

The hospital was located in the Mid-Levels area on Hong Kong Island, with a hotel-style lobby featuring marble flooring. A receptionist dressed in a neat suit assisted Ling with her luggage and checked her in. Around ten o'clock, Ling entered the doctor's room. Large floor-to-ceiling glass reflected all of Victoria Harbour, and a Swarovski crystal chandelier hung from the ceiling. There was a huge Western-style pine table next to a movable wall. On the other side of the wall was the operating room, where a purple operating table and various instruments had been placed. A male doctor in a white coat greeted Ling and invited her to take a seat. He was handsome, his hair slicked tall with wax, with big, bright eyes and thick eyebrows, and when he smiled he looked a bit like the singer-actor Raymond Lam. Ling couldn't help but do a double-take.

She thought of Master Chan. In fact, Master Chan wasn't bad-looking. Since he knew about physiognomy, why didn't he give himself a little improvement? Maybe after having plastic surgery, he'd be even better-looking than this doctor.

Forget it. Being androgynous is his own business. Getting his advice on plastic surgery is enough. When Ling had said she wanted plastic surgery, Master Chan kept mocking her, but Ling refused to leave and begged him over and over. Finally, unable to withstand Ling's urging, he had casually drawn a picture, crumpled it into a ball, and thrown it at her feet. Ling didn't get upset. She picked up the paper ball and pulled out her wallet to pay him, but he said, "I don't want your dirty money. Go away."

It was even better that she didn't have to pay anything. Whether he liked it or not was his problem. Ling took out the paper ball from her handbag, unfolded it, and handed it to the doctor. The doctor understood at a glance and explained it to her briefly, then took a photo of Ling and inputted it into the computer. Her face on the screen was outlined with countless contour lines, as though it were covered by a tight net. The doctor moved the mouse up, down, left and right, easily elongating and widening her eyes, ears, mouth, and nose. A moment later, the printer spat out a face, a new face, fuller, with big eyes and a high nose bridge, more attractive than she was ten years ago. Ling nodded in satisfaction.

After he finished his explanation, the doctor pulled out a folder and asked her to sign the surgery consent form. She carefully read the terms and conditions—facial bone contouring could cause sagging of the cheekbones, double-eyelid surgery could cause corneal detachment and, more seriously, general anesthesia could affect lung function, leading to a stroke or heart attack. It was as though plastic surgery were a one-way ticket to the afterlife. In fact, Ling had long been well aware of these side effects, having scoured the internet for countless information; afraid that she'd become worried, she had deliberately watched plastic surgery clips on YouTube. On the screen, red rubber tubes were threaded in and out, and bloodstained custard-colored surgical gloves were cutting and snipping. There were knives, electric drills, and needles.

At first, watching these videos was a little gruesome, but gradually Ling became numb, and they even reminded her of the National Geographic programs her mom regularly watched. Animals devoured animals, the same blood flowed like rivers, but under various kinds of hunting and slaughter, the strongest animals still survived generation after generation. So, what was so scary about plastic surgery?

Seeing that, after a long while, she had yet to sign, the doctor smiled and said, "Actually, the chances of complications are slim. We have extensive experience. I myself have undergone facial bone contouring, double-eyelid surgery, and autologous fat transplantation."

Ling wouldn't have imagined that the doctor himself had undergone plastic surgery. She'd assumed he was naturally handsome. She studied the doctor: his double eyelids looked natural, and the contours of his cheeks were soft, as though he really were Raymond Lam himself. Ling hesitated for a moment, then signed her name.

After receiving the consent form, the doctor instructed Ling to go to the dressing room and change into a vest and shorts provided by the hospital. Afterward, he used a marker to draw on her waist and thighs where liposuction was to be performed, and then drew on her face. Gazing at herself in the mirror, Ling realized the body could be divided into so many parts, like a robot composed of different pieces. Once she was ready, a nurse helped Ling put on a surgical gown, wrapped her hair, and asked her to lie down on the operating table. The operating lamp shining from above caused Ling to squint. The doctor put on blue scrubs, a surgical hat, and gloves. Two nurses took her blood pressure, connected a heart rate monitor, and disinfected her . . . At this point, another masked doctor came in. The attending doctor told Ling, "This is the anesthesiologist who will administer general anesthesia to you shortly." Hearing the word "anesthesia," Ling remembered the consent form she'd just signed. Now that she was on the chopping block, she couldn't help feeling a little worried. Noticing she was nervous, the anesthesiologist asked, "Who referred you to us?"

Ling felt a mosquito bite on her wrist. "My colleague."

"Name?"

"Ivy."

"Surname?"

"Ma."

"Ah, Ivy Ma. Many of our clients were referred by her. She earns a commission of hundreds of thousands of dollars per year. In the future, if you refer clients to us, you can also earn commission . . ."

Heavy drowsiness washed over her. She closed her eyes, and soon lost consciousness.

LING AWOKE FROM a dreamless sleep, feeling weak and tired. She wanted to continue sleeping, but the nurse kept talking to her and wouldn't let her fall back asleep. After a while, she began to regain some clarity. She realized she was lying in a bed, her head tightly bandaged, unable to move from the neck up. Her eyes were covered with gauze, leaving only a narrow slit for her to see through. The nurse raised her bed, and through the small opening in the gauze, Ling could see the twinkling lights of Victoria Harbour outside the window. The surgery had been performed at noon. Now it was evening, but she didn't know what time exactly. The nurse brought her some thin congee, instructed her to use a thick straw to drink it, then explained a few precautions and left.

Was the surgery a success or failure? She didn't know yet, but at least she hadn't died. Ling really wanted to see what she looked like now. Through the weave of the gauze, she saw a full-length mirror on the left side of the room, and propped up her worn-out body to walk over to it. In the mirror, her head was wrapped in gauze, revealing only her eyes, nostrils, and two blood transfusion tubes in her mouth.

She thought of Wai. If Wai had been saved, would she also have her head wrapped in gauze like a giant glutinous rice ball? She heard the person in the mirror mocking her. "You—" Ling stroked the surface of the mirror, the icy coolness seeping into her fingertips. It was her in the mirror, no mistake, it was only her. In her mind, Ling told the person in the mirror: "Save it. I'm not as stupid as you were. At least I'm still alive." No, why was she speaking Cantonese? She should be speaking Mandarin! She repeated herself in Mandarin. "Save it. I'm not as stupid as you were. At least I'm still alive." She felt her Mandarin was fluent. Had she really cast off her old body and transformed herself? Or was it all in her head? She silently recited a few more sentences in Mandarin—it seemed as though she really had a Beijing accent! Ling stared at the person in the mirror: beneath the white gauze head was a red hospital gown, hands holding two blood bags, and even her slippers were red. This person before her wasn't Ling or Wai, but her Mandarin teacher. The teacher smiled at her. *Yes, you speak very well.* Ling smiled back, and as she did, her wounds throbbed. How foolish, talking to herself in front of the mirror like a madwoman.

The room resounded with the vibrating sound of her phone, which the nurse had thoughtfully placed by her bedside. Ling walked to the bed, picked up the phone, and saw it was the credit card company calling. She let it ring until they hung up. The screen showed four missed calls. The first two, from her mom and Ivy, she had missed while she was in surgery. The latter two were from the credit card company. Ling then checked WhatsApp and found a message from her mom: Remember to follow up on the renovations when you get back. Then there was a message from Ivy: Are you awake? I wanted to tell you . . . The principal hired the girl wearing Céline, but she didn't say anything about firing anyone. Relax. Also, if any of your friends are interested in plastic surgery, you can tell them to get in touch with me . . .

The anesthesia hadn't yet worn off, and heavy drowsiness came over her again. She turned off the phone and lay on the bed, looking out the window at Victoria Harbour. Compared to the strip of seaweed-like sea at home, this was an unbeatable ocean view. But now only a narrow slit remained, Victoria Harbour flattened by the white gauze, the texture of the gauze dividing the entire sea into horizontal and vertical lines, the lights all contained within white square after white square, perpetually neat, perpetually spotless . . . Ling closed her eyes, mumbling to herself, "Everything will get better," slowly sinking into dreamland.

Translator's Note

THE HORRIFIC EVENTS that transpire in *Tongueless* are inspired by the increasing pressure for Hong Kong secondary schools to integrate Mandarin-language education into the curriculum. As contract teachers, Ling and Wai must navigate a cruel and ideologically charged battleground, resulting in dire consequences. Although the novel was written prior to the 2019 anti-extradition protests and implementation of the National Security Law, it presciently engages with critical issues facing Hong Kongers during a pivotal juncture of quickly shifting realities, exposing the precarious plight of teachers in Hong Kong.

As a novel centered on the loss of language (the title literally means "lost speech" or "lost language"), Hong Kong's unique linguistic landscape of two written and three spoken languages features prominently throughout the book, culminating in a scene toward the novel's end where Ling stands on a street corner in Mong Kok, overwhelmed by the dissonance of hearing songs simultaneously sung in Cantonese, Mandarin, and English. Occupied by Britain from 1841 until 1997, when the territory became a Special Administrative Region of China (with a four-year period of Japanese occupation from 1941 until 1945), English was exclusively the official language in the region from 1883 until 1974; Chinese was only recognized as a second official language in 1974. Presently, under Hong Kong Basic Law, both English and Chinese remain official languages, though what form of Chinese is unspecified.

There is in fact no one monolithic "Chinese" language. Standard written Chinese serves as a written language that unites speakers of various Chinese languages, using a standardized set of characters and grammar, as its name implies; thus, someone who speaks Mandarin, Cantonese, Shanghainese, Hokkien, or another Chinese language will typically be able to use standard Chinese for reading and writing, though there may be slight lexical differences among various regions. The characters themselves can be written in either traditional or simplified forms—Hong Kong, Macau, and Taiwan use traditional Chinese characters, as opposed to the simplified characters commonly used in mainland China and Singapore, while Malaysia uses a mix of both. Given the fact that the grammar and structures of standard written Chinese are based largely on Mandarin (also called "Putonghua," meaning "common tongue"), there is a huge gap between this "standard" written language and the form of Chinese spoken most commonly in Hong Kong: Cantonese.

Cantonese, a Sinitic language that allegedly almost became the official language of mainland China, is the most widely spoken language in Hong Kong, used by the majority of the population in their daily lives. Whereas Mandarin originates from northern China, Cantonese originates from Guangdong province in southeastern China. Spoken Cantonese is distinguished from Mandarin in terms of not only grammar and lexicon but also its pronunciation and tones (depending on the regional variation and definition of "tones," Cantonese can have six or more, versus four main tones in Mandarin). A speaker of Cantonese who has not learned Mandarin will largely find the spoken language unintelligible, and vice-versa. Additionally, written Cantonese contains characters, grammar, and expressions that deviate from standard written Chinese and may not be understood by speakers of other

Chinese languages. Although some sentence structures in written Cantonese may align with standard written Chinese, there are many instances where they differ due to the influence of spoken patterns. Whereas standard written Chinese ostensibly serves as a unifying written language, written Cantonese captures the specific nuances and expressions of the Cantonese spoken form. As such, there is a notable difference between using Cantonese to read aloud a literary work in standard written Chinese versus using Cantonese to read aloud a literary work originally composed in Cantonese. Generally speaking, in Hong Kong, standard written Chinese is used in government documents, media, education, formal communication, and literature, while written Cantonese is found in more informal contexts, such as comics, dialogue in literature, online discussion forums, text messages, and local newspapers or magazines, though there is an increasing body of literary works written in Cantonese, at least partially motivated by an impulse to preserve the local language and culture.

In 1998 the Hong Kong government implemented a "trilingual and biliterate" language education policy to enable students to become conversant in Cantonese, Mandarin, and English and to read and write standard written Chinese and English. Despite the promotion of Mandarin, the official spoken language of the People's Republic of China, Cantonese continues to flourish in Hong Kong and remains one of the top twenty most spoken world languages by population. While Mandarin is still less commonly spoken in Hong Kong than Cantonese, it is becoming more prevalent in business settings and among younger generations, including in schools, which either use English as a medium of instruction or Chinese as a medium of instruction. Previously, Chinese as a medium of instruction constituted using standard written Chinese for the written language and Cantonese for the spoken language. As the local Hong Kong government has become more closely aligned with the central mainland government, however, there increasingly have been discussions about replacing Cantonese with Mandarin in the classroom. Consequently, Chinese-language teachers may find themselves required to exhibit competency in standard Mandarin by taking the Mandarin Language Proficiency Assessment for Teachers (LPAT), and in some cases, the Putonghua Proficiency Test (PSC). Passing these exams not only requires speaking Mandarin in a "standard" accent but also demonstrating fluency in using Mandarin in teaching. It is among this changing linguistic landscape that *Tongueless* is set, and the inspiration for the title of the book, *Tongueless*. The novel reflects real-life anxieties of Mandarin eventually eclipsing Cantonese as the predominant Chinese language in Hong Kong, thus reducing Cantonese to an "inferior" and "vulgar" "dialect" and threatening to erase a distinct Hong Kong identity that, for many, is deeply rooted in the Cantonese language.

As the novel's title suggests, the anxiety of losing one's language is a key theme in the book. Lau Yee-Wa deftly captures Hong Kong's rich multilingualism by weaving together standard written Chinese, Cantonese, and Mandarin, also incorporating the occasional English phrase. Most of the narrative is composed in standard written Chinese, while the novel's dialogue is either in Cantonese or Mandarin, with bits of English scattered throughout. The majority of the dialogue is written in Cantonese, which is depicted as the natural, default language. This is the language spoken by clever-tongued Ling and her colleagues, and Ling and her mother. In contrast, Wai primarily speaks poor and awkward Mandarin, stumbling over words and using the wrong tones, often to comedic effect, resulting in strange-sounding expressions. One finds Wai's language struggles mirrored in the secondary character of the sex worker from mainland China, who similarly mispronounces Cantonese.

One of the most challenging aspects in bringing the novel into English is the focus on language itself, an obstacle I have strived to overcome by attempting to recreate similar effects in English. For example, I have aimed to reproduce the lexical variations of the source text by drawing on the differences between UK and US English, such as "aubergine" versus "eggplant," or "rubbish bin" versus "garbage can." There are also several instances of wordplay in the novel, such as a saying used by Ling's mother that capitalizes on the fact that the Chinese character for official contains two "mouths," while the character for boss contains three. Because a literal translation of "an official has two mouths and a boss has three" forgoes the pun and makes little sense in English, I have translated this phrase as "I always say, a two-faced official talks from both sides of the mouth, and a boss gives you the third degree—three strikes and you're out." Similarly, I have devised creative solutions to highlight the various languages and the characters' differing language proficiencies. As the standard written Chinese narration and Cantonese dialogue in the book are largely unmarked (with the exception of the mainland sex worker's poor grasp of Cantonese), I render them into unmarked English, translating the Cantonese dialogue spoken among the staff members at Sing Din Secondary School, or between Ling and her mother, into fluent, colloquial English. Meanwhile, I convey Wai's clumsy command of Mandarin through faltering, stutter-filled English, using incorrect words to evoke the strangeness of her Mandarin, employing a similar strategy for the mainland sex worker's halting Cantonese. For example, throughout the novel, Wai frequently laments in her bumbling Mandarin that being a teacher is "xianfu," a mispronunciation of "xinku," which is often translated into English as "hard work." To illustrate both the intended meaning of the phrase and also Wai's mispronunciation, I have translated this term as "horde lurke."

Indeed, as the novel shows, being a secondary school teacher in Hong Kong is hard work, with teachers facing an enormous amount of pressure. In addition to their daily teaching responsibilities, the Education Bureau frequently revises the Chinese-language curriculum, forcing teachers to invest a lot of time in preparing their lessons, on top of tending to numerous administrative tasks at school. Moreover, many teachers are employed on a contractual basis to save money. Long-term teaching positions are difficult to come by, making the situation for teachers precarious. As contract teachers, Ling and Wai resort to extreme measures to ensure their job security, which ultimately leads to tragedy.

Aside from addressing the harsh and exploitative working conditions of secondary school teachers, the novel also sheds light on other urgent concerns facing Hong Kong residents in the past decade, including political apathy, the housing crisis, immigration, mental health, workplace bullying, and the absurdity of pursuing luxury and status. The original Chinese-language version of this book was published prior to the anti-extradition protests. Although the anti-extradition protests galvanized many Hong Kongers, a large number of the city's residents remain either pro-establishment or politically indifferent. *Tongueless* is one of the rare contemporary Hong Kong literary works that delves into the mindsets of such people, exploring the origins of their political apathy.

Finally, there are certain cultural nuances that resonate throughout the novel in both its language and unstated assumptions. Readers may be curious why Ling's mother, who emigrated from the mainland, speaks to her in Cantonese instead of Mandarin. Though it is not stated explicitly in the novel, like many mainland immigrants to Hong Kong, Ling's mother is from Guangdong province, the birthplace of the Cantonese language. While in the present-day, the use of Cantonese is dwindling in Guangdong province, during the period in which Ling's mother grew up, it was much more widespread, and thus it would be natural for her to raise her daughter in a Cantonese-speaking environment. Readers may also find it curious that Ling still lives with her mother at the age of thirty-four; however, living with parents as an adult in Hong Kong is not uncommon. On a practical level, the city is known for its exorbitant housing costs, plus the environment is densely populated, making it challenging to find afford-able and spacious accommodations. Moreover, as a contract teacher, Ling's income is lower than that of teachers with more stable employment. Financial constraints aside, in Chinese culture, multiple generations often live under one roof, and moving out is frequently associated with marriage, instead of reaching adulthood or gaining employment; with adults getting married later in life (if at all), adult children have been remaining at home longer. This is not to say, however, that all unmarried adults in Hong Kong live with their parents, but the confluence of economic and cultural factors explains why it is not unusual for Ling or Wai to live with their moth-ers. Additionally, living with and helping to take care of their mothers reflects the concept of filial piety, a core virtue that has served a foundational role in the family and social dynam-ics of many East Asian societies, emphasizing the importance of familial respect, loyalty, and duty. On a similar note, in the book, there are several instances of gift-giving, a practice deeply embedded in Chinese culture that conveys respect, cultivates relationships, and demonstrates appreciation, carry-ing an underlying expectation of reciprocity. Toward the second half of the novel, face reading, or physiognomy, also plays a crucial role. It is a tradition that has been practiced for thousands of years, based on the belief that a person's individual facial features can reveal aspects of their personality, fate, and overall journey. People may turn to face reading for guidance and insights, especially in making significant life decisions and overcoming personal challenges.

Right now, the world is watching Hong Kong, wondering if it will become just another mainland city or retain its individuality. I am excited to bring *Tongueless* into English at this critical juncture when so much of what is integral to Hong Kong's uniqueness, particularly its language, is at risk of being silenced.

—Jennifer Feeley
December 2023

LAU YEE-WA is one of Hong Kong's most exciting up-and-coming fiction authors. Lau began her literary career writing poetry at the Chinese University of Hong Kong, where she obtained her BA in Chinese language and literature, and her master's degree in philosophy. Lau's short story "The Shark" won the prestigious Award for Creative Writing in Chinese in 2016.

JENNIFER FEELEY is the translator of *Not Written Words: Selected Poetry of Xi Xi*, *Carnival of Animals: Xi Xi's Animal Poems*, the White Fox series by Chen Jiatong, Wong Yi's chamber opera *Women Like Us*, and *Mourning a Breast* by Xi Xi. She holds a PhD in East Asian Languages and Literatures from Yale University and is the recipient of the 2017 Lucien Stryk Asian Translation Prize and a 2019 National Endowment for the Arts Literature Translation Fellowship.

More Translated Literature
from the Feminist Press

La Bastarda by Trifonia Melibea Obono,
translated by Lawrence Schimel

**Blood Feast: The Complete
Short Stories of Malika Moustadraf**
translated by Alice Guthrie

**Grieving: Dispatches from a
Wounded Country**
by Cristina Rivera Garza,
translated by Sarah Booker

Happy Stories, Mostly
by Norman Erikson Pasaribu,
translated by Tiffany Tsao

Human Sacrifices by María Fernanda Ampuero,
translated by Frances Riddle

In Case of Emergency by Mahsa Mohebali,
translated by Mariam Rahmani

Panics by Barbara Molinard,
translated by Emma Ramadan

The Singularity by Balsam Karam,
translated by Saskia Vogel

Sweetlust: Stories by Asja Bakić,
translated by Jennifer Zoble

Violets by Kyung-Sook Shin,
translated by Anton Hur

The Feminist Press publishes books that
ignite movements and social transformation.
Celebrating our legacy, we lift up insurgent
and marginalized voices from around the
world to build a more just future.

See our complete list of books at
feministpress.org